$ $ THE DEVALINO CAPER $ $ $ $

$ $ $ $ $ $ $ **A. J. RUSSELL** $ $ $ $ $

$ $ THE DEVALINO CAPER $ $ $ $

 . . . RANDOM HOUSE . . . NEW YORK

Copyright © 1975 by A. J. Russell

All rights reserved under International and Pan-American Copyright Conventions. Published in the United States by Random House, Inc., New York, and simultaneously in Canada by Random House of Canada Limited, Toronto.

Library of Congress Cataloging in Publication Data

Russell, Andrew Joseph
The Devalino caper

I. Title.
PZ4.R9593De   [PS3568.U7655]   813'.5'4   74–26506
            ISBN 0–394–48999–3

Manufactured in the United States of America

9   8   7   6   5   4   3   2

First Edition

123095

"Life is a pile of horseshit, and everybody's
scrambling over the pile hoping to find a pony."

$ $ $ **THE DEVALINO CAPER** $ $ $ $

CHAPTER 1

One Sunday afternoon not long ago a small plane appeared out of a stone-gray sky and landed on a dirt field in Indiana. The man known as the Indian sat on the fender of a 1970 Mercury and watched it stir dust. When it had taxied to a stop, he slid off the fender, punched his fists into the pockets of a gray suede jacket, and shambled out to meet the lone passenger.

"Dev?" the Indian asked.

Joe Dev nodded. Sunglasses to shoes, the modest but splendid bulk of him—five feet ten, one hundred and sixty pounds—spoke of elegance. He and the Indian strode briskly across to the Mercury. The Indian lifted the trunk lid. Joe Dev tossed in his suitcase. They drove off.

Many minutes passed before either of the two men spoke. Joe Dev stared out the car window with an expression of grave wisdom, and the Indian thought he understood why. For the better part of the year the twenty miles between the private airport and Uniontown has no grandeur in it. The landscape— dreary and unendingly flat—professes no great attraction until early summer. Then it is tasseled by fields of ripening corn, relieved, now and then, by distant farmhouses and barnyards lying cool and inviting in groves of greened-up trees. The Indian was prompted to hold to the silence; it was a sight to give a man a tingle, especially if the man is city-bred and is seeing it for the first time. He waited. Five miles later his passenger straightened in his seat and adjusted a cuff link with manicured fingers.

"Fucking lot of corn," Joe Dev said.

The Indian's handsome features, always inexpressive, did

not break precedent. He leaned over the wheel and looked fleetingly skyward. "Been making up to storm all day," he said. "Tornado weather."

Joe Dev remained silent.

"People in the East think very highly of you," the Indian said.

Joe Dev nodded pleasantly. "Tell me something about the job," he said.

"I'm only your reception committee," the Indian said.

"They told me it could go better than a million," Joe Dev said.

"Your reception committee," the Indian said.

Joe Dev frowned and stared him down. "Hey, what is this, a funny sketch or something?" Although he'd lived in the United States for ten years, Joe Dev's thought processes were still generated by his native Italian and then translated into New York gutter English. "You make a remark about people in the East and then you play the dummy. If you got to talk, talk. You got nothing to talk about, don't start up. All of us, you know, we got two eyes, two ears, but only one mouth. There's a reason. It's to use the mouth only half as much."

"Conversation," the Indian said. "I was only being friendly."

"Don't bother," Joe Dev said. "I got as many friends as I can handle."

"I'm also the listening committee," the Indian said. "If you have something to say, now's the time to say it."

"I'll talk to the boss," Joe Dev said.

"Mr. Anson wants to be sure," the Indian said. "About you, the setup, your being here."

"Maybe you want my Social Security," Joe Dev said. "Goddamn sketch, that's what. I'm the one should listen. I'm the one should be sure. Somebody mentioned to expect a piece of a million. So far all I got is conversation and a ride in a condemned machine."

"The car's low-key," the Indian said. "Mr. Anson doesn't want to attract attention."

"Low-key, fine," Joe Dev said. "But don't danger my life in a fucking heap like this."

The Indian saw no reason for this belligerence. It was deliberate and unnecessary and he was about to say so. Joe Dev cut him off.

"I'll talk to the boss," he said.

The Indian nodded.

The landscape was now under sporadic attack from the artifacts of man. A few miles more and the rape was complete: factories, used car lots, shopping centers, Uniontown.

A gas station flawed the corner of Stetson and Lynch. The Indian drove into the interior and braked the car over one of the hydraulic lifts. He honked the horn. A mechanic hunched over a car motor responded with a turn of the head, registered disinterest and continued with his work.

A large man came out of a door marked "Office." He was about fifty, top-heavy, but he moved gracefully on feet too small for the rest of him. He wore black alligator shoes, a well-tailored suit, blue shirt and blue tie. A cigarette was scissored between his fingers. One of the fingers was studded with a diamond ring. He looked tired.

The Indian opened the back door on his side. The large man dropped the cigarette on the garage floor, crushed it underfoot and got in the car. The Indian backed off the lift, swung deftly around. He nosed the car toward the street.

The large man didn't speak until they had entered the flow of traffic. "I'm Bick Anson," he said. His speech was colored with a Midwestern localism. "Appreciate your coming, Mr. Dev."

Joe Dev half turned to him. He nodded, stared, said nothing.

"They tell me you're temperamental," Anson said.

"All artists are temperamental," Joe Dev said.

"How old are you?" Anson asked.

Joe Dev smiled and remained silent.

"Trying to make a point, is all," Anson said. "Let me guess. About the age of the Indian, here, I'd say. Twenty-nine going on thirty." He reached into his pocket for a cigarette, and said, through the lighting of it, "You'll get to be thirty only if it's okay with me. Try to hassle me and you won't be around any longer'n a beer head."

"My stop line," Joe Dev said. "When?"

"After you look," Anson said. "We're headed there now. Just this side of Indianapolis."

"I'll look," Joe Dev said. "If it can be done, I say yes. No, I take my expenses and walk."

"And forget today," Anson said.

"You got a good recommend, didn't you?" Joe Dev asked.

"Appreciate your cooperation," Anson said. "Acting in good faith, we owe that to our mutual friends. Maybe they told you, I've got a long arm. This is my town. Not because I say it's mine. People want me to have it. I do more for this town than any Washington politician ever could. No crime here, no strikes, none of that crap, picketing, sit-ins, and especially no goddamn welfare rolls. Everybody eats and eats tasty. Taxes are low, property values high, and the school system's the best in the state."

"Your trains run on time?" Joe Dev asked.

"Your paisan was a dumb shit," Anson said. "I'm not. Okay? We understand each other? We do, and I'll get on with the telling of this thing of ours."

"Happy birthday to me," Joe Dev said.

"Appreciate your attitude," Anson said. He lowered the car window and released the cigarette stub to the wind. "Now, we're talking, you and I, about a million, maybe a million one or two, about. Give you a little background.

"A few weeks ago a bonded messenger was walking down Beaver Street, New York. Had a briefcase handcuffed to his wrist. Guy with a machete comes along and leaves the poor sonofabitch's hand in the street. Takes off with the briefcase. A hundred and fifty thousand, negotiable securities, cleanest paper you can put your hands on. That's one day. Another day a guy in a brokerage house of Frish and Frish, San Francisco, leaves four hundred thousand—same thing, negotiables—on his desk and goes to the can. When he gets back to his desk . . . understand, I can tell you anything you want to know about these people, what that guy did in the can, who he's married to, who he's screwing. I can even deliver the freak that swung the machete. What I've got invested in information regarding this thing'd put a lot of pone in the pan.

"What'd I get for my money?" Anson asked. "This. A half

dozen different people, a half dozen different jobs, all negotiables, understand, and all of it goes to one man, one million, and spares, cheap, because this man knows how to handle it, he's big enough to handle it."

Joe Dev smiled. "You had it, you'd know how to handle it too, huh?"

Anson nodded. "I had it, I'd know how to handle it too."

"Who is this man?" Joe Dev asked.

"Name's Cugarman," Anson said. "Dan Cugarman. That's it for now. Next, you'll take a look at his place."

The Cugarman estate commanded attention because of its size and not because of architectural skills applied at the time of its conception. Three of its sides were visible from secondary roads, the fourth faced the main highway. They drove around it, ten acres squared off by a ten-foot-high brick wall. There was only one opening in the wall—the entrance—and that was barred by a wrought iron gate. At one point the road dipped slightly. Joe Dev looked ahead and saw that the top of the wall glistened with chunks of broken glass bottles.

"This is an old place," he said. "The glass, that's left over from the old days. For kids climbing over to steal apples or something. Got to be different, now."

"Place is tight," the Indian said. "How're you on flying?"

Joe Dev said, "You got a knack for saying the wrong things, Mister Indian."

"Place is tight," the Indian said. "I know."

Joe Dev said, "Keep working. Something'll come out of your mouth nobody knows."

"Little misunderstanding here," Anson said. "The man's not my chauffeur, he's my associate."

"I don't need remarks," Joe Dev said. "I don't fly. It's not my style. You want something that flies, get a bird. You want a burglar, don't send for me."

"Noted," Anson said. "And no offense."

"Okay," Joe Dev said. "Now look, anybody tries to go over that wall needs a head doctor. Glass in the old days, you can imagine now. I got a pretty good idea, but we see, huh?" He turned to the Indian. "Stop when I tell you."

Joe Dev studied the roadside until he spotted a fallen tree branch. "Here," he said. "Keep the motor running."

The Indian pulled over onto the shoulder of the road. Joe Dev got out, raised the hood of the car and pretended interest in the engine. He waited for a break in the flow of traffic. When the road was momentarily clear in both directions, he picked up one end of the branch and dragged it to the wall. He lifted the thick end—it was about four inches in diameter—and rested it against the weathered brick barrier. Then, cupping his two hands under the slender end, he hoisted, balanced it into an upright position and heaved it over to the other side. Glass went with it.

He walked slowly back. He slammed the hood shut. He got into the car. "We go," he said to the Indian.

Tires screeched as the Indian gunned the Mercury back onto the highway. Joe Dev looked at his watch. Bick Anson reached for another cigarette. They drove on. Two minutes and two miles later, Joe Dev said, "Okay, let's go take a look."

The Indian decelerated, waited for a hole in the oncoming traffic, U-turned, started back. He had scarcely regained the former speed before the trooper's car bore down on them. It came from behind and zoomed past, whirling flasher and penetrating *whoop-whoop* demanding that its haste be served.

"Fast," Joe Dev said. "The alarm's gotta be connected right to headquarters to be that fast. What they call a capacitive-type alarm. Wires strung up on the other side of the wall. Weak electric charge, very weak, almost nothing. It's like you touch it, you don't feel it, see? But the thing is you never get to touch it, no sir. You go three, four feet near those wires, the current steps up and sets it off." To the Indian, "Flying wouldn't help."

Traffic slowed to a crawl as they approached the Cugarman estate. A trooper was waving the rubberneckers by. Behind the trooper, off the road, three police cars had converged. Several uniformed officers were standing by the wall in caucus with a burly civilian who gesticulated wildly as he racked up verbal points.

"That Teague?" Anson asked.

The Indian nodded. "Cugarman's chauffeur. Does double duty, wheel and gun."

Joe Dev said, "Gotta be an ex-con, the way he talks out of the side of his mouth."

Anson nodded.

Rounding the corner from the secondary road, in the near distance, a white-jacketed figure came jogging toward the others. His pace was set by two large dogs straining at their leash.

"Donnet," the Indian said. "Houseboy. Army sergeant. Did twelve years, four in Vietnam."

"How many people working in that place?" Joe Dev asked.

"As many as a football team, I'd say," Anson said.

The Indian said, "Never heard of greyhounds being used for attack."

"Greyhounds, my ass," Joe Dev said. "Greyhounds've got short hair all over. Use your eyes and look, you'll see those've got hair around the feet and the end of the tail. Baluchi hounds. You order a Baluchi to fetch a bottle, and he fetches it. That's the kind of a dog he is. Dogs don't like to pick up bottles, you know that. Bottles're slippery, got no grab. Any dog tries says fuck it. Not Baluchis. You order a Baluchi to fetch a basketball and he'll bring it to you. A guy I know can tell you about Baluchis. Almost chewed off his gun arm, one of them. And when he dropped the gun the goddamn thing started for his fucking throat. Sonofabitch talks to you now, sounds like he's grinding coffee down there." He added, sotto voce, "The trooper."

The trooper was crossing the traffic lane to the dividing line. He kept growling, "Move it."

Bick Anson leaned back in his seat. The Indian checked traffic over his right shoulder. Joe Dev said loudly, "The guy takes three balls and one strike and then he—"

They crept past the trooper. Once beyond the Cugarman estate, the traffic speeded up. A gust of wind swept through the car. It was damp-cool and it promised rain. The sky grew darker.

"Goddamn sketch," Joe Dev said. "This guy Cugarman, what's he need all that protection for?"

Anson shook his head and shrugged slightly. "The man's a high-flying financier, got all sorts of things going for him, not necessarily legitimate, but legal. Couldn't tell you what he's afraid of. His life? I doubt it. Travels all over, no bodyguard, ever. Money? No way. Losing a million'd mean no more to him than a pound of neck-beef. No reason for him to be afraid of anything."

"I dunno," Joe Dev said. "What you tell me about him, a man like that, he's afraid all right."

"Of what?"

"Of being fooled," Joe Dev said.

"Interesting," Anson said.

Joe Dev asked, "The securities, you're sure they're in that house?"

Anson nodded. "Part of the information I paid for. In there someplace. Just where, I couldn't say, but in there. And maybe not for long. Cugarman's in Chicago now. I'd guess he's fixing to convert the stuff to cash or property or whatever the hell."

"He comes back when?" Joe Dev asked.

"The thirty-first," Anson said.

"You're sure?" Joe Dev asked. "It's important you're sure."

Anson nodded. "Comes from Cugarman's secretary. She's forty-six, thirty pounds overweight, varicose veins, and the guy's been screwing her the past two weeks is twenty-nine and the county longcock. Would she lie to him? She's with Cugarman in Chicago. She won't come back with him because she'll be on vacation, but any change in plans, and she'll let us know."

Joe Dev smiled. "Friends all over, huh? You got friends in the telephone company?"

"We'll make some," Anson said. "Just tell us what you need."

"The thirty-first," Joe Dev said. "That means—what?—twenty-seven days."

"Any change in the date and we'll let you know," Anson said. "Right now I'd like your opinion of things. What I've heard about you, not only could you cop the Mona Lisa, you'd get away with selling the damned thing on the installment plan."

"Hey, I just remembered," Joe Dev said. "You don't mind, huh? I gotta make a phone call. My mother. She worries when I go up in a plane. Take two minutes to tell her I got here okay."

"Pignuts," the Indian muttered.

Anson said, "Fella shouldn't worry his ma."

He placed the call from a booth outside a short order restaurant. The Indian stared. Bick Anson lowered his eyelids and slept.

Joe Dev heard the operator say, "I have a collect call for anyone from Joseph Devalino. Will you accept the charge?"

Toni said, "Yes," and when the wire went quiet, she said, "Joey?"

"Yeah," he said. "Look, I know he's asleep, but wake him up."

"Joey," Toni said, "it's less than an hour since he closed his eyes."

"Wake him up."

"Joey, I haven't got the heart," Toni said. "Joey, you don't know. They came, six of them, last night, from Jersey City, or Lodi, I don't know. Two o'clock in the morning, just when he's getting ready to close up. Six of them."

"I know," Joe Dev said. "He was expecting them. Look, get him on the phone."

"He wasn't expecting them two o'clock, just before he's closing. Joey, they started at the top of the menu, like, you know, they owned the place. Drinks, three, four rounds of drinks, appetizers. You believe anybody could eat three orders clams oreganato—to start? I never seen such a belly squad. They went right down the menu, special orders, all of them. Eight bottles of Bardolina. Four A.M. and they're still asking for brandy and Fernet Branca. Two hundred and seventeen dollars, the tab, and nobody picks it up, nobody signs. 'Say hello to Joe Dev,' they said, and they blow. They don't even tip the waiter."

"Look, Toni," Joe Dev said, "I appreciate that you bring me up to date. But, you know, give some consideration I got enough on my mind that I don't need that. I mean, I know what the crunch is, it's not necessary to, you know."

"I'm only explaining why Bruno can't come to the phone," Toni said. "All day long he's been trying to sleep, but how do you, you know, with all his troubles you don't fall asleep that easy. It's less than an hour that he closed his eyes."

"Screw that," Joe Dev said. "Wake him up."

"Joey, don't curse," Toni said.

"Wake him up," Joe Dev said. "And don't start with the incense and the Hail Marys. Goddamn sketch, Jesus Christ Almighty."

"Joey," Toni said.

"Wake him the fuck up," Joe Dev said.

He waited.

"Yeah, Joey," Bruno said.

"Look," Joe Dev said, "I know that they came and I know what they ate. What did they say?"

"I got one of them aside," Bruno said. "The guy they call Frankie Shoeshine, you know? He's got a direct to the old man. I offered it to him again, the forty and the restaurant. He says they don't do business that way."

"My mouth hurts from laughing," Joe Dev said.

"I'm just telling you what he said," Bruno said. "He swears by his mother that he talked to the old man, and the old man says no dice, the whole hundred or nothing. So, like they're rooting for you to come up rosy, you know?"

"Yeah sure, rosy," Joe Dev said.

"If I could get to the old man myself, I could explain," Bruno said. "But I can't. They say no, and who's gonna cross them if they say no, huh? My father knew the old man on the other side, I told you. I could explain to him I'm not trying to deal, I'm not holding out, that I haven't got it, I haven't made it. Jesus, they know business is shitty all over. Like yesterday, Saturday, the regulars, you don't see them for dust, they head for the country after Friday lunch. The fucking summer visitors, you depend on them and you go dry. They stand in line for two hours in front of the Music Hall, with their fingers up their ass, and after the show they go eat a steak for ninety-nine cents."

"Bru, listen," Joe Dev said. "Before I say yes or no to these guys, it's definite, huh? No way?"

"They want the money, Joey," Bruno said. "The investment and the profit, like I promised, cash that they can fold up and run with. They're desperate, Joey. You know what's going on. The niggers are squeezing them out, and they can't do anything about it, they're shitting green, they gotta take it and run. You talk about assets and they say balls. They got no interest in assets, they want the bundle so they can clear out. They don't want to hear that I've put the restaurant up for sale, they won't stand still for that. Too long, they say. Bastards."

"Okay, okay," Joe Dev said.

"Hey, what does it look like there?" Bruno asked.

"Gonna take a Houdini," Joe Dev said.

"You're better than Houdini," Bruno said. "Better. A thousand times."

"He died a natural death," Joe Dev said. "I had my way, this wouldn't be my next job. I'd be in L.A."

"What are you saying to me, Joey?" Bruno asked.

"I'm saying that this thing's not without worries to me, that's what I'm saying. I'm not gonna have any freedom to move. These people, they look different, they talk different. You believe it, a goddamn Indian's the number two guy? Me, I stand out like the fucking white in those Oreo cookies your kid's always eating."

"What can I tell you, Joey," Bruno said. "When they left, they said, 'Regards to Joe Dev.' That's all. 'Regards to Joe Dev.' Like, you know. So what can I tell you?"

"All right, look, I gotta go, they're waiting," Joe Dev said. "Just in case, though, these people here, I don't trust them. I'm not sure they'll let me walk when I'm finished."

"The guys in Jersey'd mob them," Bruno said.

"The guys in Jersey maybe got a deal with them, they take my share or something, you understand? Like you said, they're desperate. Maybe they're not doing you a favor by putting me on to this so you can pay them off. I know people, Bru. I got a feeling about people when I meet them, you know that. Anybody connected with this thing so far, I swear to God, I wouldn't trust one of them with a fucking box of Chiclets."

"Look, Joey, if it's like that, fuck it, back off."

"My sister's too young to be a widow," Joe Dev said.

Bruno said, "Joey, look."

"Just listen, okay?" Joe Dev said. "Go ready, understand? Something happens to me, don't go hollering hindoo or anything like that. Don't fight it. Shut the goddamn door and clear out. Get my sister and the kid out of there."

"Joey," Bruno said, "I'd do anything, you know? What you're doing for me, who's got the words?"

"Yeah, yeah," Joe Dev said. "Who knows? Maybe I'm working myself up over nothing. I'm used to walking alone, picking and choosing my own jobs, and all of a sudden I'm punching the clock for a Jersey mob, an Indian and a guy sounds like Old MacDonald. Jesus."

"Stay cool, Joey," Bruno said.

"Nobody's cool," Joe Dev said. "Never. Not until they're dead, then they're cool."

"Well, look it, I mean," Bruno said. "I hope you look it."

Joe Dev hung up. He returned to the car.

A beginning rain made pinpoints on the windshield. The Indian stared through them and asked, "The airport?"

Anson smiled at Joe Dev. "Reassure your ma, did you?"

"Yeah," Joe Dev said. "You know how they are."

"My plane's standing by at the airport," Anson said. "Anybody eastbound's still in time to fly ahead of the storm."

"We've got to discuss," Joe Dev said. "It's not easy, what you're asking. I didn't expect it'd be easy when I came, though. It's never easy, but there are other considerations."

"One hundred thousand," Anson said. "Ten percent."

Joe Dev shook his head. "You're not discussing what I want to discuss," he said. "Look, you bring me here and you say to me, 'This man has something I want. You get it for me, I give you a share.' Well, you know, I don't have to be a gypsy to guess who's got things. All over the place people got things. New York, Miami, San Francisco, Rome, Paris, all over. You peruse the goddamn newspaper and you find out that so-and-so of such-and-such a place is rich. Why? Because you see a picture of his house, you see the diamonds hanging around his wife's neck, you see his car, his chauffeur. So why don't I go to such-and-such a place and take from so-and-so. And no split. I keep the whole shooting match for myself. Why, huh? Because I don't go in a place has only one door. I go in, I got to come out, no? Even a dumb animal lives in the ground has a hole to go in and one to come out. Right now I got only one door. And if somebody locks it, what? That's the consideration, Mr. Anson, and that's why I come to do your job instead of I go to such-and-such a place."

"In this territory," Anson said, "I can fix anything."

"Thank you," Joe Dev said. "That's what I wait to hear you say. That's my second door."

"Just don't kill a cop," Anson said.

"Have the confidence that it won't be necessary," Joe Dev said. "I don't carry no heat. I never had a gun in my hand. I don't know how to use it. I use what God gave me. God didn't make guns. God made brains."

"You simmering some notion regarding the job?"

"How can I answer?" Joe Dev asked. "I don't work the same way every time. First I study. I learn about the way of the people and the things around me. Like for instance, you're lost in a strange forest and you're naked. What do you do, eh? What can you do? You use what you find. You study around and you discover a way to keep warm and what to eat, and then you give part of your brain to the question how you gonna get out. It's the same if you are lost in a desert, or like your ship sinks and you are left in a small boat in the water. You study. You learn. That's what I do here. I study and learn and then I go in.

"You think I've got twenty-seven days. No. I got a day, two, maybe, after Cugarman gets back. I got to figure he's the only one knows where those securities are stashed. Say I'm stupid enough to go over that wall now, and I'm lucky, and I get past the Baluchis, and I don't trigger the alarm in the house. What? The securities. You think they're in the top right-hand drawer of the guy's desk? No. I gotta wait for Cugarman, understand?"

"I understand," Anson said. "Reason you're here is, this sort of thing's not in our line. Too good to pass up, though, if the right man's available. You saying you're willing to give it a try?"

Joe Dev looked at the Indian, and said, "Any horse's ass can *try*. I *do* it."

The Indian stared at the pinpoints and remained silent.

"So now we go like this," Joe Dev said. "You leave me alone. When I get this paper, these securities, I'll bring it to you and you give me one hundred thousand, cash. Write down for me your telephone number so I can tell you when I'm coming."

"Pignuts," the Indian said.

"I don't brag," Joe Dev said. "It's no use to complicate things, that's all."

"You said something about the telephone company," Anson said.

"Yeah," Joe Dev said. "You get for me from the telephone people a line record map of Cugarman's neighborhood. Won't be easy. A line record's confidential." He said to the Indian, "Better write that down. A line record map."

"I heard you, goddammit," the Indian said.

"The line record map and some equipment to climb the poles, and that's all," Joe Dev said.

"Need anybody to help?" Anson asked.

"I thank you, but I need help I arrange it myself," Joe Dev said. "I choose. Nobody knows I'm in this town. We let it stay like that. That's important. I got my ways and I like to stick to them. What you do for me now is, you take me to people you can trust, where I can stay awhile and they give me food and a place where I can throw myself down, and they leave me alone and do what I tell them."

"How about the Stocker woman's place?" the Indian said.

"Harriet Stocker?" Anson said. "Why send him there?"

"Harriet Stocker's okay," the Indian said. "I hid out there myself, once. It's clear out of town, got a room upstairs away from the action, back entrance. It's perfect."

"Get moving," Anson said. "It's a piece to go before dark."

CHAPTER 2

Harriet Stocker, soft and fat and black, half dozed and half listened to the storm sounds and to Alice, who was saying, "It was my first trick for money. I was eighteen and the guy gave me fifty dollars."

The others, too, only half listened. Because common calamity had brought the four women together after serving long apprenticeship in going downward, backward glances—by any of them—were necessarily dulled by familiarity; tales twice told. Julia's attention remained hyphenated by the newspaper, and Helen's by her sewing.

A loose shutter banged noisily. Alice paused and made a face in anticipation of another assault by the wind. Gently, as if turning the page of a precious and tattered volume, she brushed a wisp of hair from her face. Her hair was long and blond and it cascaded past sparsely freckled cheeks and slender neck to shoulders that were entirely feminine. A gentle melancholy had matured in her eyes; they persisted in reflecting sadness even when she smiled.

The gust of wind came. It tangled with trees in full leaf, whined itself free, slammed into the house, thudded, swirled and rattled the old place to the joists.

"Jesus," Helen said. She started the motor of the portable sewing machine. It was set atop the black enameled bar, and she was settled on one of the stools. "This won't bother you," she said to Alice, "not with that howling out there. I'm going to finish the goddamn dress or else. Who knows when it'll rain again."

Alice smiled. The dress was a long-term project, a time-killer when activity in the house was sluggish. Alice liked Helen. Helen was sweet; she cared about people. Not like that bitch Julia whose consuming interest was her invested capital. Look at her. Look how those eyes of poisonous green devoured the stock market quotations. From the smug look of her she'd probably racked up a few bucks. Money. Money was number one for Julia, in all things, in all ways. Bitch. If somebody in downtown Cleveland were to bounce a quarter on the sidewalk, she'd wake up from a deep sleep and oil her twat.

Helen said, "Fifty bucks wasn't bad, Al. Not bad at all."

"Sure changed my life," Alice said. "If only I'd known."

"Yeah?" Helen said.

"The way it happened was," Alice said, "I was six months pregnant when my husband and I were married. Both of us were in college, and it seemed only, you know, sensible, he stay and graduate, and me, I play house. His people'd send us a few dollars now and then, and he'd haul garbage when he didn't have classes. Didn't near crack the nut, though. Christ, you got any idea what a pediatrician gets every time he pats a baby's ass? Anyway, what with all the expenses and us going backward instead of ahead, I figure I could make out better if I pay somebody to sit with the kid, who's a year and a half by now, and I find myself a job."

She took a sip of her bourbon and Seven-Up. "So there I am, hacking around trying to beat the cost of living and coming out in the red every day—no job, carfares, lunches and all—and like who's in bad trouble, you know? Jesus, I mean who needs it? I was really squirrely about my husband, sure, the reason I'm breaking my ass like that, but what good's it if you can't make the numbers come out right?" She reached for a cigarette. "Know what I mean, Jule?"

Julia placed the green eyes on Alice. She had thick red hair, her face was bone-prominent, her body tall and elastic. She wore green slacks, and a yellow cashmere sweater against which her nipples protruded saucily. "Yes, love, I do, y'poor thang," she said, too sweetly. Her voice was South-soft and sugared, a tranquil chant. "Rats and rattles but it takes a heap of doing to stay on the sunny side of the woodshed nowadays."

Harriet opened one eye, the one which put Alice and Julia in her vision. She studied them warily. She wasn't deceived by their saccharine exchange of words. You can't keep a lid on a boiling pot. She anticipated a brawl. It was in the making.

Fire and water, those two, cats snarling over a fishhead, or a thirty-inch dwarf, to be precise. Harriet chuckled inwardly remembering how and why a personality conflict had grown into a feud. He'd come in about two weeks ago, the dwarf, and Julia'd gotten hold of him. That Julia. Really something, that Julia. What a time she give that little guy. Tossed him around her bed and played with him like he was a baby doll, and the rest of them sneak-peeking in the door and near busting apart laughing. Dwarf when he came in, yeah, but when he left, Julia had him thinking he was King Kong. Generous, too. Julia asked him bold as you like for a hundred dollars, and he handed it over like it was no more'n bus fare.

He'd come back the very next night, all the way from Fort Wayne, too. Julia'd been busy with Kelsey, the gas station owner, so Alice had that little fella upstairs quicker'n a wren can make to the honeysuckle. Julia didn't like that, losing a hundred dollars, uh-uh. Dwarf was her property, she felt. Ever since then it'd been needle and stab and jab and looks like a scythe coming down on grass.

"The idea of putting out for a price never crossed my mind," Alice continued. "It was always, you know, strictly for good times, until this day when I have this trouble with this white-bread bitch in the employment agency, and I leave there boiling mad.

"To show you how things happen: I'm standing on a corner waiting for a bus and trying to get back my cool, when this guy pulls up in a nice car. 'Hi,' he says, 'you sporting?' And I say, 'Yeah.' Because now I've really had it with the whole sonofabitching deal, you know, the job bit? 'Yeah,' I say. Dumb me, never even realizing it could be one of those bastards from Vice, me not knowing about those things then. 'Yeah,' I say.

"We go to this guy's apartment, which is not bad, a doorman and all, and it isn't five minutes before I got a number on him. Sick. Got the instincts of an itinerate flea. And he *knows* what he is because he asks me to come back again, and the only way he's going to get me to do *that* is to really green off. Which is what he did, without my even asking. Fifty dollars.

"From then on things're going pretty good. I tell my husband I got a part-time job as a cocktail waitress, with good tips, which he doesn't like much but says okay, and twice a week I go to this guy's apartment for the trick, and then run home in time to put on the potatoes.

"This guy doesn't make it easy. I mean, I earn every nickel. But I put up with it until the time comes I don't need him any more. Man, it was a real pleasure saying goodbye.

"Him, though, he's all shattered. Jesus, how he goes on. He's fallen in love with me. I can't do it to him. He'll blow his brains out. A whole pile of sick crap. He begs me, please won't I come just a few more times so he gets used to the idea of losing me.

"Even if I know what the sonofabitch is up to, I don't know what I could've done about it. He was always doing sick dumb things, and I don't see why it should be any different now. To show you: The next time I go to see him he says he wants to pull this gag on a friend, and he'll give me an extra fifty if I play along. All I have to do is sit there in the apartment and have lunch with him, only we'll both be mother naked. You see what I mean about sick?

"What's supposed to happen is, this friend of his is coming to see him, and this friend is a real soft-ass fairy. When he walks in and sees us sitting there, it's gotta be like screams, right?"

Harriet opened both eyes. Into their blankness there came an expression of astonishment.

Alice made note of the look. "Hah, see?" she said. "Why didn't I think of that? Okay, I didn't. Never figured it."

Helen asked, "Never figured what, Al?"

"I never figured what this guy is up to," Alice said. "What he does is, he gets in touch with my husband and says he's fucking me regular, and if he doesn't believe it, how about coming over and seeing for himself."

"Jesus," Helen said.

"And this fairy friend isn't a fairy friend at all, it's my husband, who stands there in the doorway like his intestines're going to dribble out. Poor guy just stands there and looks. He turns around and walks out. He stops. Takes another look over his shoulder like it can't be. And me, I'm sitting there in my bare ass, holding a forkful of cottage cheese."

"Jesus," Helen said.

"Well," Alice said, "by the time I get through telling this guy what I think of him—his doing what he did being his idea of good times, you understand—and I get dressed and rush home, my husband and the kid are gone."

She puffed up her cheeks and forced out air. "At first I, you know, was going after him. Only what good would it've done. He had me, you know, cold. Cold."

"You should have," Helen said. "Gone after him, I mean, and given your side of the story."

Alice shook her head. "He had me cold."

"That sick guy," Helen said. "God'll punish the sonofabitch."

The phone rang. Harriet fought her way up and out of the upholstered chair. Breathing heavily from the effort, breasts flopping on her pendent stomach, it was only great resolution that took her to the hall. "Hello," she said into the phone. "Oh, Mr. Holly. Yessir, I do remember you, very well, Mr. Holly."

She turned and looked at Julia, indicating that the call concerned her. "*Mister* Holly," she said, "you looked overhaid? It's a terrible night to ask Julia to go out." She listened a moment, then laughed. "Now you talking from a position of *strength*, Mr. Holly. I knows you'll be very generous and treat my Julia right." She cradled the phone. "I'll pack you a li'l overnight," she said to Julia. She began the slow ascent to the second floor, shifting her full weight on every tread.

Alice said, "Hey, I remember him. Jim Holly. The one with the crooked eyebrow."

Julia remained silent.

In Julia's bedroom Harriet packed the essentials in a black leather bag. Julia came in, undressed, then went into the bathroom and turned on the water in the shower. Harriet followed.

"Something bothering you," Harriet said. It was not a question.

Julia shrugged. "Sunday in this cheap labor town. Supper in the middle of the afternoon, then television, then bed, the whole damned town. And just let it rain! Goodness. Just let a few itty-bitty drops fall." She stepped into the shower and drew the curtain.

"Womenfolk likes to have their men around on Sunday. You ought to 'preciate that. Gives you a little time to do your own thing," Harriet said. "But that ain't what's bothering you. Why you keep carrying spite in your heart for Alice?"

"Spite?" Julia said. "Why, Harriet, what a thing to say. Spite? For Alice, poor thing? Why, nobody has more sympathy for the girl than I have. Such a tragic unhappy life. Did you see the dress I got at Larkin's yesterday?"

"Saw it," Harriet said. "Loved it."

"I just knew you would," Julia said. "Who could resist that print, so delicate and lacylike. Maybe I'll wear it tonight."

"No you won't," Harriet said. "You'll wear the uniform."

"Shoot," Julia said. "This Mr. Holly, did you notice that he has a crooked eyebrow? Imagine Alice noticing a crooked eyebrow. It uncomforts me the way the girl gets so involved with men."

"Your tongue's real pointy tonight," Harriet said. "Something been raw-assing you. I been noticing. A couple of weeks now, I been noticing. Ain't Sunday and it ain't the rain and it ain't Alice."

"I'm going in the real estate business," Julia said.

"Shit, honey," Harriet said.

"I'm going to do it," Julia said. "Soon's I get everything right, I'm going to do it." She drew the shower curtain aside. Harriet was grinning and shaking her head. "Don't you think I won't," Julia said.

"I don't think you wanna," Harriet said.

Julia snatched a towel from Harriet. "No, you don't think I wanna," she mimicked. "That's why I've been looking into it and all, how to learn about it and get a real estate license, because I don't wanna. Lost my senses, have I? That what you're thinking?"

"Depends on why you doing it, Jule," Harriet said. "You looking to be free, you free now, better'n any woman's free. The real estate business mean you goan be in a one-man bed."

"Hah," Julia said.

"Ain't good, a one-man bed, Jule," Harriet said. "Give it free to one man in trade for kitchen privileges and the time come when your one-man bed goan be half empty because he be off buying himself a fresh piece. If you selling and he give you question about it, you can tell him to fuck off. You picks up and retires with what you made offa him in the past. But, if you be home in a half-empty bed, you just a big bother to him, you his slop bucket, somebody he got to snow and bullshit, and if you complain, he goan break your face. You no more welcome to him than dog shit on the sidewalk."

"I'm not stupid," Julia said.

"I say you stupid?" Harriet asked. "I say that? No, I say you don't know yo'self, and if you don't know yo'self you don't know what you wants, and maybe real estate ain't it atall, 'cause you looking for something and I don't think real estate's it."

"It isn't a man," Julia said.

"You watch yo'self, Jule," Harriet said. "Just watch yo'self and learn about yo'self. Dangerous for a person not to know herself. And you be careful about changing your life for a man.

You don't sweeten your mouth by saying honey. I know. I been there."

"You?" Julia asked. "You mean married? Harriet, no! Really?"

"Killed the motherfucker," Harriet said. "Skivered his throat with a billhook and made off. Laughing, I was, too, goddamn."

Harriet went back downstairs. In the living room Helen and Alice were peeping out the window through a slit in the drapes.

"There's a man out there," Helen said.

"They is?" Harriet said. She sounded disinterested.

"Yeah," Helen said. "Just standing there, in the wet. Dumb cock."

"The shy kind, I guess," Alice said. "Getting up his nerve to come in. Jesus, a tornado, almost. How shy can you get?"

When Julia appeared she was wearing the uniform of the Uniontown Community Visiting Nurse, a navy blue. The hat, soft and helmet-shaped, was piped in a lighter blue, the blouse was white, the black shoes flat-heeled. She clutched the black bag in one hand.

"Honestly," she said. "Do I have to wear this tonight?"

"Yes, you have to wear it," Harriet said. "Bick Anson give protection in the house, outside a woman gotta fix up her own de-fense."

"But there won't be a soul on the streets, not in this weather," Julia said. "Damned ugly old thing. I feel ugly and I look like a sweet-ass."

"That's the idea," Harriet said. "Nobody goan mo-lest a sweet-ass. You goan wear the uniform and you goan ride with your car windows locked."

"The way they gawk when you walk into a place," Julia said. "I can just see the look on Mr. Holly's face when I present myself."

"Take it off in the vestibule," Helen said.

"You shut, you pagan," Julia said.

"Girls," Harriet said.

"Pagan?" Helen said. "What's this pagan shit?"

"You know what I mean," Julia said. "All that candle

burning and those—those idols. Stinking up the whole of the upstairs with those guttering candles."

"Girls," Harriet said.

"Idols?" Helen said. "Jule, it's the statue of Jesus Christ, for Christ's sake. I burn a candle before Jesus Christ."

"Well, it isn't right," Julia said. "God's in church, not in your bedroom."

"God in my bedroom is better than yours in church," Helen said. "I know your kind. You go to church five o'clock in the afternoon, eat a ham and bean supper, sing a few songs and you think you go home blessed. You go home constipated."

"Oh, shut," Julia said.

"Girls," Harriet said.

From the window, Alice said, "What do you think, Har? Go out and coax him in?"

"No," Harriet said. "Could be the gentleman Mr. Anson called about. If it is, you remember what I tole you. Treat him proper and don't ask no questions."

"Who is he?" Alice asked. "What's he doing here?"

Helen said, "What *could* he be doing here if he's teamed up with Bick Anson and the Indian. He's here to organize a charity drive."

"How long'll he stay?" Julia asked.

"Guess you all didn't hear," Harriet said. "No questions and no rapping about it."

Julia rummaged through the hall closet for an umbrella. She found one. It didn't belong to her.

"It's mine," Helen said, "but you can use it. And don't say thank you. No shocks, please."

Julia made no answer. She left.

Someone—Harriet, probably—turned on the porch light and she saw the man in its glow. Neither of them spoke. He stared earnestly; her gaze brushed him briefly but thoroughly. He was handsome, interestingly so, but there was something about his face . . . It wasn't the black-as-can-be black hair, now wet and flattened against scalp and forehead by the rain, nor the angular features that reminded her of a picture of a young Caesar she'd seen in a grade-school book. The hair, skin coloring and chiseled face called for dark eyes. His were blue-purple, like two muscat grapes.

She scurried past him to the car, head down and shielded by the umbrella. She lowered the window and looked back. Despite the knowledge that the distance between them rendered a smile meaningless, she smiled.

Hatred of Alice spread like a coffee stain. Alice would come down on him like five o'clock traffic, leave it to Alice.

"Damn," Julia muttered as she drove off. "Damn Jim Holly and his big belly and his hairy shoulders. Damn Alice. God-damn the bitch."

CHAPTER **3**

Unmindful that the rain filled earth and sky, Joe Dev placed his suitcase on the porch and walked slowly around the house. The house was three stories of hopeless ugliness, its height so disproportionate to its width that it resembled an upended shoe box. He slogged through the weedy grounds and studied doors, windows, the roof line. In front again, he wiped his eyes with the palms of his hands and, forearm shielding his face, surveyed the area. The torrent blurred his vision and its sting made him wince, but he persisted with the patience of an animal until he'd seen what was out there—the dead-end turnaround, the falling-down, abandoned frame structure opposite, the woods beyond, the lights of the nearest house.

He returned to the porch. He stamped mud from his hundred-dollar shoes, picked up the suitcase and pressed the chimes button. They rang out "One Enchanted Evening."

Harriet opened the door. He entered the hall.

"Mr. Dev?" she asked.

Joe Dev nodded. With a shuffling motion, he wiped his feet on the mat. The hall floor was covered in linoleum tile. Imprinted on every square was a pair of dice, each pair showing a combination of seven.

He followed Harriet into the living room. His eyes swiftly

recorded the assertive details: Harriet's black and orange print muumuu; Alice, seated, long legs curled under, dress barely covering loins; Helen, the sewing machine, her see-through blouse, the bar; the strawberry-red upholstered chairs clustered around an imitation marble-topped table; drapes the color of overripe limes; flowered wallpaper with orchid background; creamy shag rug; simulated crystal chandelier.

"I'm Harriet Stocker," Harriet said. "This here's Alice. That's Helen."

"Hi," Joe Dev said, looking from one to the other. "Jesus, this place, all this beauty. A guy walks in here it's like an electric shock."

"Anybody wet as you are, an electric shock is dangerous," Helen said. "Where'd it hit you?"

"You know where, baby," Joe Dev said, "you know where." They all laughed.

Harriet led him up the back stairway to a room on the third floor. It was tiny, barely large enough for the double bed and a dresser. A toilet adjoined it.

"No bath here," Harriet said. "Bath downstairs." She saw that he looked past her and that his eyes narrowed. "That's my room down the hall," she said. "I uses it only for sleeping. Days."

Joe Dev winked and made a noise with his teeth. "Lock your door," he said. "I'm the type guy, my blood talks for me."

Harriet chuckled. "Snow in Ju-ly. Towels in that chifferobe."

He stripped to his waist and dried himself. "I thank you for your hospitality," he said. "You can expect from me a hundred dollars a day for every day I'm here."

"In that case," Harriet said, "I hopes you enjoys our Christmas dinner."

"Hey, food," Joe Dev said. "How about it?"

"I can scramble you some eggs," Harriet said. "May be some jowl in the 'frigerator, too. I'll see."

"What is it?" he asked.

"Jowl? Pig," she said. "You around here long enough you eat a lot of it. Folks this part of the country figures you doing good or bad by the amount of pig fat you 'cumulate in coffee cans." She started out, sighing wearily. "What I need's an elevator."

"You got it," he said. "A present from me—if you scramble the eggs soft."

She showed her teeth through a smile. "Dev, huh? Short for devil, maybe?"

"You want to see my tail?" He unzipped the wet trousers.

Harriet hurried off, her laughter climaxing like a glissando.

Alice brought the tray. "Harriet isn't much on stairs," she said.

He enjoyed boldly all of her that was physical, the long bare legs, the manner in which she tossed her hair back when she leaned over to put down the tray, the liquid motion of her breasts under the dress. "You're really something, you know that?" he said.

She smiled. "Thank you," she said, and started to go.

"You got time, stick around a minute," he said. "Sit down, sit down."

"I can't," she said. She remained in the doorway.

He sat and sliced into the thick bacon. She watched the muscles of his arms and chest. They rippled gently, like water giving way to an insect darting across the surface of a still pond. A scythelike scar ran from his left breast to the middle of the abdomen. Surgery had not been skillful. Stitch marks showed, white and pointed; they gave the scar the look of a palm frond.

"Alice, huh?" he said. "That's a nice name. Sit down, sit down."

She shook her head. "No, I'd better get back down." She tarried a moment longer, then said, "You should hang up that wet jacket. It's a very good-looking jacket."

"From London," he said. "All my clothes are made in London. I don't buy anything in the United States. You buy United States made and you buy junk. Anything—automobiles, furniture, bread toasters, toothbrushes, junk. No tailors here any more. The young people, they think being a tailor is a low job. Here everybody wants to be a boss, with a box on the desk that you push a button, and say, 'Miss Jones, come in and take a letter.' These people, they have no brains but they want to go high." He laughed. "They like a lot of pig fat, eh?" He emphasized his next point with his fork. "You don't go high unless you've got brains," he said. "You can get rich, sure, like you rob a bank, but you don't go high. So what happens if you haven't got the balls to rob a bank? Huh?"

"Everybody hates drudgery, I guess," Alice said.

"Correct," Joe Dev said. "Hey, sit down, please, huh?"

"Well, a minute," Alice said.

"So," Joe Dev continued, "whatever your work is, you hate it, you don't give a goddamn about the quality when it comes from the machine. But you know what the crazy part is? You listening to me? The crazy part is that *you* got to buy it. You hand your baby a piece of shit and you say, 'Here's a toy, play.' Boy, I'm telling you, anything comes out of the United States is like something falls from a cow's ass."

Alice giggled.

Joe Dev said, "The trouble is, people here don't experience real bad times, that's the reason, I think. When I was a kid—hey, you wanna know about bad times? After the war, people went to the Borghese Gardens—that's in Rome—and they don't go to walk, to enjoy it. They went and they tore up the grass and took it home and cooked it, I swear to God. If you grew anything yourself, you used your own crap for fertilizer."

"You're kidding," Alice said.

"I mean it," Joe Dev said. "I was only about four years old but I still remember. My mother had a little garden, and when me and my brother had to go, we went in the tomato plants. Laugh? Boy, I'm telling you. It was a sketch. You like kids, huh?"

"What makes you ask that, suddenly?" Alice said.

He shrugged. "When I talked about giving a baby a toy, you got a funny look in your eyes."

"You must be an athlete or something," Alice said.

"Naggh," he said. "I keep in shape, that's all. Listen, a body and mind, they're the only thing that's yours. A body and a mind. So it's wise if you keep both of them in good shape."

He didn't drink the coffee.

"Would you like a glass of milk?" she asked.

"I don't want to make a bother," he said.

"It's okay," Alice said. "I'll be right back."

"Hey," he said.

She turned.

He said, "Maybe you stay, huh?"

"Maybe," she said. "Sunday and the rain and all." She laughed. "Maybe you'd like to come downstairs. The work rooms're something you've got to see. I've got a bed shaped like a swan. And when I switch off the lights, stars twinkle in the ceiling."

"It's more better up here," he said. "Besides, I already been laid in a swan. In Amsterdam. The Dutch are big on swans."

When she returned he had stripped down and was brushing his teeth. "I'll drink the milk later," he said. "It doesn't mix good with the toothpaste." He beckoned to her. "Now come over here and let me touch you, because you're so beautiful, I swear to God you raise my blood just to look at you."

She approached him with professional cool, but when she felt the heat of him, felt him rising against her loins, she lifted her face, and, with a low lingering sigh, parted his lips with hers.

He started to take her gently, lovingly; she responded with intensity and made of the next twenty minutes a violent and savage ritual.

"Jesus," he said. "I thought the Chinese invented fireworks."

"Fireworks're my downfall," she said.

They were silent for a time.

"I didn't bring cigarettes," she said.

"I quit smoking," he said. "Sorry."

"I wish I could quit," she said. "When did you?"

"When they told me it could kill me, for Christ's sake," he said. "When." He lifted himself to one elbow and reached for the glass of milk. "You don't talk like these people," he said.

"I'm from Boston," Alice said.

"Alice from Boston," he said. "Unhappy Alice from Boston."

"I'm not," Alice said.

"I noticed," Joe Dev said. He sat on the edge of the bed and fondled her. "You're an educated person," he said.

"You notice everything, don't you?"

"You mix up your talk," he said. "Sometimes educated, sometimes low."

"You pick up other people's speech patterns," she said. "Mmmm, that feels good."

"You shouldn't hide your education," he said. "It's a sin. I never had many chances in my life."

"I've got a feeling you'll make out fine," Alice said.

He stretched out beside her. "How do you spend your time when you're not working?" he asked.

"Don't stop," she said. "My free time? Weather's nice, I walk. Shop. I go to the movies. I really let down in the movies. It's like, well, you know, dark, and quiet, and you release yourself from yourself."

"Maybe you'll do me a favor," Joe Dev said. "I like to know about this town. Maybe you'll get me newspapers that go back, a month, two months."

"No problem," Alice said.

"And you'll rent a car for me, huh?" he said. "Nothing flashy, a small car. Black. Across the street from here there's a tree—you know, on the empty lot?—the kind of tree that stretches down."

"You mean a willow?" she asked. "I never really noticed."

"It's there," Joe Dev said. "You park the car under that tree and you lock it and you give me the key."

"Anything else?" she asked.

"Maybe," he said. "By and by. Okay?"

"Harriet said Bick Anson's orders are that you're to get whatever you ask for."

"Sure," Joe Dev said, "but what you do for me it's personal and private, huh? Between us. Nobody has to know our business, correct?"

"Correct," Alice said.

"Fine," he said. "Now we shoot off more fireworks, and then you sleep. I'll put my arms around you and you sleep, and you don't be unhappy. Okay?"

"Okay," Alice said.

CHAPTER 4

Detective-Sergeant Wendell Cooney, a heavyweight whose dissipation materialized in the low belly, slid ungracefully out from behind the wheel of his Pontiac, removed a sodden cigar from his mouth and said, "Fill it up," to the gas station attendant. Then he moved heavily through the downpour to the station hut.

One arm raised to form a tent of his raincoat, the attendant unscrewed the cap of the gas tank and inserted the hose nozzle. He waited, facing the station. Through windows clouded with condensation, he could see his customer dialing a number on the pay phone. The tank filled, he replaced the cap and hopscotched rain puddles back to the station hut.

"Damn, sweetheart," Cooney was saying, "is it my fault? It's raining hammer handles or hadn't you noticed? Goddamn slow going . . . let's see . . . it's twelve-thirty . . . another hour at least. I'm still in Liberty Center." He balanced the cigar stump on the edge of the telephone box, and momentarily dividing his attention, dipped into his pocket for money to pay for the gas. He came up with a crumpled fifty-dollar bill. He held it out to the attendant. The attendant stared at it and made a face. Cooney said into the phone, "All right, all right, drive nails through my hands, okay?" He seemed unaware of the attendant's hesitation.

The attendant took the bill and crossed to a display of pyramided oil cans. He reached into the display for the can that held his hidden cash. He removed the lid.

Cooney stopped talking.

The attendant heard a *click*. He turned and stared at the cocked gun. He froze, can in one hand, lid in the other. "Goddamn," he said.

Cooney jerked the telephone wire free of the instrument. The cigar went back into his mouth. He reached into the can and clutched a handful of bills, his fifty included. "Move," he said. "It's the gun talking, boy." He gun-prodded the attendant out and around to one of the washrooms. He held up the money. "How much here?" he asked.

"About three hundred," the attendant said.

"You willing to die for it, boy?" Cooney asked.

The attendant shook his head.

"I dunno," Cooney said. "You look like a fucking hero to me." He forced the barrel of the gun into the attendant's half-opened mouth.

The attendant said something. It was "Please, no, mister," but the plea was unintelligible.

"Come to think of it," Cooney said, "you don't *sound* like a hero. You stay put, hear?"

The attendant gagged; the oily smell of the gun and the cold metal on his tongue caused his stomach to heave and warn that its contents were surfacing. Cooney withdrew the gun and stepped quickly back to avoid the ejection and to give the attendant room to turn to the wash basin.

Slowly, unhurriedly, Cooney lumbered back to his car, started the motor and dug out. An hour later he was pounding at Harriet Stocker's door.

"I told you the last time, you ain't welcome here," Harriet said. "You're not goan break up my place again."

Cooney stiff-armed the door and sent it crashing against the wall. "Don't fuck with me, Harriet," he said.

She trailed him into the living room, her posture defiant, the gleaming whites of her eyes betraying fear. Cooney shrugged out of his raincoat and tossed it contemptuously at her. She let it fall to the floor. He wore a short-sleeved sport shirt. It was darkened with perspiration around the shoulders and armpits. A waistband gun holster, handcuffs dangling from the band, encircled his overhanging belly. The grip of a blackjack jutted out of a back pocket.

"You don't go, I'm goan call Luke Bishop," Harriet said.

"Goddamn it," he said, "I'm not going to make trouble. Only one reason I'm here. Only one."

"Houses is for living in, not for breaking," Harriet said.

"I said I'd pay for the fucking damage, didn't I?" He dipped a hand into his pants pocket and came up with the fistful of bills. "Didn't I say that?" He threw the bills into her face. "Where's Helen?" he asked.

"Asleep," Harriet said, "and I ain't goan wake her up."

"Fucking right you ain't," Cooney said. "I'll do that myself. You get me a drink. Move your black ass. I said *move* it. Guy comes in here wet and with his balls all swole and you stand there looking like a busted sofa somebody put on the sidewalk for the trash man."

He drank a half-tumblerful of whiskey in one gulp. Fired by it, he clomped noisily up to the second floor and crashed into Helen's bedroom. "Hi, sweetheart," he said.

Helen sat up in bed and watched him turn the key in the door. She genuflected. "Mother of God," she said.

A few minutes later Harriet telephoned Luke Bishop. "He goan kill her," she said. She sucked in breath, turned and looked up the stairway as Helen shouted for help.

"Hell, he won't do anything like that," Luke Bishop said.

"He will, he will," Harriet moaned.

"You always take on more'n you should," Luke Bishop said. "Besides, you looking for me to come over there and heave him out? I do a thing like that, we'll have trouble and more trouble."

"I pays you good cash," Harriet said.

Helen screamed, in anger now. "You hit me again and I'll . . . Stop it, stop it, goddamn hillbilly, goddamn hillbilly trash."

Luke Bishop said, "I do a thing like that and he'll get back at us sure."

Harriet said, "Bick Anson say you take care of me and my property."

Helen yelled, "Bugger your sister. No hillbilly bastard's going to plug me."

Luke Bishop said, "We won't have no more chance'n a crow in the gutter, I do a thing like that."

Cooney bellowed, "You shut your cunt mouth. Don't you put my sister's name in your cunt mouth."

Helen screamed.

Harriet said, "Jesus, God."

Luke Bishop said, "I can't mess with Wendell Cooney. Whyn't you just let him screw himself dry?"

Luke Bishop hung up.

Joe Dev and Alice left their bed and went out to the third-floor landing. They remained there listening to, identifying, interpreting the sounds they heard: Cooney's fist against Helen's flesh, her shouts—alternately of anger and pain, like the whine and the roar of the storm winds outside—shattering glass, unintelligible word-filth excreting from Cooney's mouth, all against the pitiable rhythm of Harriet's fists pounding the locked door.

"The police come?" Joe Dev asked.

"He *is* the police," Alice said. "Motherfucking sonofabitch. I hope his asshole festers." She looked at him. "We ought to do something," she said.

Joe Dev turned and went back to the bedroom. Alice followed. He sat on the bed, hunched over, elbows resting on his naked thighs, and thoughtfully contemplated the floor.

"We ought to do something," Alice said.

Joe Dev remained silent.

"It's okay," Alice said. "I'm scared too. I don't want to go down there either. I know Cooney."

"Your mouth is prettier when it's closed," he said. "Keep it like that and let me think. I didn't say I would not go down there. I can't show myself to him, understand?"

Alice slammed the door shut against the sickening shouts. The volume lessened but not the horror. Presently a new sound was introduced. Harriet had gone to the kitchen for a meat cleaver and was hacking away at the door. Helen stopped calling to Harriet for help and was calling to God.

"If he heard a man's voice, maybe," Alice said.

Joe Dev said nothing. He stayed focused inwardly for some invaluable minutes. Then he sprang to his feet.

"Where is the electricity box?" he asked.

"What? I don't know," Alice said.

They went below to Harriet.

"It's in the pantry," Harriet said.

"Go throw the switch," Joe Dev instructed Alice. "The main one that puts out all the lights. Stay there and keep your hand on the switch until I say put the lights on again. You take your hand off the switch and you won't be able to find it again in the dark. Understand?"

Alice left.

Harriet kept hacking away at the door. "Git him out here," she said. "Git him out here and I'll chop his head up so small it'll squeeze into a pickle jar."

Joe Dev pointed to the far end of the landing. "There," he said. "And stay there, quiet."

She obeyed unquestioningly.

The lights went out.

"What the hell," Cooney said from behind the door. "Harriet, what's happened to the goddamn lights." He roared in pain; Helen had found his face with a blunt object. He stumbled around trying to find her and could not. Frustration mounting, he said, "Harriet! Goddamn nigger cunt." A response denied him, he blundered his way to the door and unlocked it. "Harriet," he shouted.

He must have sensed the peril before he felt the smooth hand on his naked arm. He struck out. His fist met nothing. The hand slid down his forearm to his wrist, it jerked him out of the doorway, tearing shoulder from socket. His cry protested the obscenity of the attack. He was about to seek the floor for comfort, but now someone was behind him. He felt something snap in his chest, and when he lifted his good arm—to defend himself, now, not to attack—the hand found his wrist, spun him about, released him. He cried out again, this time more like a hysterical woman than a wounded bear. His knees went tallowy. The last sound he heard was the crunching of his cheekbone when it hit the floor.

Helen was crying, "It's my punishment, it's my punishment. Let me die, please God, let me die, I've had enough."

CHAPTER **5**

With the passing of the storm the air became warm and still. Bick Anson stared out the window of his bedroom and scowled at a rosy dawn. He looked around for his robe, muttered an oath when he didn't find it and another when he did, knotted in the bedclothes. After brushing his teeth and swallowing diet pills, he padded across the deep-pile carpet to the hall and knocked on the door opposite his. "I'm putting the coffee on," he said. There was no answer. "Come on," he said irritably.

Nurturing the thoughts that had brought the scowl to his face, he went down to the kitchen and plugged in the electric coffeemaker readied by the cook the night before. He eased himself into one of the breakfast-nook chairs and opened a fresh pack of cigarettes. The scowl remained on his face. The coffeemaker began chugging almost immediately. He listened and scowled.

The phone rang, several times before he could get to it. "Yeah," he said into the instrument. He listened for almost three minutes, eyes darting covertly, but offering no comment. Then he said, "Appreciate it, thanks." He cradled the phone and returned to his chair.

The Indian entered. He was foggy with sleep. "Jesus," he said. All he had on was a pair of tight white pants.

"I'm going to change my room," Anson said. "Over to the other side of the house. You see that damn sun? Fucking sun's up at four-thirty these days. Who in hell's supposed to sleep with all that goddamn sun crashing in at that hour?"

"Ever consider pulling the drapes?" the Indian said.

"Nothing goes right," Anson said. "Nothing's any good if you don't sleep. Christ, you'd think I'd get used to it. I remember when I was a kid, reading about this guy who gets shot up in the war—the first war, I'm talking about—gets shot up and the bullet hits something in his head that causes him never to sleep again. Pictures of him in the Sunday section, bright-eyed and fat as a sheep's tail. Wearing a flower in his lapel. Doesn't lose weight and waste away like you'd expect, either. Absolutely normal except he can't sleep, and doesn't have to."

"Sounds like something somebody made up," the Indian said.

"You wouldn't believe a fart if you were downwind of it," Anson said. "For Christ's sake, I saw a picture of the guy and all. He prowls around all night long doing things, you know, working, reading, whatever. Never has to lay down or anything either. Went years without sleeping and he looked better than you and I do now."

"For me there's a reason," the Indian said. "These hours're killing me."

Anson said, "Aggh."

"Jesus, Bick," the Indian said. "What good's it I'm here sitting across the table? You talk, talk, talk at me, but I'm dead for sleep, I don't hear you."

"*You're* dead for sleep," Anson said. "I heard you snoring, you sonofabitch. It's all I had to listen to all night, you and your snoring and the water heater going on and off, and the refrigerator. I didn't shut my eyes, not for one fucking minute. *You're* dead for sleep."

"All right, all right, all right," the Indian said. "But look, Bick, I can't keep doing it. Lydia, she's always on me for not hitting home base. I mean, if you want to be fair and consider her side of it, Jesus, staying up with you till all hours and sleeping over and all. I tell her it's because you're an insomniac, she gives me that look. 'I'm not here just to slop the hogs,' she says."

"You don't know what it's like," Anson said. "You keep punching pockets in your pillow and starting all over again, and something in your brain says, 'The hell with you, buddy, suffer.' "

"Take a pill," the Indian said.

"I'm not going to start that," Anson said.

"A woman, then," the Indian said.

"I want to sleep, not screw," Anson said.

"Get one that's a good talker and talk," the Indian said. "I know just the one."

"Look, let's just drop the goddamn subject," Anson said. "Okay? Okay?"

"Well, don't get raspy," the Indian said.

"I said let's drop it," Anson said.

"Okay," the Indian said. "I'll just sit here. Even though I'm useless."

"Don't be useless," Anson said. "Fry me a few eggs."

"Beautiful," the Indian said. "A cook in the house, drawing good cash, and I'm up at dawn frying eggs."

"I don't like the way she fries them," Anson said. "She burns them around the edges."

"Dust her ass and get one that doesn't," the Indian said. "Jesus." He sighed wearily and went to the refrigerator for a slab of bacon. He set it on the cutting board and cut thick slices from it. "I hear the phone?" he asked.

"It was Little Neffie," Anson said. "He said Stacy's on his way here."

"Get ready for some hundred-proof Kentucky bullshit," the Indian said.

Anson said, "Little Neffie says Stacy and Wendell Cooney're holding hands."

The Indian stopped in the middle of a cut, and said, "What?"

"They've got somebody tailing Cugarman, in Chicago," Anson said. "Another thing. That trip to New Orleans Stacy took last week? It wasn't New Orleans, it was L.A. He had meetings with Hagerson and Consentino."

"I don't know Hagerson. He an importer too?"

"Better'n half of it, on that end. He's going to supply Cooney and Stacy."

"You're sure about this?" the Indian asked.

"You know Little Neffie. Thorough. Been watching Stacy for two months."

"How come?" the Indian asked.

"Routine," Anson said. "Everybody takes turns being watched."

"Me too?" the Indian asked.

"Did I say everybody?"

The Indian completed the cut. "Crazy bastards. Only reason we're doing good here is that you can't buy that shit. Probably figure on those kids in the black district peddling it. Once that starts, the rest'll start, too. Mugging, rape, burglaries, killings. You're sure about this, Bick? Sounds wild. I mean, Cooney's a psycho, you can expect anything from him. But Stacy, he's, I dunno, Bick. Jesus, he's too goddamn smart to think he could get away with that kind of thing. Right under our noses?"

"Forget your nose," Anson said. "You get a bullet up your ass it'll be with his compliments."

"Wait a minute," the Indian said. "You talking about a takeover, complete?"

Anson nodded. "You and me and any of us they know wouldn't go along with them."

"Christ," the Indian said. "Stacy. Ambitions. I thought all he cared about was pussy. His headwaiter says he has a girl come around every two hours."

"He won't die from that," Anson said.

"Oh, he'll die," the Indian said. "Don't worry about that. He's as good as dead this minute."

The red light on the coffeemaker lit up. Anson poured a cup. "Even the coffee doesn't taste right this morning," he said. "Nothing's any good if you don't sleep. I swear, if I knew what happened to that guy in the war, what the bullet did to him, I mean, I'd ask the doctors to do the same to me. A flower in his lapel. Imagine. I'm in shape for a fucking wreath."

"You'll feel better as the day wears on," the Indian said. "You always do."

"You put your mind to this Stacy thing, hear?" Anson said.

"Fast," the Indian said. "I'll take care of both of them."

"Take your time and do it good," Anson said. "Stacy, he's no big problem. Cooney, though, he'll take some fancy figuring. Cops get to thinking we take them out whenever we damned please, they're not gonna like it. They feel safe dealing with us, now. So don't fuck up. No cop killing."

"Won't look like a cop killing, I promise you," the Indian said.

"It's got to be good enough for Chief Yoder to take. You put your mind to it, but let me know what before you do anything, hear?"

"I was figuring on that anyway, Bick," the Indian said. He turned squarely to him. "Christ Almighty, you know that."

Anson grunted.

The Indian arranged bacon slices on the griddle. "Okay," he said, "let's go to the top of this heap of shit. They've got somebody tailing Cugarman. Reason for that's obvious. The securities. You expect him and Cooney know about this wop being here?"

Anson shrugged. "Couldn't say."

"I had a nightmare," the Indian said. "I strangled to death in a swimming pool full of spaghetti."

Anson remained silent.

"I don't like him, Bick," the Indian said.

"Don't like or don't trust?" Anson asked. "The first, nobody gives a shit who you like or don't like. Second, what's to trust? His friends guarantee him. He makes off with our goods, they'll waste him. He knows that."

"He's all sparkle," the Indian said. "More mouth'n anything else."

"Know anybody who could do what we've asked him to do?" Anson asked.

"You don't know that he can," the Indian said.

"I'll lay eight to five he does," Anson said. "He's the type guy, you hatch him in the right place and he grows up to be chairman of the board. Grow him in the gutter, force him to live by his instincts, and you've got an animal with chairman-of-the-board brains. Pretty good combination. Come to think of it, I'll make it nine to five."

"Maybe that's what bothers me about him," the Indian said. "A guy doesn't like what's happening to him and he decides to fight the system, that's okay, that's natural. He fights the system and he makes out or maybe he mudfoots it. This wop, I mean, Bick, Jesus, does a guy train to be a thief? Study? And like take a fucking postgraduate course in lip reading? He's unnatural, that's what bothers me."

"You're sure talking a streak this morning," Anson said. "Remember I like my bacon limp."

"We don't need him," the Indian said. "It's a simple job and we're complicating it. Know what he brought in his suitcase?"

"That Stocker woman snooping for you?" Anson asked.

"So he'll tap Cugarman's phone. Pignuts. We could've done that a long time ago," the Indian said.

"Why didn't we?" Anson asked.

"For Christ's sake, is Cugarman going to tell somebody

over the phone where those securities are hidden? Let's talk sense."

"Talk it," Anson said.

"Like I said, it's simple. Sooner or later Cugarman's got to move that paper, especially if he's making a deal now, in Chicago. We watch him. We watch his place. When he moves it, we step in and say 'Gimme.' Don't you see how beautiful that is?"

"Brilliant," Anson said. "You redskins've really got savvy."

"Well, if that's the way you're going to be," the Indian said. "What's wrong with doing it my way?"

"Everything," Anson said. "You don't plant a field when the government's willing to pay for a cover crop. Cugarman ever got the notion he was being watched, he'd get an armored truck and fifty guards." He shook his head. "I dunno. You make this Dev guy sound better all the time. Trouble is, you wasted your time playing baseball when you were a kid. Your first arrest—what?—a stickup. Twenty bucks from a milkman. Dev was probably screwing the dairy owner's wife and getting paid for it."

"Okay," the Indian said. "He's Superman."

"By God, for a minute there, you sounded almost mad," Anson said. "You losing your redskin cool, Iron Face? You know how this guy learned to read lips? Listening to guys like you telling him how great you are. Only he discovers that compared to him you're a fucking idiot, so he turns off the sound."

"You're in a great mood this morning," the Indian said.

"Goddammit, I didn't sleep," Anson said. "Do I have to tell you in Algonkian?"

The Indian remained silent. He flattened the bacon with a spatula and turned it over.

They heard the crunch of automobile tires on the loose gravel of the driveway. Anson wrenched his body around and peered past the window screen behind him. "It's him," he said.

Stacy, thirty-five and handsome, favored striped suits and string ties. His suit was wrinkled and he needed a shave. He said good morning and made straight for the coffeemaker. "Hot," he said. "Good. What a rain last night, hey? You believe it I'm chilled? And in this heat? Only living thing's had its ass in water more'n me lately is a mallard." He joined Anson at the table. "Been ramshacking around this town the better part of the night. Never made it to my bed."

"Screw every last one of them, did you?" Anson said.

Stacy smiled. "Trouble, massuh, trouble. You know Jory Brewster? State trooper, one of Finch's boys. Coming south on 205 last night and he spots a stalled car on the side of the road. Hazard lights flashing. Speculates it's some poor bastard broke down with wet wires or something." He added sugar to the coffee. "What he finds is Wendell Cooney. On the back seat. Naked's a possum tit. Clothes all wrapped up in a bundle on the front seat. Gun and holster, too, blackjack and that stuff." He divided the sentences between Anson and the Indian. "Isn't dead, though. Appeared to be, until the ambulance. Now you lean over and listen, man. That mean sonofabitch—and don't you go asking the obvious because I don't have the answer— turns out that mean sonofabitch's got a busted arm and a chopped collarbone. Like to mangled."

"You brighten my morning," Anson said. "Whoever did it, I'm sorry they didn't shove a canal pole up his ass."

"Let me finish," Stacy said. "You going to let me finish? I go to the hospital. You ought to see. Cooney's a-setting there, in bed, with one arm in a cast and the other wired, and he's holding it up like this, like he's saluting and saying hello, you know? Gonna walk funny for a while, too. You ought to see. He's got a look on his face couldn't scare you more if he were toting a scatter gun.

"Isn't talking. Isn't saying a word, not to anybody. Just sets there with that look. I nears up to him and says, 'Wendell boy, what happened, Wendell boy? Want to tell old Stace about it?' Nothing. Turns those raisin eyes on me so mean I couldn't help backing off, even with him all mutilated and helpless."

"What happened?" Anson asked.

"I don't think but Wendell Cooney can tell you that, and the people did it. Logical to say 'people,' isn't it? Knock him out, carry him to the car, naked, and make off? One man going to violate Wendell Cooney like that? No way, no day. Maybe

Harriet Stocker can answer your question, just maybe, couldn't tell you." He sipped the coffee. It was hot and it burned his tongue. He made a face.

"Will you get the fuck on with it?" Anson said. "What's Harriet Stocker got to do with this?"

Stacy crossed to the refrigerator. He poured milk into the coffee cup. "If you'll allow me to tell it my own way, you'll get a better hold on the whole story.

"I saw Cooney early on, last night. He was in the Room. Drank up his money for an hour or two, and then takes to gaming. Drops fifteen hundred at the dice table. I remind him nice-style that that's his credit limit. He gives me a little trouble, usual thing, you know, borrows a fifty and grumbles off. I know where he was headed, too. Never been a cat like Wendell Cooney for whore hopping. Sonofabitch's got a rag on every bush."

"Some guys are like that," the Indian said.

Stacy seemed not to hear. "But all of a sudden," he went on, "two, three months ago, he takes uncommon liking to one in particular, one of Harriet Stocker's gals. From Cincinnati, peaches-and-cream number been vacillating twixt the whorehouse and a nunnery ever since she started to take growth. Wendell's got more'n a hard-on for this gal. Screwing won't do it for him, he got to beat the fuzz off her skin. Awful things. Spread shit on her if he had it handy. So I'm not surprised when Luke Bishop calls me, two in the morning or thereabouts. Seems the Stocker woman's drawers are running brown because Cooney's there and having at this gal again, and she expects him to do something about stopping it. He passes it on to me and asks what I want him to do about it. Well, I slither away from that one, even though it put me to the blush. Got your interests to think of, Bick, ours. Cooney keeps the whole detective squad in line, got the balls for it. Hard man to replace. It's a good business situation and I wasn't about to stir him up."

"Who bobtailed the bastard?" Anson asked.

"I can tell you what I saw, what I did and what I heard, period," Stacy said. "After I checked out Cooney, I got my ass over to Harriet Stocker's. Doc Selkir's there, patching up the gal.

My God, you ought to see. Blood all over the room, teeth on the floor like somebody's been kerneling corn, gal's face is the color of the Legion flag, rib snapped and God knows what-all on her insides."

"A canal pole," Anson said.

Stacy said, "I nears up to Harriet and asks her who coldcocked Cooney. Got to be that. You just don't walk up to the man, you know? Not Cooney. But Harriet's not talking, either. 'What'd Sergeant Cooney say happened?' she asks. Answers me with a question. So there you are. Who *did* coldcock the bastard? Wasn't Harriet or one of the gals, that's certain. Got to be another hog in that wallow—a man—or men. Question is who."

Anson and the Indian exchanged a look.

"That it?" Anson said to Stacy.

"Complete," Stacy said.

Anson scowled for a moment. "First," he said, "you enjoy your work and the money you make doing it?"

"Beats cotton," Stacy said.

"Then you'd fucking well better *do* your work," Anson said.

"You referring to this Cooney thing," Stacy said, "I made a judgment."

"You make a judgment or twitch your asshole it's the same to me, except one doesn't do me damage," Anson said.

The Indian intervened. "Hell, Bick, what'd you expect Stace to do? The way I see it, he exercised good judgment."

"You just keep frying the goddamn bacon and listen, hear?" Anson said. "It's a tossup which one of you is the biggest shit-for-brains."

The atmosphere fouled with Anson's anger, they remained silent and listened to the bacon sizzling.

The Indian said, "I'd've done the same thing Stacy did."

Anson looked at the Indian, and then he turned to Stacy. "I'm sorry," he said. "Had one of those nights."

"Sure, Bick," Stacy said.

"Thing is," Anson said, "I depend on you, Stace. You, me, the Indian, it's the three of us, right? No number one, no number two or three. It's the three of us together."

"Appreciate that, Bick," Stacy said.

"Thing like that happens again, you call Chief Yoder," Anson said. "Cooney's his problem, not ours. Yoder's taking, we're handing it out. He can't keep Cooney gentle, he's not earning the money. Now, I want you to make things right with the Stocker woman before word gets around we don't take care of our people."

"I'll do that, Bick," Stacy said.

"And that girl took the walloping," Anson said. "Her too. And be generous."

"Damn if that isn't like you, Bick," Stacy said.

The Indian said, "Stay to breakfast, Stace. How many eggs'll you have?"

He fried a dozen, served six to Anson and divided the remainder between Stacy and himself. They ate wordlessly. Stacy and the Indian knife-and-forked bacon and eggs into tiny pieces and shoveled mass to mouth with a fork. Anson carefully trimmed off and ate the whites of the eggs, leaving six small suns on his plate. These he consumed in six bites.

When Stacy had gone, the Indian poured hot coffee. "You hear him—hinting, asking, talking about another hog in the wallow? Bastard. Testing us, looking to see what we'd say about the wop being there."

Anson remained silent.

"May work out just fine," the Indian said. "Taking Cooney out, I mean."

"You put your mind to it, hear?" Anson said.

The Indian nodded.

CHAPTER **6**

He proposed to go ready, as always. At dawn, amid the gradual crescendo of birdsong, he dressed and padded quietly out of the house. He drove southward on the expressway in the car Alice had rented for him, a Dodge Dart. He wore denim shirt over jeans, the bottoms of the jeans stuffed into work boots.

He arrived in Indianapolis in time to be absorbed into the

morning traffic. A man-made haze imprisoned a hateful humidity below and made the motorist, and consequently the traffic, peevish. He drove slowly, choosing his course with deliberate randomness. When he had familiarized himself with the pattern of the main arteries and off-streets, he swung west on Raymond and headed for the airport.

At the airport he sought out a stand-up lunch counter. A waitress asked, "Coffee?" and added to the question a glance charged with animal interest. Joe Dev nodded and said nothing. He spoke to no one, looked at no one. The coffee only half finished and aware of the waitress's lingering interest, he left.

He studied flight-departure schedules. When done, he had recorded in a little book an escape chart from Indianapolis to Chicago, Newark and St. Louis for all hours of the day. By midday he was northbound again. He circled the Cugarman estate twice at half-hour intervals, decelerating slightly when he drove past the main gate to note all in his field of vision. Convinced that the place was not susceptible to forced entry, he returned to Harriet Stocker's and spent the afternoon poring over back copies of the *Uniontown Call-Bulletin.* Shortly before dinner a messenger delivered the pole-climbing equipment and the telephone-line record map he'd asked for.

Ten o'clock that evening he headed southward again. Approaching Back Trail Road, he turned, slowed and began counting off the telephone poles silhouetted against the moonlit sky. The details of the line record map were securely deposited in his memory bank. A congruent figure indicated the central telephone office and a thin line emanating from it marked the route of the main cable. The cable originated from the distributing frame. A variety of symbols established the size of the cables, the placement of conductors and the poles to which were attached the terminal boxes. Pole 101 was the twenty-first on the left.

He ran the car deep into shrubbery and switched off motor and lights. He opened the trunk and reached in for a body belt from which dangled an assortment of tools, then a safety strap and a set of gaffs. He secured belt and strap around his waist, the gaffs to his boots.

A length of wire ringing his shoulder, he crossed the road to

pole 101. The equipment made chinking noises. Digging the
gaffs into the pole, he climbed until the terminal box was at eye
level. He embraced the pole, locked the safety belt, leaned back
and, pencil flashlight between his teeth, attached the wire to the
terminal box. On the way down he stapled the wire to the pole,
keeping it taut and vertical.

He returned to the car for a tape recorder. It was carefully
wrapped in plastic sheeting. A wire protruded from it. He mated
the wire with the one originating from the terminal box. He
placed the tape recorder among roadside weeds. He left. Start to
finish, the work took exactly fourteen minutes.

He returned the equipment to the car trunk, then drove to
the rear of the estate. He counted off telephone poles until he
found number 213. At the base of the estate wall, directly
beyond the pole, he dug a hole and buried in it a small
aluminum suitcase.

It was past midnight when he arrived back at Harriet's.
Someone had left the pantry door open and he could see
through the kitchen to the living room. Alice was sway-dancing
with a man, his face buried in her neck, his hands cupping her
rounded bottoms. Head music made a din, but Alice and the
man were oblivious to it, they just held on to each other and
swayed.

He climbed the narrow stairs to his room but did not enter.
On one knee, he looked for the black cotton string he had strung
at ankle length across the doorframe. The string was broken.

He knocked softly on Helen's door, then inched it open.
Through the slit he saw her turning in the ridiculous swan-
shaped bed. Swelling had put a fat woman's face on her slender
body. He went in.

"How do you feel?" he asked.

She answered that she hurt all over. "Inside and out. My
bones, my flesh, even my mind aches, Joe. Oh, dear God, Joe. I
wish I could die."

"Hey," he said.

"Die or save myself," she said. "No third answer. Die or
save myself. I called the priest. I asked him to come and hear my
confession. He said no, I'd have to go there, to the church. You
ever hear of anything like that? He wouldn't come."

Joe Dev shrugged. "What's a priest? A stranger."

"He's supposed to come," Helen said. "No matter what, you call them and they come. I read once how one of them went down into a sewer because a workman was hurt and dying. A goddamn sewer, Joe. No matter what, you call and they come. First he said yes-yes, and then when I told him where, he started up with the no-no, like coming here'd put strawberry marks on his belly or something."

She moaned. Clutching his forearm for leverage, she gingerly shifted position. He brushed the hair from her face and applied a fresh compress to her forehead.

"You have good hands, Joe," she said. "You should've been a doctor. Or a healer. You got them kind of hands." Despair routed the wan smile from her face. "That priest. Prick. He could've come. He's supposed to. It's the whole goddamn reason he's a priest."

"You know him?" Joe Dev asked.

She shook her head. "I've never been to church since I came here, more'n a year ago, a year and a month, now. I never even done my Easter duty. I don't know him."

"He knows you, maybe," Joe Dev said.

"What?"

"Listen," Joe Dev said, "even a priest gotta get laid."

"Jesus," Helen said.

"Figure it," Joe Dev said. "First yes-yes, then no. Why? Because you tell him where you are."

"You mean he's been here?" Helen said.

"I don't say for sure," Joe Dev said. "Maybe. It's not a big town."

"Jesus," Helen said. "Without the collar, huh? Is that what you mean, he's been here without the collar? Sure. He's been here without the collar and he's scared to come back with it on because somebody might recognize him. Yeah. You've got a lot of shrewd, Joe. Wouldn't that be something, huh? I mean, if I balled the guy and then I ask him to come hear my confession. The prick could've been sporting right here in this bed."

"Who knows?" Joe Dev said.

"Mother of God," Helen said. "What a rotten world, what a

rotten world. He's supposed to intercede for me. That's really something, huh? Intercede my ass."

"Goddamn sketch," Joe Dev said.

"You know what, Joe," she said. "I haven't been around too long—only twenty-three years. But I learned a lot. I learned what it's all about. Life is a pile of horseshit, and everybody's scrambling over the pile hoping to find a pony."

She freed tears. "I gotta save myself, Joe. Find a way to make it right. I've got to make a fresh start and stay with it or I'll wind up in hell, sure. Cooney. Wendell Cooney. You know why he beats up on me? It's because I'm bad. He's said things to me, nice things, you know? About love. But I never pay attention to what they say, these johns. Christ, they come in here, who pays attention? It's like a thousand voices in the bus depot and on top of that there's a voice on the loudspeaker you can't even understand. But I remember, now, him, Cooney, saying nice things to me, and then, all of a sudden, pow, it's like somebody poured hot grease on him and he lets out a yell and starts cursing and hitting and trying to do dirty things to me."

"Hey, come on," Joe Dev said. "You think crying's gonna save you?"

"You're right, Joe," she said.

"Hey, look," Joe Dev said. "Somebody goes to my room and they snoop around my things. I got signs to know, understand? Personal and private between us, you maybe listen and watch, huh? And you find out who it is."

"Sure, Joe, anything," Helen said. "For Christ's sake, anything. Who do you think it is?"

"Who come up with the idea to bring me here?" Joe Dev said. "The Indian. Why? Because somebody in this house, both of them, them and the Indian, they wash each other's back. You know? Harriet, maybe. Julia, Alice. One of them's got me in their eyes. One of them for sure."

"What about me?" Helen asked.

"Not you," he said. "Somebody went up there tonight, while I was out. You couldn't make those stairs. You haven't got the legs."

"Honest, Joe," Helen said, "the way you figure things out, it's like you go right inside people's heads."

"You don't get along in this world if you don't learn how to
do that," Joe Dev said. "Because everybody is a bastard and a
sonofabitch and they're looking to get you before you get them.
Everybody's got a gun on you. From the top to the bottom,
they're all the same. You got to walk around with your fucking
hands in the air every minute. If you don't go inside their heads,
I swear to God, Helen, you got nothing but danger, I mean it. A
long time ago, I learned that."

He said, "My grandfather was the stingiest sonofabitch ever
walked the face of the earth. Boy oh boy, he was the king, the
emperor of the family, and you better treat him with every
respect. When he walked in our house everybody stands with
two feet in one shoe, that's the kind of respect he got. Okay. One
night it's Christmas Eve, and the cocksucker shows up with a
bottle of wine. This is his gift to my family. The way he carries it,
so gentle, so careful, you think maybe he's bringing a liter of
Saint Peter's piss. And what is it? The fucking new wine he made
in October. Nine people in the family and he walks in with one
lousy liter of wine. And that ain't enough, either. Before he
finishes his visit, he drinks half a bottle of our anisette. Then he
says 'Buon Natale' and me and my brothers and sisters we kiss
his hand, because that's the way we learned to do for respect,
and he goes."

Joe Dev shook his head. "Jesus, that pissed me off. It's like I
gotta do something to get even, you know? So what do I do? I go
inside the old fart's head. Stingy people, you know, they're not
stingy because they want to hold on to their stuff, it's like they
got power, that's what makes them like that. Okay. He likes to
be king, right? I fix the sonofabitch. I give him time to get home,
and then I run over there screaming and hollering blue murder. I
beg him to protect me because my father's going to kill me."

Helen laughed. "What the hell, Joe?"

Joe Dev was laughing too. "Listen, listen. I run and hide
under the bed and I won't come out for nothing. 'No, no, no,'
I'm yelling, 'my father finds me it's the last day of my life.' 'I'll
protect you,' the old bastard says. 'No, no,' I say, 'even an
emperor can't protect me, my father's so mad.' Well, finally I let
him coax me out, and by this time I got tears the size of chick
peas. He asks me what's the matter, and I tell him that I dropped

the bottle of wine he gave us, and it broke, and I'll never be able to go home again because my father's looking for me, and if he finds me, watch out, because it wasn't any old bottle of wine, it was *his* wine, a gift from the emperor."

"I get it, Joe," Helen said. "He gave you another bottle of wine and you took it home."

"Took it home, shit. I sold it."

Laughter brought pain to her sore flesh. "No more, Joe, please, it hurts."

"Better than crying," he said.

"Give me a hand up, huh?" she asked. "I gotta tinkle."

He helped her to her feet and led her to the bathroom. When she returned she said, "Talking to a friend's just as good as a priest."

"Sure," he said.

She said, "You know what bothers me most? The money. Almost nine hundred dollars. My mother—God, it feels like my heart's in a plastic baggie every time I think of it—like suffocating, you know? My mother saved it to start a grooming parlor for dogs. We always had dogs around the house, like twenty or more, sometimes. They were in and out, in the backyard, all over. The place smelled like I don't know what, every inch, you couldn't get away from it, no matter where you went. You walked from one room to another and you crunched dog biscuits under your feet."

He helped her back into bed.

"For my mother," Helen said, "raising a good show dog was like winning the lottery, only she never, couldn't make it. The next best thing was a grooming parlor. She tried to like me, I know, it wasn't that she didn't. It was the dogs, that's all. The dogs were her future, see? Understand? She never had to worry about me. Because ever since I could remember, I don't know who decided what or how, I was supposed to take holy orders. Me, I'm thirteen years old and I'm tickling myself under the covers at night and I'm crazy to find out about boys and I got this nun thing hanging over me. Come the right time, that's it, I go behind the walls, bride of Jesus.

"I don't know why, Joe," she went on. "The dogs, the smell, the being afraid of taking orders, my mother . . . when I was sixteen I stole the money and ran off. Now, what I'm getting now, it's my punishment."

"Aggh," Joe Dev said. "You believe that crap? Everybody got what was coming to them, you know what would happen? Boy."

"It's my punishment, Joe," she said.

"You better get some sleep," he said. "It's late."

She said, "Joe, listen. Maybe you oughta ask Harriet to call Doc Selkir."

He said, "Hurting bad?"

She said, "Something's awful wrong with me. With my insides."

<h2 style="text-align:center">CHAPTER 7</h2>

"Cugarman residence." A girl's voice.

"Mrs. Crawford, please." A basso.

"One moment, please."

A pause, then the girl again: "Mrs. Crawford says who's calling?"

"Mr. Bogen. I'd like to send some girls around for her to interview."

A pause.

"Mr. Bogen?"

"Yes?"

"Mrs. Crawford says she'll come there. Tomorrow afternoon. Two o'clock. Okay?"

"Very well, yes, thank you."

Click.

Click.

Anticipation placed Joe Dev at the intersection of Back Trail Road and the highway. At one thirty-five a strip of chrome spangled out behind him like a mirror in sunlight. The limousine turned from the Cugarman driveway into the road. Joe Dev started his motor and front-tailed it to the expressway. There he allowed it to overtake him. As it zoomed imperiously past the Dart, Joe Dev caught a glimpse of an elderly woman seated beside Teague, who was in chauffeur's uniform. Joe Dev noticed that the woman wore a fussy gray outfit of watered silk and that her face, pockmarked and generously lined, resembled starched lace yellowed with age. She stared steadily and concentratedly ahead as though a strong will—suggested by her angular features and compressed lips—lent necessary assistance to the vehicle's horsepower.

The limousine's destination was a two-story brick building on a deteriorating commercial street in Indianapolis. Teague scrambled out from behind the wheel and jack-rabbited around to curbside to open the door for his passenger. She entered the building. Joe Dev parked the car and followed her up a flight of stairs to the office of CUSTER'S EMPLOYMENT AGENCY–THE BEST IN DOMESTICS. She preceded Joe into a smoky room littered with forlorn job seekers and vintage dirt. One corner of the room, boxed off by a hip-high partition, separated the man in charge.

The man's stony expression softened when the woman in watered silk entered. He leaped to his feet and came forward. "Ah, Mrs. Crawford, come in, won't you?" To Joe Dev, he said, "Take a seat."

Joe Dev remained standing until Mrs. Crawford settled in a chair to the right of the man's desk, then positioned himself so he could see both of them.

"I regret that you had to make this trip, Mrs. Crawford," the man said. "No problem sending people out to you, you know."

"Mr. Cugarman doesn't like strangers traipsin' in and out," Mrs. Crawford said. "Got a likely prospect, have you?"

"Two of them," the man said. "Waiting."

"References?" Mrs. Crawford asked.

The man nodded. "The best. Been living in, both of them. Nice families, good homes."

"Young?"

The man nodded again.

"And white, of course," Mrs. Crawford said.

The man shook his head. "Black," he said.

"Won't do," Mrs. Crawford said.

"I beg your pardon?" the man said.

"Reckon you heard me," Mrs. Crawford said. "Blacks

won't do. Mr. Cugarman doesn't want blacks around the place. Young, white and pretty is what he wants. I thought I told you that. I'm sure I did."

"I don't believe so," the man said.

"Think I did," Mrs. Crawford said. "But no matter. Mr. Cugarman won't have 'em."

"Mrs. Crawford—" the man began.

"Young, white and pretty," Mrs. Crawford said. "Mr. Cugarman needs somebody young, white and pretty to do the serving, somebody who won't go spilling and breaking things."

"Mrs. Crawford—" the man said.

"I wouldn't come all this way to look at some nigger," Mrs. Crawford said. "I'm sure I told you that."

"Experienced waitress—" the man began.

"Don't go telling me there aren't any around," Mrs. Crawford said. "Young, white and pretty ones. Don't go telling me. 'Cause I won't believe it."

"Experienced waitresses won't accept live-in jobs," the man said. "They do much better in restaurants and cocktail bars, some make as much as two hundred a week."

"Wouldn't pay that," Mrs. Crawford said. "Not near that. Nobody but cook gets near that."

"I suggest that you engage—" the man began.

"Young, white and pretty," Mrs. Crawford said.

"—a maid and train her to serve," the man finished. "Now any one of these two girls—"

"Young, white and pretty," Mrs. Crawford said. "I'm sure I told you that in the first place. You didn't pay me no mind then and you're not paying me any mind now. Young, white and pretty. Don't tell me there isn't a decent girl around who wants a decent home. You find her."

"I can't promise to—" the man began.

"And don't go trying to push niggers into my house," Mrs. Crawford said. "I won't allow it. Mr. Cugarman's sensitive about things like that. Nobody's going to push—"

A man with a cigarette clipped between two fingers stepped into Joe Dev's line of sight and asked for a light.

Joe Dev shook his head.

He went out.

CHAPTER 8

"Cugarman residence." It was a man's voice.

"Hello, could I talk to Mr. Teague?" A woman. The accent suggested she came from southwestern Indiana.

A pause.

"Yeah, this is Teague."

"Hah're you doing?" the woman asked.

"I ain't died a winter yet," Teague said. He sounded belligerent.

"Tonight's fy-un with me," the woman said. "Eight o'clock?"

"Well, well, well," Teague said.

"Y'sound funny," the woman said.

"S'at right?" Teague said.

"Something wrong, honey?" the woman asked.

"Look," Teague said, "you ain't ordering up a pound of liver meat, you know. Calling me up any goddamn time you please."

"Honey, I just wish you wouldn't," the woman said. "Honest. I cain't help it. I cain't always get in the clear."

"Yeah, I know," Teague said. "It's a long line."

"Honey, honest, don't," the woman said.

"I'll see if I can make it," Teague said.

Slam.

Click.

Joe Dev followed Teague from the Cugarman house to the Holiday Inn, just outside Wabash. Teague arrived there at a quarter past eight in an oversized black limousine. He parked it, a beetle among ants, and entered the lounge. He joined a woman who was about twenty-five and pretty, the prettiness abused by a too-flamboyant hairdo and eye makeup. The fingers of her two hands embraced a ginger ale highball.

A hostess glowing with implausible enthusiasm appeared and started toward Joe Dev. He avoided the encounter and sought a place at the bar which would put Teague and the woman in his sight line. The bartender approached. Joe Dev muttered, "Beer."

A waitress stepped up to Teague's table, took an order and left. Teague lit up a cigar. He twirled it between his lips like a pacifier.

Joe Dev saw the woman say, "Like what?"

"Some stuff in the attic," Teague said. "Place is jam-packed. You could open an antique shop. There was this clock. I called"—Joe Dev couldn't make out the name; it ended with an "e" sound—"and described it to him. Said it could be a Simon-something clock and I should check to see what kind of ornament's sticking out of the top. An eagle and he'll give me a hundred, an acorn he'll go maybe a hundred and a half."

"What is it?" the woman asked.

"What the hell else?" Teague said. "A goddamn eagle. My goddamn bad luck. All's I got to do is get out of bed in the morning and there it is, waiting to have coffee with me."

The woman said something as she lifted the glass to her lips.

Teague said, "In the trunk. I'll drop it off at 'e's' in the morning."

The woman said, "Kitty isn't growing too fast, hon."

Teague said, "I got a case of booze, too. Some canned goods, linens, couple of snow tires. Comes winter I'll order another pair. He'll never know the difference. I gotta stop with the linens, though. The old lady's startin' to wonder. Turn pure ferocious if she caught me."

"No sign of the cash," the woman said.

Teague shook his head. "No, but I ran into John Wayne. Sonofabitch."

"What?" the woman said. "Who?"

"Cugarman," Teague said.

"What do you mean, you ran into John Wayne?" the woman asked.

"Forget it," he said.

"Honestly," she said. "Why do you do that?"

"What'd I do?" Teague said.

"You *say* things," she said. "And then you say it's *nothing* and to *forget* it. What'd you *mean*, you ran into John Wayne?"

"Forget it," he said.

She sighed. "Hon, maybe it just ain't there," she said.

"I'm telling you I watched from the sidewalk outside the bank," Teague said. "I stood there and watched. They was two stacks, with bands on them, better'n an inch thick. They put them in an envelope for him."

"Maybe he took the envelope with him when he left," the woman said.

"No way," Teague said. "When I drove him to the airport I rubbed him down—when he got in the car and when he got out. He didn't have it on him and he wasn't carrying no briefcase or anything. It's gotta be in the house, a safe, a strongbox, something. I've been over every goddamn inch of the place."

The woman said, "We're wasting here, that's what. Wasting. Now, I've been talking to my friend again—the one in Columbus? She says her husband's taking on real bad, sousin' before breakfast even, and getting up in the night for it. She cain't run the store alone. If we gave her a down payment—"

He silenced her with a sneer. "I already done time in prison," he said. "I ain't about to serve another stretch slicing Swiss cheese in some goddamn delicatessen."

"You always look to make something sound bad," she said. "It's a grocery. And they make out real good."

"I'm staying right here until I hit it good," he said. "Meantime, I ain't doing too bad."

"Not too bay-ud?" she asked. "You'll be down to the brass doorknobs soon. You call that not too bad?"

Anger glowed neon-pink in his face. "Paddan me, but let's just get one thing straight. You're the one's always looking to be loved up. You're the one always comes prowling. Me, I got a wide field. If you want to do without, that's okay with me. Get somebody else to lay his weight into you."

"Honey, I just wish—"

"I ain't the first you throwed yourself down for, so don't go making out like I'm supposed to figure on no life contract. Onliest reason you're hanging in there is I got what fits you real good, you not being so goddamn tight-tailed no more."

"Honey, you're being just awful," she said. "Just *aw*ful. I'm gonna shut my ears to that kind of talk."

"Aw, drink your goddamn drink," he said. He pacified

himself with the cigar. The waitress returned with his drink—a straight shot with beer chaser. The waitress left. Teague downed the whiskey.

The woman said, "You know I wouldn't split."

"That's up to you," Teague said. "Just so's you make up your mind one way or the other and stop kickin' at my hucklebones."

The woman was silent for a time, then she said, "If you do find the safe, d'you think you can get into it?"

"Did George get into Martha?"

Joe Dev watched the woman thrill her tongue with a sip of the highball. "Way-ull," she said, "like Mamma used to say, 'It takes time and patience before a mulberry leaf turns into a pair of satin bloomers.' Why'n't you go check us in, honey?"

"Settle up here," he said, and went out.

Once alone, the woman's eyes roamed idly over the drinkers and diners. They wandered past Joe, stopped, returned and lingered boldly. He looked away, as if unaware of her presence. Turning, he saw the man again—the big, red-faced, nearly bald man with the thick eyebrows. Tonight he was wearing brown—brown suit, brown shirt and tie and size-thirteen brown shoes. The slight bulge around his middle gave him the look of an El Producto. He stood at the far end of the bar pretending interest in the sports pages of *The Indianapolis News.*

Joe Dev bristled. Goddamn. We'll fix the sonofabitch one-two-three.

He paid for the beer. He went into the lobby. He found the men's room. He chose a stall adjacent to the urinals. He entered and locked the door. He kicked the toilet seat and cover down. He sat. He waited.

For the next ten minutes Joe Dev stared at the tiled floor and watched a footwear show. Shoes came onstage—between the proscenium provided by the base of the toilet-stall walls—all sizes and colors, entrances and exits. He was confident that the brown ones would appear before long. If he, Dev, were tailing a guy who didn't show for ten minutes, he'd start scratching, too. You never know when a toilet's maybe got another entrance or a window or maybe your bird gave you the slip.

Less than a minute later the brown thirteens made their

appearance. Joe Dev stood up and flushed the toilet. The sudden sound stopped the brown shoes in center stage, hesitant, considering a hasty retreat or advance. Joe Dev forced the decision: he flicked the door lock open noisily. The shoes advanced toward the urinals.

When Joe Dev came out of the booth the man was in the act of peeing, and for a fleeting moment Joe Dev was behind him, presumably on his way to a wash basin. A fleeting moment was all Joe Dev needed. Up came his knee, in a pistonlike motion, and smashed into the man's coccyx. The man grunted. His head jerked back, met the heels of Joe Dev's hands, and was forced forward. Forehead crashing against tile wall produced a dull metallic sound.

Joe Dev left.

The man tried to stay on his feet and could not. He slid slowly down, the remnants of consciousness frantically shouting to him, advising that he clutch the water pipe, and, missing that, the urinal flusher, then, on his knees, the urinal itself. As consciousness abandoned him, it called his attention to the final ignominy: he was staring into his own waste. He loosed his hold.

In the lobby Joe Dev found a public telephone. He dialed a number.

The Indian said, "Hello."

"It's me," Joe Dev said. "Let me talk to the boss."

"He's in the tub," the Indian said.

"Okay, I talk to the underboss," Joe Dev said. "You got some joker tailing me. Two days now. Call him off."

"Some kind of mixup," the Indian said. "No information about that."

"He gets in my way, Mister Indian," Joe Dev said. "You don't call him off, I chop him up like something you put ketchup on."

"Like you did Cooney?" the Indian said.

"Some kind of mixup," Joe Dev said. "No information about that."

"Oh, sure," the Indian said.

"Look, you want me to do my job or you want to play games?"

"Don't fuck with Little Neffie," the Indian said. "He's dangerous."

"Please," Joe Dev said. "My mouth gets all out of shape from laughing too much. Maybe you *want* me to take care of this creep, huh? Maybe you figure if he ain't smart enough to tail me without his ass showing to me, he's no fucking good anyway. That's what you want? Okay. I accommodate you."

"I'll call him off," the Indian said.

"Right now," Joe Dev said. "Come get him. The Holiday Inn. Route 15. In the toilet. Bring medicine."

"Sonofabitch," the Indian said.

CHAPTER **9**

Harriet kicked off her house slippers, and she and Joe Dev strolled across the scraggly backyard lawn toward a stand of walnut trees. It was Harriet's favorite time of day. The approaching twilight, the cooling down, the twittering of birds as they settled for the night, restored the mind and spirit and prepared her for arrival of clients.

Joe Dev said, "Hey, terrific meal. Thanks."

"Not near good enough for you, Joe," she said. "I'd like for you to remember me. Ain't much to remember as is. What you looking at is almost sixty years old and ugly and fat enough so's she has trouble tubbin'. So if I can *do* something for you, you can remember what I *did* and forget the *me* part of things."

"Among friends it's not necessary to do special things," Joe Dev said. "Friendship is enough."

She made a shield of her hand against the sun and stared at him. Their smiles formed simultaneously. Harriet said, "Don't snow me, handsome. You wants something and you a-scared of asking 'cause you doan want me to know what it is you wants to know."

"Aggh, come on," Joe Dev said. "We're just conversing."

"Conversing means two," Harriet said. "You just listening."

"You were speaking of your home," Joe Dev said.

"Right on," Harriet said, "if that be the way you wants it.

Home. You build a wall fifty feet high around Ole Miss and that'd be just fine with me—just so's I be on the outside of the wall." She leaned over the flower bed and clutched at weeds which triumphantly displayed their insignificant blooms. The effort yielded no satisfaction; roots held tenaciously to the earth. "Damn," Harriet said, "can't pull them up without I pull petunia." She laughed. "Happen that way with me, Joe. Inched my way north, out of Ole Miss, north where I got rights was the idea. Didn't go north enough, that's for sure. They's still trying to disturb my roots. Somebody give me question, and say, 'Harriet Stocker, this here your property? This here your house? This here your yard? Them your greens?' I say no. *Nossir.* I'm a weed, see? And a weed don't belong in no garden. You understand, Joe?

"Indiana? Garden? Good Jesus, hold my hand. Not for Harriet Stocker, no garden. I has to put out that I'm cook and maid and bottle washer and that somebody white over yonder employ me to supervise things here. I puff up and say the truth, that I'm legal owner and taxpayer, ain't many white girls goan work for me, not unless'n they's from the North, and I mean *North.*"

Her eyes widened with outrage. "And the po-lice. Before Bick Anson give me protection they crash in here expecting a piece free of charge, just like they's snitching an apple off'n a fruit stand. Wouldn't do that in no white woman's house. Uh-uh. Bick Anson, he put a stop to that shit. Any law and order in this town, you thank Bick Anson."

"You must carry a lot of respect for Mr. Anson," Joe Dev said.

Harriet came alert. "You want to know about Bick Anson? That it, Joe?"

Joe Dev laughed. "Harriet," he said.

"Yeah, I know," she said. "Conversing, just conversing. Yeah, I thinks a heap of Mr. Anson. I ain't saying he turn Uniontown into heaven, but how's a body to know about heaven before her ass feel the heat of hell? Mr. Bishop, now, he come here and give me five hundred dollars to make up for the damage what Cooney did. And he give Helen a thousand, tide her over till she can get back to work. *And* he goan take care of

Doc Selkir's bills. You goan get that kind of justice from anybody legal, by the democratic pro-cess? Nossir. Justice ain't swift and it sure ain't worth a meadow pancake. Woman needs a petticoat to keep her ass warm, it ain't goan cheer her none to promise her lace trimmin's before you gives her the petticoat. Outside Bick Anson's territory it be years before any judge'd give his ear to my grievance, and if something be raw-assing him when I'm standing there looking up at him in his high place, what you think he goan see? A woman been abused? He goan see a whore madam and a nigger one at that. Shit, I be walking out that courtroom with my haid full of blibbety-blabbety and no satisfaction. Nothing wrong with Bick Anson's justice, nossir. Uniontown's just fine with me. Don't take much to make a bird sing."

They sat in old willow chairs. The chairs were weathered to a silvery gray and they squeaked. Harriet lifted her face to the sun, acknowledged its presence and gave thanks for its warmth.

Joe Dev said, "Your girls like you, Harriet."

She said, "Okay, let's converse about the girls. Yeah, when they gets to know me they don't mind my being nigger. Ain't nothing really matters but they has good times. Something about girls takes to whoring's all the same—good-timers. They loves the good times. Some folks inclined to pity and pray for them, they thinks these girls they's been stomped on by condition and ain't no other way they get food to mouth 'ceptin' they sells themselves for cash money. Ain't so. Ain't so at all. Good times is what it's all about. They loves the good times comes from whoring."

Joe Dev smiled. "You speak of all women, Harriet."

"Yes and no," Harriet said. "If every woman could go a-pickin' and a-choosin' her customers there be more whores around'n the sky could rain on. Pleasure gals, that kind, they wants a man's got to be tall and handsome and no fat on him. Pleasure gals disgusts at the idea of putting out for *any* man come along with cash and a stiff stick, they disgusts at the idea of old men and drunks and trash. You think a pleasure gal goan want any part of a mean mother-rapin' shit like Wendell Cooney? Uh-uh. Pleasure gals is different from good-timers. Good-timers try to joy themselves no matter who come along."

This premise sparked the recollection of Julia and the dwarf. Her laughter a half shriek, and groaning for mercy, she told him about it. "She toss him around her bed like he was a baby doll, and all of us sneak-peeking in the door and near busting. Thirty inches high when he come in, and when he walk out he feel like King Kong."

Joe Dev said, "Julia's a very smart girl."

Harriet came alert again. She turned to him, her eyes showing all their white, and questioning. Joe Dev remained expressionless.

"Julia ain't sure of herself," Harriet said. "I'm mindful of a puppy dog walking along with a bone in his mouth. He look down, see the shadow, the shadow bone look bigger'n the real one, so he drop the real one. Been with me a good spell, Julia. Got a nice piece of money tucked. She be okay 'cepting for them shadows. Real good-timer. Southern gals, they's the best good-timers. Dunno why, but they is. Southern gal come to work for me a piece back. Wildcattin' on her own, she be, over Gary way. Come for one reason only. Bad night come along once in a while and she don't turn a trick, she be obliged to hustle a job next morning before she could get breakfast. Didn't like that. Uh-uh. No fun hustling a job before you had your morning coffee. No fun atall. They likes the good times, these gals.

"I recollect my ma had two goats. I didn't pay them no mind, they was just creatures crapped up the yard and the porch of the shack. Didn't pay them no mind until one night I wakes up hearing a sound like some spooky spirit be tap-tapping the ground. Well, sir, I goes to the window and looks out, and damn, there's them two goats a-jumpin' and a-leapin' and a-frolickin' in the moonlight like nothing you ever see. Them goats, they puts me to mind of my gals on a big Saturday night. Good-timers."

She focused on something in the near distance. She smiled. "Watch, Joe, watch," she said.

Joe Dev followed her gaze. Beyond a mock orange bush and a wire-netted fence, he could see a newspaper boy cycling up the street. The boy rode no-hands and sailed newspapers onto front porches with expertise. When he reached Harriet's house, he braked to a halt, propped up the bike and started to the front door, newspaper in hand, furtive anticipation in his eyes.

Shrubbery denied them the remainder of the drama. They heard the boy's step on the porch, the opening of the door, a voice.

"That'll be Alice," Harriet said. She chuckled. "A hellion, that one. Real good-timer. Wanted to go to the door bare-ass, once, really treat the boy. I say nossir. She do that, go to the door bare-ass, you imagine how many kid's goan be ringing my doorbell? She got the sad look, Alice, lots to be sad about, too, but she's a hellion and a good-timer."

Face flushed, his step springier for the experience, the boy came back into view. Harriet laughed. "Look like Alice open a couple buttons of her blouse when she hear him coming. That boy goan starch his bedsheets tonight for sure. A hellion. Ain't no man ever goan go short on her mattress." She nudged Joe Dev with her elbow. "Guess you know that. You been joyin' her pretty good, eh, handsome?"

Joe Dev smiled.

Harriet's eyes rolled and showed their whites again. "If you wants to converse about Alice, I can tell you she's got her stuff together. All her shit's in one bag, Joe. Person can depend on Alice. Smart. Quick. Steady. 'Specially if she got a good feeling for you. Bad feeling, watch out. Trouble. Hellion in her gives two ways. I hopes she don't get in no scratching match with Julia. I sees it coming."

Joe Dev said, "They don't get along?"

Harriet leaned aslant and appraised him. "Man, you blind? You got eyes can see through walls, so don't tell me you don't see what's goin' on 'tween those two."

"I don't," Joe Dev said.

"You *don't?*" Harriet said. "You don't know Julia got the hots for you? Now how'd that 'scape you?"

Joe Dev shrugged. "She told you this?" he said.

"No, but it stick out like a dirty deuce in a new deck," Harriet said. "Oh, she gone for you all right, Joe. Only, she ain't sure if she got the hots or the hates." She laughed. "That's Julia for you."

Joe Dev appeared confused.

Harriet said, "Ain't I already tole you? Julia ain't sure of herself, she ain't sure of anything, 'cepting maybe loving money and squirreling it away. Right now she ain't sure if she want you because she *want* you or because Alice is joyin' you. Understand, Joe? That's what I mean by the hots or the hates."

Joe Dev nodded.

Harriet said, "You want to converse about that?"

"No," Joe Dev said. And then, "Hey, you know who's a nice guy? The Indian. Real nice.fella."

"Don't know the man," Harriet said.

"He was telling me what a good time he had when he was living here," Joe Dev said.

"Didn't mix none," Harriet said. "Never got to know him atall."

"I guess maybe the girls mentioned it," Joe Dev said. "They were here then, no?"

"Seems they was, yes," Harriet said. "But me, I can't converse none about the Indian. Didn't mix. Never got to know the man. Something special you want to know?"

Joe Dev shook his head.

"You do, and I try to find out for you," Harriet said.

Joe Dev shook his head.

"All this conversing," Harriet said, "I say something to help you, Joe?"

Joe Dev laughed and said nothing. Harriet *had* helped him. She'd helped him eliminate Alice from his plans.

"Did I, Joe?" Harriet asked.

Overhead, the raucous cry of blue jays interrupted the birds' melodic repertoire. Harriet and Joe Dev looked up into the leafy thickness of the walnut trees and saw a crow flapping heavily off, a featherless songbird scissored in its bill. Screeching and squawking threat and accusation, the jays pursued the bandit in its flight, but the crow flew unconcernedly on. Distance silenced the jays and brought the drama to an end.

A past in which she had been badly used had left Harriet disenchanted with God's mysterious ways, and she was quick to classify as evidence anything which would serve to justify her diminished faith. She thought, If He goan give a creature a shitty deal like that, how come He make the creature in the first place?

New baby bird, no bother to nothing and nobody, just waiting so's to grow up and sing. That any way to do? Don't make no sense. No sense atall.

She was about to observe that if He were for real He would not allow a thing like that to happen. But then the door chimes rang out "One Enchanted Evening."

CHAPTER **10**

They were alone. Joe Dev, sprawled on the sofa, said, "Listen, I don't say a woman's got to get married just to put something between her legs. I'm not, you know, a fool. There are many considerations."

Julia slapped the red queen on the black king. She crushed her cigarette in the ashtray, rose and headed for the kitchen. Joe Dev altered his sprawl to keep her in his vision.

"So okay," he said. "You go out and you sell a big important piece of real estate and you make a high commission and then at night you go home and who's there? Nobody. Silence. Shh."

Julia reached into the refrigerator for a can of beer. "Gonna have a cat," she said.

Joe Dev said, "Aggh. Meow-meow. Ridiculous. Cat. You need a face, a face that says hello in your language."

"No faces, if you don't mind," Julia said. "No faces, please. Not for me." She tore the seal from the can, tossed it into the sink, and returned to resume the card play. "Lordy. Faces. Shoot. When I finished eighth grade I got myself this little old job in a candy factory. Two weeks later I couldn't stand the taste, the smell, not even the sight of candy. I thought to myself, 'Julia, honey, is *this* the way to put food to mouth? Really, honey, is *this* the way? Well, the answer to that's plain as day. Found an easier way—I *thought*, mind, *thought*, easier. Wasn't. Not a damned bit different from the candy. Candy, men, faces, I have a little old list this long of things that, you know, make me put my nose to the wind. Faces're at the top."

"Love," Joe Dev said.

THE DEVALINO CAPER . . . 67

"Business," Julia said. "Married or unmarried, business."

Joe Dev laughed. "I think you've never seen a widow crying at the funeral of her husband."

"Shoot," Julia said. "People're obliged to cry at funerals. I'll bet those widows just as soon take to a fit of laughing." She put match to another cigarette. "Mercy, how'd we ever get onto this kind of talk? We were going on about mushrooms."

"Oh, yeah," Joe Dev said, "mushrooms. Tell me. It's a big deal, huh?"

"I should say," Julia said. "Rats and rattles, you've never seen such a to-do about anything. Everybody kind of slinks, like they was doing secret work for the FBI or something. They go 'round with a paper bag folded and tucked and looking this way and that, scared as all get-out somebody'll find out where their cache is."

Julia was recalling the time of year when a probing sun mottles the floor of the Indiana woods and encourages the morel mushroom to poke up its head. "People aren't greedy, y'understand," Julia said. "They'll share with you if you don't find any y'self, but nobody's about to tell you where they found theirs."

Joe Dev's eyes flicked to his watch: almost two o'clock. He had to get her out of the house—now—before Harriet and Alice returned. An interruption would be too bad. She's ready. She's all mixed up and hoping and standing me off, all at the same time.

"Maybe you'll show me," he said.

"Now?" Julia asked. "No mushrooms out there now. In the springtime."

"You'll show me the woods," Joe Dev said. "Snap a picture of me I'll send home. 'Joe Dev in the woods.' I don't think they believe it. I never been in no woods."

Julia shrugged. "If you like. Lordy, it's so hot indoors I can scarce draw a breath."

They strolled the woods and found a swimming hole. They skinnydipped and sat in the sun to dry and suddenly Joe Dev turned to her, and said, "Hey, look what you done to me."

Julia laughed and reached out to touch him. "Y'bad boy," she said.

"Hey, you wanna?" Joe Dev asked.

"If you like," Julia said.

As they dressed, he said, "Where will you sell this real
estate?"

"Louisville," Julia said. "I'll have to, you know, get to know
the area and all."

"You'll be very successful," Joe Dev said. "No question.
You're a person who thinks much and feels little. That's a
compliment, you understand. People who think much, they
make like a funny thing. If you feel—ah. You feel too much and
you make your life a fucking heartache. Why do you laugh?"

"It don't amount," Julia said.

"Come on," Joe Dev said. "Why do you laugh?"

"Well," Julia said, "and don't you go taking offense, now,
you are *so* full of it, Joe, honest. The things you say."

"You think I speak unsincerely?" Joe asked.

"It don't weigh none one way or the other," Julia said, "not
with me. But that tongue of yours—nimble as a bee making into
a snapdragon. Now, shoot, don't go looking like that. I'm only
just talking. A girl's got to do her arithmetic startin' with one
and one makes two. You, you're going through the house like I
don't know what. First, Alice, now me. Helen gets to feeling
better, you'll be flittin' around there, too. Nobody's going to
hassle you about it. Shoot, Harriet thinks you're God Almighty,
Helen figures you for Jesus Christ, at least, and Alice, I don't
know what."

"And you?" he asked.

"Joe," she said, "if you'll only get that *look* off your face.
Mercy, we stopped to dawdle a bit, nothing more than that, and
if I choose to look at the truth of things there's no need for you
to go into a fit of the sulks."

Joe Dev remained silent. He tied his shoes—slowly, one,
then the other.

To Julia the silence promised to stretch into an eternity; it
provoked fear, panic. In trying to play it cool, to probe his
thoughts, she'd gone too far. She made a try at recovery.
"Maybe I got you all wrong," she said. "Y'talk funny. Different.
I mean the foreign part of it. It could be I misunderstood. You
know?"

He remained silent.

"May be," she suggested, "it's our different kind of talk. What I said, I wouldn't want you to think, you know, like we can't be friends."

He remained silent.

"Sulky, sulky," she said.

He leaped to his feet. He smiled. "Naggh, no sulky," he said.

She smiled, relieved.

He said, "Hey, I got ambitions too. You like to hear? I'm going to have a restaurant. In the country. Upstate New York. Listen, you never saw such a beautiful country. You don't have trouble selling that real estate, no sir. I bought a piece of land there last year, just off the main road, beautiful trees all around, a lake, you oughta see. I build there soon a restaurant is so clean you can eat off the floor, let me tell you. And the food. I bring over some of the women from the old country, none of these fakes you find here that makes a big show and gives you nothing. Those women, when you eat their food, you lick your fingers. Because all their life they cook to please their men. That's their secret—they put their heart in it. They keep one eye on the meat sauce and one eye on the old man's meat. Yeah, I'll have a fine restaurant and a good life. And when I finish my work, I'll have my woman. She'll be there. If she wants to work with me, in the restaurant, fine, sure, or if she wants to do something else—you know, an office or have a dress shop or sell real estate, that's okay. Why not? Just so she's there when I finish my work. Then we have a drink and we talk and I run my hand up her dress and we laugh together about it."

"Sounds great," Julia said. She laughed. "Not that you're offering."

"You don't think that I'm full of it?" he asked.

"Oh, shoot, Joe," she said. "Did I or didn't I say it was a misunderstanding?"

"Yes, you did," Joe Dev said. "A misunderstanding."

They started back toward the car.

Julia said, "What'd you mean about me thinking and not feeling? And don't you go claiming it's a compliment, Mr. Bad-Boy, because I don't take it that way."

Joe Dev shrugged. "Like you mention, sometimes I have trouble with the language."

Trying to laugh, she said, "I don't think it's so much the language as that tongue of yours, saying one thing when you mean another."

He shrugged and remained silent.

She said, "I'm sure Alice finds it purely entertaining."

She has no trouble with my language," he said.

"Well, well," Julia said.

"We better leave it at that," he said.

"Damn, Joe, get to the point," she said.

"No points," he said.

"It wasn't a compliment and you know it," she said. "Who's going to be complimented when you tell them they don't have any feelings?"

"Look, Julia," he said, soothing her while defending himself, "you said it yourself. Love is a business, no? You have a body, it's beautiful and you learned how to use it. Boy oh boy, let me tell you. Terrific. But what you do for a man, it's a service, that's all, a service. You know how to tickle a man's senses and you do it. Yourself, you don't permit a man to do anything to you. Love is a business. Money, that's all."

The pain born of her mistake was to be endured; the ensuing humiliation was not. She grew angry and defiant. "Well, it *is* a business for me and it *has* been for a long time," she said, "and I can't see making out that it's any different. It's Alice who'll turn on every time some joker walks into the house. Damned nymph. Ready to pop the minute she hears a footstep on the porch."

"That's not very nice to say," Joe Dev said.

"If you think Alice is so damned wonderful why're you taking up with me? I'm not Alice. And I'll tell you what else I'm not. I'm not some model looking to get her picture in a magazine or go on the television, and I'm not some dopey airline stewardess who'll give it away for dinner and a floor show."

"Goddammit, you want me to pay you?" he said. "I pay you what it was worth to me and you couldn't buy a pack of cigarettes with it."

Her palm never connected with his cheek. He grabbed her

wrist. "Don't raise your hands to me," he said. "I don't like women with long hands."

"You bastard," she said. "I treated you decent."

"Decent?" he said. "You insult me. You raise my blood, I make love to you, and what? I shove a firecracker up the ass of a corpse and I get as much as I get from you."

"Oh, Jesus Christ, Joe," she said.

"You don't like that, huh?" he said. "The truth gives you an earache. Somebody makes love to you and says nice things, sincere things, and you say 'Crap.' Somebody thinks maybe you'll remember them, with nice thoughts for them, and you say, 'No, no, Joe Dev, you're a face, a face on a list, that's all. Love is a business. Marriage is a business.' "

"Joe, listen—"

"Goddamn slot machine," he said.

She tried to storm but there was no thunder in her, only humiliation, with tears the final abasement. She ran from him like a fleet animal struck by a tranquilizing dart, stumbling, directionless.

He followed, helped her to her feet, dried her tears with the sleeve of his shirt. "I'm sorry about all the bad things I said," he said. "I give myself away, huh? Now you know. You know how I feel about you."

"What?" She searched his face.

"Yeah," he said. "I got it for you. Strong too. Very strong."

"I didn't realize, Joe," she said. "I didn't. Honest."

"Sure, sure," he said.

"Next time, Joe, huh?" she said. "Next time?"

"Next time," he said.

"I thought it was Alice," she said. "Only Alice."

He shook his head. "You, baby," he said. "I go against it, sure. I got too much to do to go falling for anybody right now, so I turn my face away from you. I turn my face because I don't want to start up. Understand?"

"You shouldn't have, Joe," she said.

"I gotta keep my eye on the target," he said. "The restaurant. It's gonna take a lot of work, a lot of doing."

"It sounds wonderful, Joe," she said. "The trees and the lake and all."

"I don't have time for other things," he said. "Especially a woman. You don't realize what I got to do."

"I'll help, Joe," she said. "I'll do anything to help. You *said* you'd have a woman. And if you feel about me like you've been saying—"

"Yeah," he said, "but not you, not anybody like you. You got to pardon me, Julia, it's not in my heart to hurt you, but the truth is the truth. I figured all the time that I go back to the old country and I find myself a girl no guy ever had his hands on her. So okay, I crash down for you. That's my heart makes me do that. My mind, that's another thing. I don't double up with you. For your own sake. What kind of life you gonna lead if I got it in the back of my head all the time what you been, all them guys?"

"Oh, Joe, none of them ever mattered," she said. "Not one, ever."

He flared. "No, huh?" he said. "None of them."

"I swear, Joe," she said. "Honest."

"How many guys you screwed?" he asked, livid now. "How many, huh?"

"I don't know," she said.

"Goddammit, I said how many. A thousand? Five thousand?"

"I don't know."

He slapped her, hard. "Tell me. A guy falls in love with a whore, he's got a right to know what he's gotta live with."

She stammered words he did not understand.

He said, "Some life you'll have with me, huh? You still want it? Like every day you gotta show me you're more better than I think? I tell you, I'm that type guy. I can't help it. I don't burn a thing like that out of my head so easy."

"Joe, Joe," she said, "please."

"Goddammit," he said. "You gonna start begging? Things ain't hard enough for me, you gonna start begging?"

"Yes, yes," she said. "Oh, please, Joe. I've been waiting. You don't know how I've been waiting for something to happen so's I could get away. And ever since that first night in the rain . . . I *will* prove I'm better, Joe. Every day. Every minute."

He sighed. "I don't know," he said. "You wouldn't be

getting no bargain, either. You, you're not good enough for me, and me, I'm not good enough for you. Maybe that's the answer for the both of us. Even-steven. Like partners in a card game."

"Yes, Joe," she said. "Partners."

"Partners, they play the hand," he said. "One of them plays for the other and the both of them they play to win."

"Yes, Joe," she said. "One helping the other. Oh, I want that so much."

"You gotta swear, Julia," he said.

"I swear, Joe," she said. "Anything."

"Maybe we give it a try," he said. "I see it don't work, it's over. It's no use to complicate."

"It *will* work, Joe," she said.

"It's gotta be like I'm God, Julia," he said. "You understand?"

"Yes, Joe," she said.

He slapped her again. "You say to me, 'Forgive me, Joe.' "

"Forgive me, Joe."

"Forgive me for being a bad woman."

"Forgive me for being a bad woman."

"I love you, Joe."

"Oh yes, yes, yes," she said.

CHAPTER **11**

The Monday night dinner had become ritual. At seven o'clock the Indian drove his 1936 Chrysler roadster into the parking lot. The antique, a dazzler the color of coffee yogurt, with wire wheels spangling and Klaxon horns mounted on its front fenders trumpeting, kindled nostalgia in the elderly and yearning in the young. The Indian ignored the eager attendant and personally chose a stall for his treasure. As always, he cautioned the attendant: keep one car space clear on either side of it and, as always, solemnized his concern with menacing tone and a five-dollar bill. He entered the Sabre Room. There George Stacy greeted him with the freshest gossip and jokes and led him to the bar. The Indian drank a sugarless cola, Stacy sipped bourbon and gave an accounting of the previous week's gambling take. A steak dinner followed.

Yawning inwardly because of the Indian's niggardly contribution to conversation, Stacy found diversion in eavesdropping on the couple seated at the adjoining table. They were young; she was pretty, he was handsome.

The low-voiced exchanges began to seep through during their first cocktail. From the young man: "Dammit, what do you expect me to do?" From the young lady: a hissing sound. From the young man: "Oh, come on, honey, that just isn't fair."

The second cocktail raised rancor and decibels. The young man: "For Christ's sake, it's my job." And then Stacy distinctly heard the young lady retort with: "Screw you and your job. How about that, huh? How about that?"

The young man's temper spilled over. Slapping his napkin on the tabletop, he stood erect and, through his teeth, said, "I wanted us to enjoy what time we had, but you just won't have it that way, will you."

The young lady also used her teeth to hush her response. "You *and* your job. Screw."

He left. The young lady stayed and stared into her cocktail glass.

Stacy turned to the Indian. "Hey, Iron Face," he said, "what kind of woman gets old Stace's peccah to doing high jinks?"

"Make it easy," the Indian said. "Ask me what kind doesn't." He followed Stacy's across-the-nose gaze to the young lady.

"Stung filly," Stacy said, "and *exactly* my kind."

The young lady stopped the waiter and asked for the bill. She reached into her purse for a checkbook and wrote a check. The waiter brought it to Stacy for his okay. It was a joint account, signed "Leslie Ranier." The other name printed on the check was "Howard Ranier."

Stacy rose and positioned himself so that his eyes could plumb the depths of Leslie Ranier's front. "Excuse me, Miz Ranier," he said. "I'm George Stacy. Manager man? How-do."

She looked at the check in his hand. "Is anything wrong?"

He chuckled. "About to ask the same question of you, Miz

Ranier. Only, I don't mean the check. Couldn't help noticing—the gentleman?—the little hassle you had?"

She wasn't about to discuss that. "He had to leave suddenly, and I don't have any cash with me," she said.

"If that's all," Stacy said, "happy to be of service." He initialed the check and handed it to the waiter. He pulled the young lady's chair back for her. She left.

Stacy rejoined the Indian. "About that top part of her . . . Mmmm . . . small, pear-shaped, with chewy centers and topped with tweakable mammilla. Lawd, Lawd, what'd a guy ever do in the days of the bra?" He sighed. "Lovely. Just right. Never cared for big-breasted women."

"If you don't mind," the Indian said, "I've heard it all before."

"Big breasts mean no muscle," Stacy said. "Like sourdough rising."

The Indian remained silent.

Stacy asked the waiter to bring him coffee and brandy. The Indian had coffee.

Stacy's beeper beeped four times. He excused himself and went out to the front entrance, where he found Leslie Ranier staring belligerently at the parking lot attendant. She had the look of a woman about to explode, into rage or tears an odds-on bet. She held a car-check stub between her fingers.

"Mr. Ranier took the car," she said.

The attendant looked worried. He remembered Ranier driving the car in. "The guy said it was okay," he said.

Stacy dismissed him. He smiled at Leslie Ranier. "Nothing to wet a handkerchief about, Miz Ranier," he said.

"Don't worry, I won't," Leslie Ranier said. There was a snap in her voice.

"Come on in and settle comfortable till he gets back," Stacy said.

"He won't *be* back," Leslie Ranier said. "He had to make a plane. He's probably on the way to the airport. I was to drive him there."

"What about the car?" Stacy asked.

She shrugged helplessly. "I guess he means to leave it at the airport until he gets back."

"Fort Wayne or 'Nap Town?" Stacy asked.

"Fort Wayne," Leslie Ranier said. "Mr. Stacy, I wonder, could I impose on you? I mean, I'm in kind of a spot. I've got a baby-sitter at home, and I promised I'd be home by nine. If you'll cash another check for me, I'll call a taxi."

Stacy said, "Where do you live?"

"La Fontaine," she said.

"If that don't beat it raw," Stacy said. "I was just about to *leave* for La Fontaine. Always go to La Fontaine sometime during the evening—to visit my poor old drunken ma."

She managed a small smile. "I couldn't, really. Thank you. Appreciate it, but if you'll just cash the check, please?"

"Be half an hour, forty-five minutes before you get a taxi out here," he said. He called to the attendant to bring up his car, a Maserati.

The road from Uniontown to La Fontaine is two-laned, untrafficked and fast. When Stacy had to make a left on Route 124, he found himself in a familiar and frightening situation. A car coming from the opposite direction prevented him from quick-turning, and a glance at his rear-view mirror warned of headlights bearing down from behind. To reduce speed and wait for the oncoming car to pass would be inviting destruction from the rear. Prudence—the custom—dictated that he pull over onto the right shoulder and come to a stop.

The headlights from behind thundered past—an oil truck doing eighty. Stacy puffed up his cheeks and forced out air. "Never get used to that," he said. "Always feel like a bear caught with his paw in a honey tree."

Leslie Ranier laughed. "The funniest expressions," she said. "Where are you from?"

"Born in Chickahominy, raised in Richmond and corrupted in Kentucky," he said. He swung back onto the road. "What was I saying? Oh yes. I envy you, Leslie. Me, I'm cotton on the wind, blown hither and thither by every fickle breeze comes up. You, you got things goin' real cozy-style. Little home, a baby, husband on his way to becoming a big noise . . . envy you, yes *sir*."

"Sounds great," she said.

Something in her tone made him ask, "It ain't?"

"Put it this way," she said. "The little home is something I never get out of. The baby? Best thing that ever happened to me, but twenty-four hours of baby-baby-baby can drive you up the walls. And the husband. Sure. Promising think-piece, one of the real IBM brighties, except that being gone three, four days a week makes it more like he's married to those initials than to me. If that's cozy-style, then I'm living cozy, yes *sir*."

"No," Stacy said. "Man gets to doin' what your hubby's doin', his rabbit's sure to die."

"That Chickahominy or Kentucky?" she asked.

"Man's rabbit dies means he's hanging slack," Stacy said.

She said, "Oh."

"That'll drive a woman up the walls faster'n baby-baby-baby," Stacy said. "Hang slack when he comes home, does he?"

"You think I'm going to discuss that with you?" she said.

"If he's hanging slack because he's pouring his best into his ambition and his business, might be a nice thing to have it on him," he said.

"Meaning?" she asked.

"Well," Stacy said, "there he is, home for only a couple two, three days at a time and hanging slack, and you, instead of suffering anger and frustration and taking it out on your baby, why, you just look at him and say to yourself, 'It's okay, Mister IBM, I've been fucked and fucked good by somebody else.' "

"My, our language is deteriorating," she said. "Could we rinse, please? You're very entertaining, George, but my answer is 'no.' "

He put shrillness in his voice. "Was I talking about myself? Did I say do it with me?"

"Not you, not anybody," she said.

"I just said you oughta, I didn't say me."

"Okay," she said.

"Okay," he said. "Sorry I shocked you."

"I'm not a la-la girl," she said. "Fidelity's a habit, I guess."

"Fingernail bitin's a habit," he said. "Everything gets to be a habit. But what *is* habit? Just memory working overtime, is all."

"Look," she said, "get it straight. It isn't going to happen. I admit I was really brought down when Howard took off like that, and you've been very nice about lifting me back up there, but it ends with a thank-you-very-much when we get to my door."

"A little conversation," he said.

"No," she said.

"Let me finish," he said. "Leslie Ranier, you are really something. That's a real low opinion you have of yourself. I don't know how you ever come by such a low opinion of yourself. Must be the kind of life you've been leadin' gives you that low opinion of yourself. Guess that husband of yours done that to you. Depressing as hell when people around you don't appreciate you for what you are."

"It's not going to happen, George," she said. She was singing it now.

"I don't deny that lookin' at you brings on dreams of glory, but you ever stop to think that I'd enjoy just talking? Isn't that what we've been doing? And ain't we enjoyed it? A little conversation goin' to hurt?"

"Not even conversation," she said. "I've got neighbors, and this car of yours isn't exactly inconspicuous."

"You've got a garage, right?" he asked.

"Yes," she said.

"But no car," he said. "Car's in the parking lot, over to the Fort Wayne airport. Well, all right. What if I were to nose this li'l old car into that garage? Who's going to know anybody's in that house with you?"

She didn't answer.

A door in the garage led to the kitchen. Leslie Ranier said, "Stay here until I pay off the baby-sitter. I'll send her out the front way." He kissed her on the neck. She said, "I feel like such a bastard doing this to Howard."

Stacy said, "Hey, you never got dinner, did you."

"The sonofabitch," Leslie Ranier said, and disappeared into the darkened kitchen.

Stacy wallowed in anticipation until he heard the front door opening and closing and a woman's footsteps fading along the sidewalk. He got out of the car and strayed in. The light from a room beyond the kitchen guided him through a hall to the dining room.

He saw Howard Ranier.

And then the gun, a silencing device attached to it.

"Hey, looka here," Stacy said. "What'd I do?"

Howard Ranier said, "Don't ask *me.*"

"Wait, wait, wait, wait, *wait,*" Stacy said. "Twenty-five thousand if you'll wait half a second. It's the Indian, isn't it? He's taking over. I've suspicioned it. He's killing off Bick's friends and Bick doesn't know—"

The bullet struck him on the bridge of the nose.

CHAPTER **12**

"La Romana Restaurant," the bartender said.

"Mr. Bruno Savino," the operator said. "Long distance calling."

"Just a minute," the bartender said.

Bruno said, "This is Mr. Savino."

"Go ahead, please," the operator said.

Joe Dev said, "Hi, Bru, it's me."

"Hey," Bruno said.

"Got a minute?" Joe Dev said.

"One problem I ain't got is time," Bruno said. "We did a three-hundred-dollar lunch. Goddamn waiters almost leaned the building into the ground. Dinner is so-so."

"I can almost smell it," Joe Dev said. "My belly's yelling for some of it."

"Whatsa matter, Joe?" Bruno said. "You not eatin' good?"

"I was, there for a while," Joe Dev said. "Now I'm running double with a broad comes from Tennessee. We livin' in a motel. She cooks a steak like we cook a veal cutlet."

"You mean fried?" Bruno said.

"That's only the half of it," Joe Dev said. "First she dips it in flour and breadcrumbs?"

"*Maron,*" Bruno said.

"Enough to make a guy puke," Joe Dev said. "But whattya gonna do?"

"To put up with that," Bruno said, "she's gotta be some piece."

"There I can't complain," Joe Dev said. "There ain't much anybody can teach this one. She started early. Poor kid, she was telling me about her old man, he's fifty years old, and counting reform school and all, he's done thirty-two years on the inside."

"That's what I call a loser," Bruno said.

"Break your fucking heart to hear her side of it," Joe Dev said. "There's this uncle, see, her father's brother? And he comes up with enough so the kids don't starve to death. Only this one, because she's growing up juicy, nice—you know?—to this one he says she's gotta fuck for him or she don't eat. She's eleven years, two months when he cops her."

"Jesus Christ," Bruno said. "The things you hear in this world."

"Hey, listen, how's Toni and the kid?" Joe Dev said.

"Okay," Bruno said. "Toni's getting water on the knee from praying, you know."

"Well, if it makes her feel good," Joe Dev said. "Me, I don't believe in begging."

"Hey, how's it going?" Bruno said.

"Well, you know," Joe Dev said. "Look, I want to tell you, you won't be hearing from me for a while. Don't worry. It's okay."

"I'm glad you told me," Bruno said. "Otherwise, you know."

"Look, you got a pencil?" Joe Dev said. "Take this down."

"Shoot," Bruno said.

"Write a letter," Joe Dev said. "Rent a typewriter, understand?"

"Yeah," Bruno said.

"Write the letter to—I'll give it to you slow," Joe Dev said. "Daniel Cugarman, C,u,g,a,r,m,a,n. Back Trail Road, Indianapolis, Indiana."

"Zip?" Bruno said.

"Screw it," Joe Dev said. "Now look, no dear sir or anything. Just the message. Like this: 'Sorry. Bond number 498653E is hot. The rest are okay.' "

"That it?" Bruno said.

"Yeah," Joe Dev said. "Don't put it in a white envelope. A colored one. But you gotta tell me now."

"Whatever you think," Bruno said. "Pink okay?"

"Fine," Joe Dev said. "And, Bru, it's gotta be mailed in Chicago. Gotta have a Chicago postmark, understand?"

"I'll put somebody on a plane if I have to," Bruno said.

"No if you have to," Joe Dev said. "For sure. Get somebody, somebody won't fuck up. Go yourself, Sunday, if you have to."

"Okay, Joe, I'll take a ride myself," Bruno said. "If it's so important."

"It's important, I tell you that," Joe Dev said. "I gotta sign off now."

"Go ready, Joe," Bruno said.

"All the time," Joe Dev said, "all the time, Bru."

CHAPTER **13**

Detective Barry Bushman smuggled a fifth of blended whiskey into Wendell Cooney's hospital room, and as they started on the third drink Bushman said, "How much longer does the Doc say you gotta be here?"

"What the hell's he got to say about it?" Cooney said. "I go when I'm ready. Soon's this thing on my arm comes off and my leg holds me up like it should. I got things to do. I'm gonna find the guy what did this to me if I have to tear up the whole goddamn pea patch."

"The guy's long gone by now," Bushman said.

"I'll find him, don't worry," Cooney said. "I'll find him and I'll kill him."

"Gonna take doing," Bushman said.

"No it won't," Cooney said. "That Stocker woman and those broads in her house, they know who it is. They was there, wasn't they? I'll kill *them* if I have to, if they won't tell me, the four of them, one at a time."

"Three," Bushman said. "One of them's here."

"What? Which one?" Cooney asked.

"Little dark-haired one," Bushman said. "I was in the precinct house when the call come through for the ambulance."

Cooney scrambled out of bed.

Bushman said, "I wouldn't, Cooney. She's a mighty sick kid."

Cooney seemed not to hear. He hobbled to the closet and found his pants.

The nurse came in. "Mr. Cooney, you get right back in that bed," she said.

He silenced her with a look as frightening as a finger on a trigger. Trying to climb into the pants—his shoulder immobilized, arm frozen in midair—inspired and brought forth the choicest from his crawling compost of obscenities, but he persevered until the belt hung balanced over his buttocks. "Buckle it," he said. And when the nurse had complied, "Zip me up."

Barefoot, the institutional johnny shirt draped over the pants, he rode the elevator to the second floor. He found Helen's room, opened the door, then quickly pulled it shut again. "Shit," he said aloud, and started to sweat.

In that flash-by moment he saw Helen, the intravenous bottle with its tubing taped to her hand, water glass, plastic straw tilted in it, basin, bedpan, washcloth, towel, paper tissues, the priest . . . And coincident with the fleeting visual experience, he heard Helen murmur, "Bless me Father, for I have sinned . . ."

He waited, marveling at his patience, and when the priest left, he entered Helen's room.

The confession had wearied her. She dozed, one cheek against the pillow. Cooney stood over her and softly called her name.

The face she turned to him wore an expression of grave attention. He smiled sheepishly.

"Motherfucking bastard," she said. "Nurse."

"Keep it down," Cooney said. "You'll snap that kidney clear off the string what's holding it."

"Nurse," she said.

He put his hand gently (for him) over her mouth. "I came

down the minute I heard you was here," he said. "I didn't know until just a while ago. How are you, kid?" He freed her lips.

She repeated, but with less zest, "Motherfucking bastard."

"I guess you know I'm sorry," he said.

"No, I don't," she said. "And who gives a shit?"

"I musta been out of my mind," he said.

"You got no mind," she said. "You're an animal."

"I don't blame you for thinking that," he said.

"You should know what I've been thinking since that night," she said. "I wish I had written it down so you could be up to date."

Cooney sighed. "That night," he said. "I'm telling you, Helen, I was like a 'coon gnawing off its own foot so's to get clear of a trap. I took the biggest notion for you, early, but I kept saying to myself, 'No, you're not goin' over there. You're no good for Helen and she's no good for you.' Well, that wasn't so easy to do, stay away, so I drank it up to get shed of you, only the more drinkin' I did, the more things began to shape up for me, until there it was, clear as a baby's cry—the answer. I said to myself, 'I'll go over there and give her a whuppin' she'll keep to mind for the rest of her natural life, and then I'm gonna take her away from that place, and me and her'll make a life together.' "

"Look," she said, "will you get out of here? It isn't five minutes that I got absolution and already you've got me cursing and thinking sinful thoughts."

"Ain't nobody knows better'n me that I'm a bad influence," he said, "but you got to give me a chance to do what I come to do. Hell, you're thinking you're all cleared up, all owings paid off, clean, because of that priest being here, but you ain't, Helen. No, you ain't, Helen, and you ain't gonna be unless you own up to the fact that I'm sorry, and then forgive me."

"You've got to forget to forgive," she said.

"Yeah, but if you forgive, it won't be any time atall before you forget," he said. "Works that way. Take me, now, didn't I forgive the guy that put me in here? Didn't I? I did and I'm glad of it. I said to him, 'Forget it. I had it comin' to me.' "

She looked at him. "You've seen Joe?"

"No," he said, "Joe dropped me a line."

"But you said you told him to forget it," she said.

"It's in this letter I wrote back," he said. "I'll mail it soon's I get his address. I said, 'I had it coming to me, Joe, so forget it. I only wish I could undo what I did to Helen,' I said. 'It's Helen I care about and nothing or nobody else. Helen.' I mean, he's gotta be a pretty decent guy to take the trouble, you know? Writing like that when he had no need to, when I was to fault?"

"They don't come any better than Joe," she said.

"Yeah," he said. "Sounds like that kind of guy."

"Wendell . . . ?"

"Yeah, honey?"

"Am I going to die?" she asked. "They won't tell you anything around this place."

He made a face, leaned back and appraised her. "Now what the hell kind of question is that to go asking? Of course not."

"What makes you so sure?" she asked.

"I talked to Doc Selkir, that's how," he said. "When I heard you was in here, first thing I did was ask the Doc about you. I left him not more'n ten minutes ago. You're gonna be okay."

Her dark eyes were now full of hope. "Not that I care," she said. "Because, you see, I've got a pretty good chance of making heaven. I'm twenty-three, that means I'll be twenty-three forever—into eternity. It's a hell of a lot better than getting up to heaven when you're ninety. Who wants to be ninety into eternity?"

"You know something," he said. "I thought you had a brain. But no. The top of your head's empty as a bird's nest in December. Didn't I just get through telling you? So why're you chitterin' about eternity? Maybe the Doc'd lie to you, but would he lie to me?"

"No, I suppose not," she said.

He took her hand in his, and said, "You're gonna be just fine, honey. Which is why you've got to get everything straight, you and me—straight and tidy. You, you forgive me like I already forgive Joe for wrecking me up the way he did, no hard feelings, no which way, and that'll make everybody feel a lot better. You know, Helen, honey, I ain't much for religion, but my ma was, and I remember—hell, I couldn't've been more than seven or eight and I still remember—I remember her reading to me from the Bible about salvation. It was something about a voice cryin' in the wilderness."

" 'Prepare ye the way of the Lord,' " Helen said. " 'Make his paths straight. Every valley shall be filled, and every mountain and hill shall be brought low. And the crooked paths shall be made straight, and the rough ways shall be made smooth.' "

"That's it," Cooney said, "that's *it*, honey."

" 'And all flesh shall see the salvation of God.' "

"Yeah, yeah, salvation! Goddamn, that's *it*. My ma read that to me over and over."

"It was Saint John saying it," Helen said.

"Is *that* right?"

" 'Heaven was opened and the Holy Ghost descended in a bodily shape like a dove upon him, and a voice came from heaven, which said, 'Thou art my beloved Son. In thee I am well pleased.' "

" 'In thee I am well pleased,' " Cooney said, a catch in his throat. "I remember, too, something about the latches of somebody's shoes."

"Latchet, you dummy," she said, "latchet. 'One mightier than I cometh, the latchet of whose shoes I am not worthy to unloose.' That's when Jesus showed up and Saint John called him the Lamb of God."

"Imagine," Cooney said, "imagine us both knowing those things and not knowing it about each other. You know, Helen, honey, I got a feeling that what happened to us is maybe all for the good. I oughta thank Joe for what he did. And I'll tell him—soon's I find out his address."

"Wendell . . ." Helen said.

"Yeah, honey," he said.

"Go fuck yourself, okay?"

"Honey," Cooney said.

"You're trying to con me," she said. "You're trying to con me into telling you where he is. I don't know what come over me, believing all that he-dropped-me-a-line bullshit, must be the sickness."

"Honey," Cooney said.

"I don't know where Joe is," she said. "I wish I did so I'd have the satisfaction. You're a prick, Wendell."

"Hon-eee," Cooney said.

"You're a prick in your heart."

His nostrils stretched wide.

"Whore."

"Hillbilly trash."

"Cunt."

"Worse than trash," she said. "From what your mother kept reading to you from the Bible you must be a Baptist."

"I'm gonna kill him," Cooney said. "I'm gonna find him and kill him."

"Watch out for your other arm, prick," Helen said.

"I'd kill you too, only I don't have to," he said.

"Prick, prick, prick."

"I don't have to because you're going to die anyway," he said, "and when you do I'm gonna laugh. I'm gonna laugh until my fuckin' ribs give out."

"Laugh while you can, prick," she said, "because in hell nobody laughs."

It happened shortly after midnight. The charge nurse went in to check the intravenous level and found that it wasn't dripping. Making the adjustment, she realized that Helen's blood no longer flowed.

CHAPTER **14**

Returning home from Custer's Employment Agency, Mrs. Crawford luxuriated in the rear seat of the limousine, and Julia shared the front with Teague. Mrs. Crawford said to Teague, "Tell her about the dogs."

Teague said, "Nothing to worry yourself about there. Donnet, he's got them trained so he like to damn near carry on a conversation with them."

"Don't swear," Mrs. Crawford said.

Teague continued, "He says to them in that crazy Vietnam gook language of his, 'This here's Julia, understand, you damned no-good killers? Julia's to come and go from here and you're not to go bothering her.' All there is to it." He turned to her; his eyes shredded her dress. "I catch your name right? Julia?"

Julia smiled. "Yes," she said.

"Nice name," Teague said. He forced his attention back to the traffic and contented himself with an occasional all-consuming side-glance.

"Get on with the telling," Mrs. Crawford said. "We ain't gathered for a social."

"Yes, mum, paddan me," Teague said.

"Don't be insolent," Mrs. Crawford said.

"Not a bit, nossir, mum," Teague said. "I mean no ma'am, mum." He winked at Julia.

"I saw that," Mrs. Crawford said. "In the mirror."

"Yes, mum," Teague said.

"Just tell her about the dogs," Mrs. Crawford said.

Teague nodded amiably. "It's the sound of the words," he said to Julia. "Donnet teaches the dog the words that say you're okay, and that's it. They don't understand the word, catch? Only the sound. Nothing to worry about after that. For a while, though, maybe, if you want to walk around the place, you'd best let me go with you."

"That won't be necessary," Mrs. Crawford said.

"Especially at night," Teague finished.

Julia smiled.

"Nobody out after ten o'clock," Mrs. Crawford said.

"Excepting on her day off," Teague said. He winked again.

Mrs. Crawford said, "On your day off, if you're not back by midnight—"

"You finish up in the ash heap," Teague said. "Right, Mrs. Crawford, mum?"

Mrs. Crawford ignored the interruption. "If you can't get back by midnight," she said, "you might's well figure on staying away until morning. Thursday'll be your day off, and one weekend a month. No Thursday this week, though."

"I don't mind," Julia said. "Like I told Mr. Bogen at the

employment agency, I don't have a family here, only my fiancé. And he can change his day off to Thursday, so that'll work out just fine."

Anticipation gushed in Teague. A guy senses when he's on his way to making out, and the vibes were registering real good. This could be his greatest score. Never had there been stuff like this in the house before, this lush, hill baby. Got to be careful, though. This one's sharp, smart, not like the others, not the kind you can just shove over. It'll take some doing.

He wished he'd showered and shampooed his hair. Friends said he looked like the movie actor Lee Marvin, but he'd noticed that the comment was forthcoming only when his hair had been washed; then it stuck up straight and the premature gray heightened. Funny thing about that resemblance. Once aware of it, the strength, virility and sex appeal of the actor rubbed off on him; people treated him differently. He could swear it was so, and occasionally he would remind himself to "think Lee Marvin" and take on the actor's mannerisms and speech pattern.

He turned to Julia with a Lee Marvin smile. She smiled back.

"Stevensville, Tennessee, must be a small place," Teague said. "Don't believe I ever heard of it."

"Why, it isn't small atall," Julia said. "Better'n two thousand people."

"Wow," Teague said.

"Most of them work for Mr. Messenger, in the furniture factory. He's the richest man in town, owns just about everything there is to own."

"He give you them references?" Teague said.

"Mrs. Messenger wrote the references," Julia said.

"Must be a sharp operator, this Messenger," Teague said.

"I'll say," Julia said. "He's even a notary public."

"Wow," Teague said.

"You're putting me on," Julia said.

"Friendly-style," he said. He squeezed her knee and stroked when he withdrew his hand.

Mrs. Crawford said, "I don't allow my people to mix. You tell him to keep his hands off you."

"Yes, Mrs. Crawford," Julia said.

"You tell him," Mrs. Crawford said. "You tell him now."

Julia said, "You keep your hands off me, Mr. Teague."

"Yes, miss," Teague said, "I'll remember. No hands."

Arriving at the front gate, Julia's spirits sagged. She felt sudden loneliness. The Cugarman house, darkly shaded from the late afternoon sun by massive elms, looked a remote and sterile domain; seemed disinterested in, and unconcerned with, life beyond its chill limits; the wall bragged of the leaden existence it encircled; the sign on the gate read, BEWARE OF FIERCE DOGS.

Teague explained that the gate was electronically operated. "You want in, you toot your horn and somebody up to the house'll cut the switch. You can open it with a key, but me and Donnet's the only ones got keys." He tooted. "Own a car, do you? Glad to drive you back'n forth anytime."

"I'll be using my fiancé's car," Julia said. "He works in 'Nap Town, so he can ride the buses."

The gate swung open and Teague drove on through. The gate clanked shut. The driveway, which forked left from the house at a deliveries-in-rear sign, ended in the back courtyard. Following Joe Dev's instructions, Julia absorbed as much as possible. She noted that a wide expanse of lawn separated the house from a garage which housed a number of cars. She counted them. Joe Dev had warned to consider nothing unimportant. Ten cars, an assortment of foreign models and Cadillacs lording it over Chevys and Pontiacs; windows above the garage, clean, curtained, someone's living quarters; beyond the garage a dense wood, wild, uncared for, deadfalls across the narrow footpath.

Preoccupied with that before her, fear attacked Julia from behind. Heartbeat quickening, she turned to identify the danger before it struck—a low rumbling sound reminiscent of a motion-picture avalanche increasing in rage and volume.

Coping queasily with terror, Julia faced the dogs. They strained at their leashes, impatient for the freedom to kill, savageness intensifying with denial. The rumbling broke into a horror of snarls and grinding throat noises; they tugged and leaped and fell back, slavering, eyes refusing to free the intended victim.

Julia's eyes darted to the man clutching the two leashes: small, wiry; bones stuck out all over his body, undulated through lean flesh and gave his rib cage the look of windswept sand dunes. Dirty uncombed hair hinted at life in its shelter. The unshaven face partially hid a lipless smile, and the eyes, shards of wet asphalt that boasted a no-quarter-given toughness, shone with a malicious thrill. He held the option of releasing death and he reveled in his moment of power and glory.

Julia paled. She inhaled spasmodically until her lungs could hold no more and found she could not release the breath. The Baluchis pulled the man toward her; it seemed he lacked the strength to restrain them.

"For Christ's sake," Teague shouted.

"No swearing," Mrs. Crawford said.

"Screw off," Teague said to Donnet.

The man ignored him. Inch by inch the dogs scratched their way closer toward Julia.

"Sonofabitch," Teague said. "Knock it off."

Now the dogs were only a few inches from Julia, rooted to the ground.

Mrs. Crawford said sharply, "Donnet." And Donnet revealed he'd been in control all the time. The dogs continued to tug and strain but made no headway.

"Exempter, exempter," Donnet shouted at the dogs. The snarling stopped but the savagery lingered.

"Hold it, cookie," Donnet said to Julia. "Just stand still, understand? Don't move. It's get-acquainted time." Leaning over and unclipping the leads from the dog collars, he said again, *"Exempter, exempter."* He laughed. "Okay, cookie, make friends."

Julia resisted the temptation to turn and embrace Mrs. Crawford. She stood motionless, swayed involuntarily as the dogs trotted to her, their slim flanks slightly off center of their withers. They circled around her, crossing and recrossing each other, one clockwise, one counter, heads down, eyes up, bodies twisting wormlike to keep her in sight. They maintained an air of scarcely concealed hostility, as if reluctant to keep in check the killer instinct. One of them, resentful of restraint, bared its teeth and growled.

Donnet's voice cut it down. *"Exempter,"* he said. *"Exempter."* He made a clucking sound with his tongue, and the dogs settled on either side of him. "Okay, cookie," he said to Julia. "Welcome to your happy home. Boy, ain't you something to look at."

Julia gulped and forced a smile.

Donnet said, "You don't have to be scared of them any more. I give 'em the word, see? Over in Nam I trained more'n a hundred of the goddamn things, used 'em to run down gooks stole stores. Once I give 'em the word, you're okay. They know you belong here." He laughed. "Hey, cookie, I got an idea. Come on over here and pet 'em, show there's no hard feelings, hah?" Julia's facial reaction sent his laughter into a crescendo.

"Stop this nonsense," Mrs. Crawford said. "There's work to be done."

Donnet delayed long enough to display contempt for Mrs. Crawford's authority, then said to the dogs, *"Couche-couche-va."* The dogs trotted off and settled under a lean-to attached to the west wall of the garage. Neatly built with shingled roof to match the parent structure, it was boarded up on one side to shield the animals from cold winter winds.

Mrs. Crawford said, "Teague, get the girl's suitcase."

Teague opened the trunk of the limousine. "I'll carry it up for her," he said.

"No you won't," Mrs. Crawford said. "She's able-bodied enough to carry it herself. You've no business on the third floor, not ever, and don't you go forgetting."

The back door opened into a hall from which a staircase elled to the upper floors. Mrs. Crawford said, "This way," and continued past the stairway into a sterile-white kitchen. A girl sweeping the floor paused in her work and hugged the broom handle as though emotionally attached to it.

"This is Louise," Mrs. Crawford said.

Julia extended her hand. "My, but you're pretty," she said. The compliment was a sincere one. The girl possessed a petite beauty, the tiny body was well formed, the large brown eyes mellow with optimism. But, Julia noticed, the compliment seemed to distress her, the eyes went vacant and she took on the look of a chihuahua lost on a summer beach. Finally Louise said, "That's a pretty dress," and the mellowness returned.

"You'll wear a uniform here," Mrs. Crawford said. Turning, she called, "Gerta."

Gerta entered from the butler's pantry shaking soapsuds from chubby hands. Her face, a fleshy girlish oval out of which glinted jewel-blue eyes, belonged on a creamery butter carton. Blue eyes and fair, wholesome skin pulsated with youthful vigor. "Yah, you be velcome," she said. She dried a hand against her white uniform and offered it. "Vot iss your name?" she asked. Julia told her, and Gerta said, "Yah, you be velcome."

Mrs. Crawford said, "You'll meet cook at dinner."

The housekeeper trudged grimly up the back stairs. Julia trailed, suitcase in hand, counting the number of steps to each landing, estimating the distance to the next ell, checking placement of overhead lights, the wall switches. Joe Dev had said, "You gotta sharpen your eyes, understand? Your eyes, they gotta be mine. Practice looking. Everybody looks but they don't see anything, they see only the one thing they're looking for. You gotta see everything. Look at things, notice, measure, use your eyes, use your head."

She planned to write it all down. Time was short, the house enormous. She grew more and more uneasy. Her hopes and fears tending to the center, fear had taken the stronger hold. She could not bring herself to believe that the plan to raid the house of Cugarman's treasure would work. The future broke cold and gray.

Four attic rooms served as maids' quarters, although only the three girls, Julia included, were now employed. Julia's room, a tiny cubicle with slanted ceiling, overlooked the back courtyard and caught the heat of the afternoon sun. A bathroom no larger than the closet had a stall shower so small it suggested skinned elbows. Because of rank and tenure Mrs. Crawford and the cook enjoyed rooms on the second floor, cooler in summer, warmer in winter.

Mrs. Crawford said, "You'll make your bed and tidy up here before you come down in the morning. I do a bit of inspecting now and then, so don't go thinking you can make a sty of the place."

"It's real cozy," Julia said.

Mrs. Crawford hmph'd. "After breakfast you're to dust the entire downstairs. Louise and Gerta, they do the hard cleaning and vacuuming, up and down, first and second floors. You'll help cook and wash windows and polish silver, whatever's asked of you. Orders'll be laid out, don't you fret none about that. After lunch you're free until four o'clock. When Mr. Cugarman is home you'll serve. That's why you're here, mostly, to serve, like I told you. Houseboy was Donnet's job, but he's too filthy to allow in the house. I reckon you saw. No better'n those beasts of his. You're to wear a white, *clean* uniform at all times. You'll find a bunch of them in the hall closet, outside your door. You any good with a needle?"

"Not very," Julia said.

Mrs. Crawford hmph'd. "Well, I'll fit it to you so you won't go looking dowdy. Mr. Cugarman likes everything to be neat and pretty."

"Yes, Mrs. Crawford," Julia said.

Mrs. Crawford turned at the door. "The girl whose place you're fillin'. I sent her away. Took up with Teague. I won't have it. Reckon you understand. I won't have it."

Julia widened her eyes to full innocence. "Mrs. Crawford, I have a fiancé. We're planning to get married soon's we've saved enough to set up housekeeping. Wouldn't *he* give me a time if I so much as *looked* at another man."

"Got a way with him, that Teague," Mrs. Crawford said. "Take warning."

"I am *so* grateful for your advice, ma'am," Julia said. "Truly I am."

Mrs. Crawford left. Julia went to the window and glanced below. Teague walked toward his garage apartment, taking off the chauffeur's jacket as he went, hooking it over one finger when he opened the door. Julia saw that a leather strap ringed the left shoulder of his white shirt. A holstered gun. Joe Dev had warned that Teague carried it. On the far end of the courtyard, Donnet, moving with the obscene litheness of a ferret, dribbled a basketball and tossed it into a hoop secured above the garage door; the dogs, stretched out under the lean-to, cocked their heads curiously and followed the motion of the bouncing ball.

A screen door banged distantly. A girl wearing a white uniform appeared in the lower part of Julia's vision: Gerta. The dogs immediately sprung into attack crouch and remained so even after they recognized the scent as exempt from their charge. The girl hugged a paper sack, and eyes glued to the dogs, placed one timid foot before the other, heading, no doubt, for the rubbish bin behind the garage. Donnet threw his head back, laughed, tossed the ball aside and took the paper sack from her, retaining hold on one of her wrists. The girl tarried reluctantly, attention split between screen door and dogs. She freed herself of Donnet's hold and retreated into the house.

In answer to a timid knock, Julia said, "Yes . . . ?" She opened the door.

Louise smiled apologetically. "Hello," she said.

Julia smiled.

"Dinner is about six-thirty," Louise said.

"Thank you for telling me," Julia said. The girl obviously sought company. Julia disliked hurting her, but visits had to be discouraged.

Louise said, "You like me, don't you." It was not a question.

"My, yes, y'sweet thing," Julia said.

"I was hurt," Louise said, quickly adding, "when I was born."

"Oh?" Julia said.

"It's only when I have to answer somebody fast," Louise said.

"What, honey?" Julia said.

"You know," Louise said.

"Yes, I think so," Julia said.

"You're pretty too," Louise said. "You have red hair. I love red hair. I wish I had red hair. I always wished I had red hair."

"It's a mess right now," Julia said.

"Oh, no," Louise said. "It's beautiful." She leaned into the doorway and said conspiratorially, "We play a game at dinner. What we do is—"

"You must tell me about it later," Julia said. "I want to rest now."

The eyes went vacant; she nodded forlornly and left.

The staff ate dinner at the kitchen table. Teague warned Julia as they gathered, "It's a drag. Eat and shuck out fast." And as dinner progressed, Julia understood what he meant. The cook, a puffy and arthritic virago of fifty-five, abetted Mrs. Crawford in all her petty tyrannies. Unable to wrest leadership from the housekeeper, total agreement with the victor served as the healing ointment that salved the sting of defeat. Conversation, when attempted, pulled heavily. Only Gerta, whose innocence transcended awareness, talked blithely on, pronouncing thickly words learned from a Berlitz reader. "Vot is the vorb 'goot' the past tenz?" she asked.

" 'Goat' ain't a verb," Mrs. Crawford said.

"Y'oughta know that," the cook said.

"No, no," Gerta said. " 'Goot.' "

"That ain't a verb either," Mrs. Crawford said.

"Y'oughta know that," the cook said.

Julia began to understand, too, the game Louise had mentioned.

Teague asked for the zucchini and said, "They say it's gonna rain tomorrow."

Mrs. Crawford said, "Nonsense."

The cook said, "Them fellers're always wrong."

Teague nudged Louise, who sat beside him. It was her turn. She suppressed a giggle and shook her head.

Donnet took up the game. He belched.

Mrs. Crawford glared.

The cook glared.

Teague nudged Louise again, goading her. Louise summoned all her courage and said inconsequentially, "I don't think I'll have any zucchini."

Mrs. Crawford said, "Eat it, it's good for you."

"Full of vitamins," the cook said.

Louise glowed at the outcome of her daring; Teague and Donnet smiled congratulations.

Teague nodded at Julia. Her turn.

Julia said, "My, this meat is tender."

Mrs. Crawford said, "Cooked too long."

The cook hesitated, then said, "Well, a little."

Teague guffawed.

Mrs. Crawford and the cook glared.

Julia's spirits picked up.

After dinner the girls gathered at the back doorstep to witness Teague giving Donnet a haircut. Donnet complained, and with reason. Teague approached the task like a felon barbering the sentencing judge. "If you don't like it, go to a pro," he said. " 'Nap Town's full of 'em." He called to the girls, "He's wanted. In California, Oregon and Washington."

"Aw, shut up," Donnet said.

Gouging skin from scalp, Teague said, "If he goes to 'Nap Town for a clipping he's scared some joker'll match his mug to the one's hanging in the post office." Louise's laughter rippled above the others'. Teague singled her out to ask, "You think I'm kidding?" Louise jumped up and down with delight. "It's why he never leaves the place," Teague said. "He'll be picked up. Couldn't ask for a better hideout than this. Nobody gets in here."

"You're full of shit," Donnet said. "Shut up."

"Jesus," Teague said. "Will you look at that. He's crawling. My God, Vietnamese bugs. Brought the goddamn things back with him."

"Easy, you bastard," Donnet said. "That hurts."

"Everybody hollered, 'Bring the boys back from Vietnam,' " Teague said. "Fine. The boys. Bugs? Hey, Donny, they from the South or are they VC bugs?"

Donnet submitted because Teague was correct in all but his geography. His escape from an indictment handed down by a Delaware grand jury a thread-thin success, good sense warned him not to blow the safety of the Cugarman estate because of slovenliness. When Mrs. Crawford complained too loudly of his appearance, he gave way grudgingly to soap and water and hair clipping.

Julia dashed up to her room for a camera. "Send them to my mama," she said.

"Hey, Donny," Teague said, "you wanted in Stevensville, Tennessee?"

"Aw, shut up," Donnet said.

Julia took several pictures of Louise and Gerta standing at the back door. A shot of Teague included a clear view of the woods behind him, another the garage and driveway.

When Julia heard the avalanche she thought she'd provoked it because of focusing the camera on the lean-to and the dogs. But the outbreak of barking that followed, like a muster cry of wolves, was not directed at her. Hair bristling, the Baluchis sped toward the front gate, their brawling cries shattering the evening quiet. Lurking dread sent the girls scurrying into the house. Julia, the last one in, looked over her shoulder and saw that Teague drew a gun as he ran. Donnet was way ahead of him, a fox chasing a rat.

They reheated the dinner coffee and tried to ignore the chilling cries. Julia asked, "Does this happen often?" Gerta threw up her hands and said nothing. The question sent Louise into tears.

A few minutes later Teague and Donnet strolled back up the driveway. Teague peered past the screen door and said, "Come on, I'm gonna finish the haircut."

Gerta said, "Nah, nah, no more."

"Come on," Teague said. "It was only kids, screwing around the front gate."

"Nah, nah," Gerta said. She spoke for all three. The moment of fun was over.

Julia excused herself early and went to her room. Suddenly aware of tears, she kneaded them dry with the heel of her hand and struggled with conflicting emotions and thoughts. Never possessed of the gift of suiting achievable ambition to constructive action, the abandonment of plans for a real estate career to join Joe Dev in the performance of a criminal act was what Harriet Stocker called "dropping the bone for the shadow." But she wanted, needed Joe Dev; that was certain. Hatred of Alice had nothing to do with her decision. Too, success of Joe Dev's plan equated with security.

She prepared for bed telling herself that relief from tension explained her soul-deep fatigue. She'd made it into the house; the first step was an unqualified success. Over past days fear had been a gleefully scornful companion—the decision to couple with Joe Dev, the fraudulent imposition on the employment agency, rehearsed and acted out under the pressure of guilt, the bogus references, the nagging thought of exposure and prison—fear had taunted, accumulated into a knotted mass that set nerves atwang. Now it was over and the residue of fear was fatigue. Sleep would cure.

She turned out the light, lay back, then immediately shot upright again. No, it was not relief from tension nor the success of the plan so far that unjangled the nerves. It was *failure* that brought rest to mind and body. Yes, of course, failure. Joe Dev's plan had to be called off. It simply would not work. The incident with the dogs, earlier, convinced her that the criminal act had progressed as far as ever it would or could. Joe Dev's instructions were detailed, precise. She'd fulfill them to the letter and report to him. He'd see for himself. Impossible. Insanity even to try. No way.

She slept.

CHAPTER **15**

The Soldiers and Sailors Monument stands in the center of the square mile on which the city of Indianapolis was founded. At the top of the memorial shaft is a figure of a woman symbolizing victory. Smaller statues represent peace and war. From 9 to 4:30 daily, for the admission price of twenty-five cents, anyone interested can rise 258 feet into the air for an unobstructed view of the city.

The Indian drove his Chrysler into Memorial Circle and braked before one of the skyscrapers clustered around the monument. Alice was waiting. She got in. The Indian started around the Circle again.

"Hi," she said.

The Indian nodded. "Lose the cigarette," he said.

Alice lowered the window and tossed it out. "How come?" she asked.

"Stinks up the upholstery," he said. "How many times've I told you?"

She said, "No, I mean how come here, making me drive all this way. Why not in Uniontown, as usual?"

"Think that's an important question, do you?" he asked.

"Withdrawn," she said.

"Start where you left off," he said.

"I told you everything," she said.

"What about the car?" he said.

"He left it at the auto rental place," she said. "Dropped the keys in the mail slot, after closing. I checked."

"So you didn't tell me everything, right?" he said. "You didn't tell me about the car?"

"No, I didn't tell you about the car," she said. "But it doesn't change anything."

"He didn't say anything that'd give you some notion?" the Indian said.

She shook her head. "He had a way of talking and saying nothing," she said. "I thought he might show up at the funeral. He didn't. Guess word didn't get to him, wherever he is." She paused a moment. "Bastard. I mean Cooney. He as good as killed her and nobody's doing anything about it."

"Nothing to do," the Indian said.

"What bothers me is the Christ," Alice said.

"What?" he said.

"Helen's stuff," she said. "The other things, the plaster saints, the holy pictures, they're creepy enough. But the Christ . . ."

A Ford truck with a racing car in tow demanded a place in the traffic and zigzagged for the west exit to Washington Street. Probably on its way to the speedway. Although undoubtedly older, the driver looked to be about fourteen, and he flaunted the cockiness that goes with the age.

"Kids've got it great nowadays," Alice said. "Just great. Only trouble is it's like they've got suicide in mind. 'Screw everybody, I'm gonna do what I want.' It's the way I felt, why I never got on with my father. He's a minister, got a parish in Braintree. Episcopalian. 'Be a good girl,' he'd say. It's what they all say, no? 'Be a good girl, be a good boy.' Helen was a good girl. I mean really good, the way *they* mean good. What'd it get her?

"I dunno. If only they'd understand. If you want a kid to *be* good, you've got to make her *feel* good. Helen never felt that kind of good, you know, happy? She was always uptight inside."

The Indian whistled her silent.

Alice said, "You sound like a traffic cop."

"You're starting another talkathon," the Indian said. "I can tell. Get to it. What's bothering you?"

"I'm telling you," Alice said. "Helen's stuff—that Christ and all, that's what's bothering me."

"All right then," the Indian said. "You have to talk me to death? Get to it."

"I don't know what to do with it, and Harriet doesn't either. Not with any of it. This Christ, it's in a bell jar, see? And he's got one hand raised like he's giving a blessing. That's okay, nothing wrong with that, but the place where the heart is, you actually *see* the heart. Now, you ready for this? A rhinestone. There's a rhinestone in it, in the *heart,* pasted there, a teeny-tiny one, and the goddamn thing *sparkles.* You believe it? You believe it? What kind of a pervert'd make a thing like that and sell it to a kid like Helen?"

"Pack it all up and take it over to the church," the Indian said.

"It's really got me, this thing," Alice said. "What a way to go—no family, no close friends, no neighbors or school pals, no nobody. Just me and my black madam standing there taking in the ashes-to-ashes bit. It's like Helen was never there. Nobody knows she's gone. I hope her religion holds up for her."

"Where was the flannel-mouth broad?" the Indian said.

"She left," Alice said.

"She *what?*"

"The day after Joe Dev," Alice said. "Louisville."

"Jesus Christ," the Indian said.

"I know what you're thinking," Alice said, "but one doesn't have anything to do with the other."

"No, huh?" he said. "You're sure."

"Yes, I'm sure," she said. "We had an argument. Harriet got peed off and belted her. The bitch got sore, packed and took off."

"Who started the argument?" the Indian said.

"What's the difference?" Alice said. "We were always arguing. Harriet was expecting her to leave."

"Pignuts," he said.

She said, "Look, I mean, what the hell do you want me to tell you? You're trying to tie Dev in with Julia. It doesn't figure. He had no use for her. He hardly ever spoke to her. If he wanted to tie up he'd've come to me."

"Louisville, huh?" he asked.

"Harriet was expecting her to leave," Alice said. "She's going into real estate, chuckle, chuckle. I can just see her, picking up an extra buck on the bare wood floors of empty houses. Reminds me of a hillbilly joke."

The Indian made no response.

"Look," she said, "if it was so vital to you, knowing what Dev was doing, why didn't you have him watched from the outside?"

"Another important question?" he asked.

"Withdrawn," she said. "And don't do that to me. Don't give me that look, don't croon me that tune. I mean, Christ."

He said, "I'm going to meet a guy."

"Who?" she said.

The Indian remained silent.

"Yes, master," she said.

"There are times," he said, "when you're a pain in the ass. Like today."

"You're not always the jolly green giant, either," she said. "My excuse is I'm a manic-depressive and I'm in the down cycle. Heavy head, pressure on the bladder, distorted outlook, etcetera. I wake up and find myself sleeping in a fetal position, that'll give you some idea. What's your excuse?"

The Indian swung into the parking lot. As they walked toward the monument, he said, "You hear anything from the greaseball, let me know."

"No, I'm gonna keep it a secret," she said.

"Good to you, was he?" he said.

"Where are we going?" she said.

"Top of the monument," he said.

"What for?" she said.

He looked at her.

"Withdrawn," she said.

"I'll only be a few minutes," he said.

"And then?"

"Anything you like," he said. "Name it."

"Some joker in Vincennes claims he spotted a UFO last night. Drop me in the vicinity. Maybe one of those spaceships'll scoop me up and take me the hell off the goddamn planet."

"Your second request," he said.

"I'd like for somebody to be nice to me," she said. "I mean, *want* to be nice, for no other reason than that they want to."

"You could be talking about me," the Indian said.

"Outta sight," Alice said.

"Lunch? Then the races? Dinner?" he said.

"Outta sight," Alice said.

The Indian bought two tickets and they took the elevator to the top. The Indian looked around and spotted Eugene Bang-Jens, a big redhead with eyes the color of swimming-pool paint. He wore a transparent sport shirt over slacks. The pocket of the shirt sagged under the weight of a mechanical pen and pencil.

"Enjoy the view," the Indian said to Alice, and left to join Bang-Jens.

Bang-Jens said, "Hi," and then his eyes darted to Alice. "Nice stuff."

The Indian remained silent.

Turning into the wind, hunched up and cupping a match, Bang-Jens lit a cigarette. "Why the hell did you pick this place," he said.

"Anybody we know spend a quarter to come up here?" the Indian asked.

"It's like that, huh?" Bang-Jens said. "For a while there I was nowheres. I mean, I wasn't expecting a call, not from you."

The Indian nodded.

"Goddamn swindle for all these visitors," Bang-Jens said, looking out. "Can't see anything for the fucking haze. You can just about make out the Capitol, and it's how far? I could spit and make a splash." His eyes darted to Alice again. Her dress, a shimmering splendor in the breeze, punctuated every angle and line of her. Bang-Jens stirred within.

"Drive down, did you?" the Indian said.

"No," Bang-Jens said. "A guy I know's got his own Beechcraft. Salesman. Rubber products, tires mostly. He come down for the day. I'm gonna meet him at six, and we'll go back."

"Where'd you say your place was?" the Indian asked. "Angola?"

"Outside," Bang-Jens said, "near Pokagon Park. Second home, is what you'd call it. Me and the wife go up for my vacations, and off-season, too. She's nuts about fishing. Throws a hook so it lands right in the fucking fish's mouth."

"Your vacation's over the end of the week, right?" the Indian said.

"Yeah," Bang-Jens said. "How'd you know?"

"Pokagon Park was named after an Indian, you know that?" the Indian said.

"No, I didn't," Bang-Jens said.

"The government screwed him out of a million acres," the Indian said. "Gave him three cents an acre for the area that takes in what's now Chicago."

"No shit," Bang-Jens said. He laughed. "That why you took me away from my fishing?"

The Indian squinted into the haze. "Much of a mortgage on your place?" he asked.

"Hey, now what the fuck business would that be of yours," Bang-Jens asked.

"Enough so that I know the answer," the Indian said.

"You seem to know a lot," Bang-Jens said. "Why take the trouble?"

"I need a favor," the Indian said.

"Step right up and ask," Bang-Jens said. "You don't have to pave the way with bullshit. Ask."

"Ever take out a guy?" the Indian asked.

"Call that a favor? Christ." Bang-Jens paused a moment, then said, "Bick know you're asking that question?"

The Indian nodded.

"You don't want me," Bang-Jens said. "Detroit, Los Angeles, maybe, New Orleans. Not me. I can put you in touch with a guy in Nashville, connected with the New Orleans crowd, but lays back, you know? Only goes out when . . . well, a specialist."

"You," the Indian said.

"Uh-uh," Bang-Jens said. "No way."

"Definite?"

"Definite."

The Indian nodded. "I understand. And it's okay. Sorry. I didn't get you here to press, only to ask." He reached into his pocket for an envelope and handed it to Bang-Jens.

"What's this?" Bang-Jens said.

"Five hundred," the Indian said. "For your trouble, for taking you away from your fishing and to forget I asked the question. What're you going to do until six?"

"I don't know," Bang-Jens said. "Hit a few taverns, I guess."

"The girl's got nothing to do either," the Indian said. "Why don't you keep her company?"

"What?" Bang-Jens said. "I thought—"

"Live it up," the Indian said.

"Look, wait a minute," Bang-Jens said. Indicating the envelope, he said, "Look, you don't have to do this."

"It's Bick's style," the Indian said. "Ever know him to do different?"

"No, but just the same, it's pretty fucking decent," Bang-Jens said. "Important to Bick, is it, this thing?"

"If it wasn't I'd've called Detroit or L.A. or New Orleans, not Angola."

"Well," Bang-Jens said, "I could at least know more about it."

"Pignuts," the Indian said.

"Yes or no, you mean, huh?" Bang-Jens said.

The Indian nodded.

"What if I say yes?" Bang-Jens said. "Where do we go from there?"

"You'll know as much as you know now," the Indian said.

"I'm nowheres," Bang-Jens said.

"The only way to move," the Indian said. "You wait."

"Who?" Bang-Jens said. "Who do I take out?"

"It won't be your grandmother," the Indian said.

"When?" Bang-Jens said. "Can you tell me when?"

"Day's notice, maybe," the Indian said. "Maybe less, maybe only five minutes."

Bang-Jens scratched his hair. "I don't believe it," he said, "I don't believe what you're telling me. Boy. A setup like that, a guy could get his nuts cracked. You're asking me to be in the right place at the right time, and you'll finger the guy and that's it—kachoo?"

"Something like that," the Indian said.

"No planning?" Bang-Jens said. "The innsey-outsy of it? Nothing? For Christ's sake, if the old lady asks me to go down to the supermarket, I make a list. You're not asking me to fetch a can of beans, you're asking me to waste a guy."

"The planning's been done," the Indian said.

"Plans get fucked up," Bang-Jens said. "Especially if the guy carrying the load doesn't know if his ass is in front or back."

"Bick doesn't fuck up," the Indian said.

"This why you asked about the mortgage?" Bang-Jens said.

The Indian produced another envelope. "Down payment. Five thousand."

"Clean?" Bang-Jens said.

"Came from the Uniontown Savings and Loan less than two hours ago."

Bang-Jens smiled. "Uniontown Savings and Loan operates out of Bick's pocket. Guys who know better never accept a twenty-dollar bill that comes from Uniontown Savings and Loan." The Indian looked at him in a way that made him add, "I'm only kidding, for Christ's sake. You say it's clean it's clean. No question."

"Appreciate that," the Indian said.

"That mortgage *is* breaking my fucking back," Bang-Jens said.

"You won't get hurt," the Indian said. "I promise you that myself."

"Well," Bang-Jens said, reaching for the envelope, "if you and Bick're standing behind me."

"Come on," the Indian said. "I'll introduce you to the girl."

"Appreciate this," Bang-Jens said.

CHAPTER 16

Night came softly that Thursday. In room 301 of the Plains Motel, Joe Dev and Julia lay breathless from lovemaking. It was her first day off and their first reunion.

"Was it all right, Joe?" she said.

"I never had it better," he said, "not even with Scarlett O'Hara."

"Oh, you," she said.

"Honest, I'm not kidding," he said.

"Really, Joe?" she said. "I take this sudden fright now and again, like none of it's true. Was it really all right?"

"Holy Jesus," he said. "For the rest of our lives you gonna punish me? Okay, what I said that day, I meant it. But this is love, that makes it different."

"I do love you, Joe," she said. "Lordy, I love you s'much my teeth hurt. You turned me on the minute I saw you standing there in the rain. Funny thing is, Harriet'd been telling me things about myself and I kept denying it. And here I am in a one-man bed."

"Make sure you keep it that way," he said.

"Shoot, you'd better believe it," she said. She kissed him. "Joe, you will be careful."

"I'll be all right," he said. "You just do like I told you with my sweater."

She nodded.

He looked at his watch. "It's time," he said.

"Won't it seem funny?" she said. "My getting back so early?"

"You said they lock up at ten, no?" he said. "So it's more better before they lock up. People feel looser before the lockup, understand?"

"Yes," she said, "I expect that's so."

They talked as they dressed. He said, "This is it for us, baby. The restaurant, our life, everything. You're okay, huh? You remember everything?"

She nodded. "Joe . . ."

"There you go again," he said. "Joe. With the big worry in your mouth."

"Joe, I *am* worried," she said. "I can't help it."

"Look," he said, "I listened to every word you said, like how the whole thing's impossible, no?"

"Yes," she said.

"Then you gotta trust me," he said. "You're wrong. It's gonna work and you're gonna see that it works. Believe me. I know about people's brains. It's like some guy's got an ear for music, understand? So take the big worry out of your mouth."

She said unconvincingly, "All right."

He said, "Julia, you gotta get it in your head that I wouldn't move unless I was sure. People act in certain ways. They got habits, especially when they're working. Habits make the work more easy, understand? You told me about those people in the house, so I know how they're gonna act. Only the girls no, them I haven't figured yet. To me they're strange."

"Joe, they're the easiest to understand," Julia said. "Louise is simple, sweet as May and simple. As for Gerta, why, she's a child, got no more guile in her than a loaf of bread. She's an innocent. When Donnet says dirty things, she blushes. Blushes, Joe."

"Anybody's a hundred percent innocent don't blush," he said. "You blush, you gotta know what the hell you're blushing about. You see, Julia? You don't have the ear for it. I have. But that's okay. Take my word for it. Take the big worry out of your mouth. I know how they're gonna act. I even know how *you're* gonna act."

Her eyes narrowed. "And how's that?" she asked.

"Fine, baby, just fine, terrific," he said.

Julia bit her lip.

He said, "Hey, you still got time to back off. You haven't got the heart, okay, I don't push if you haven't got the heart."

"Oh, no, no," she said. "Joe, I'd follow you if you went into hell after the devil. But shoot, you can't blame me for being scared."

"Sure you're scared," he said. "But what else's anybody got to live with in this life? Fear and hope. Fear, that's the father and the mother of everything bad. You gotta kick it in the ass and tell it to stay the fuck away from you. Once you do that, it leaves what? Hope. Hope helps you go ready."

"Go ready?"

"One move at a time," he said. "No second move until you're sure number one is locked up tight. Like for instance, when you pull up to the gate, you stop, but that isn't enough. Stopping isn't enough. You stop, sure, but you put the car in reverse. That's what I mean by you go ready. Something goes wrong, zoom, you back off and fly. You give yourself a little edge, see? Edges add up. It takes a lot of stones to build a wall. Make sure you got the edges before you leave yourself open, otherwise you got nothing but danger."

"I'll remember," she said.

"The people in this world, they're monkeys fighting over the goddamn banana," he said. "I don't know, maybe there's nice people around someplace, but I never met them. You can't trust anybody."

"I trust you," she said.

"Me and you, that's not the same," he said. "Me and you, we gotta make our own world, a small one, no bigger than what we can put our arms around." He embraced her. "Everything else, everybody else—out. With anybody else you go ready."

"Joe . . ." she said.

"Yeah, baby," he said, touching her. "Jesus, you got a nice ass. We had the time I'd start all over again, honest. No time, okay. I settle for a little rubbing and a kiss. Like that."

When he drew away from her, she said: "Joe . . . ?"

"Yeah?" he said.

"How much money is there?" she said.

He laughed. "See?" he said. "That's hope, baby. The answer is plenty. Plenty."

"Yes, but how much?" she asked.

"Who knows?" he said.

She smiled. "Y'wouldn't be going ready, would you, Joe?"

"What?" he said.

"By not telling me how much," she said. "I don't mind. If you have a reason, if you think I shouldn't know, why, all right. Shoot, it was a no-account question."

"Look," he said, "I got no reason not to tell you. I don't know. Whatever it is, it's ours. So what's the difference? Once we got it we'll sit down and count it—together. Okay?"

"Sure, Joe," she said.

"Okay," he said. "Now it's time to go."

When Julia drove up to the wrought iron gate and tooted the horn for admittance the Baluchis, which were permitted to roam free after dark, charged forth ki-yi-ing, all fang and ferocity. Because the ki-yi-ing indicated something was wrong, the gate did not swing open. Instead Donnet came running down the driveway. Recognizing Julia, he just stood there, perplexed.

The Baluchis continued the frenzied barking. Now Teague came jogging down the driveway, the gun holster swinging loosely from his shoulder. "What the fuck," he said to Donnet. "I thought you trained them to recognize her."

"They do," Donnet said. "It must be something else."

"You trained them," Teague said, "and the first time she goes out they make a fucking idiot out of you."

"I'm telling you it's something else," Donnet said. "Another scent. In the car."

Julia's heart slipped on an icy sheet of terror. Confusion flooded her brain; she questioned that she was equal to what lay ahead. Fighting the temptation to back off and fly, as Joe Dev had said, took all her resolve. Teague further assaulted her composure when he switched on the floodlights. The light centered her in its glow and left men and dogs in a downstage darkness, the dogs leaping spectral blobs of unmanageable cruelty, the men luminous-eyed searchers.

Julia silently echoed Joe Dev's instructions. Talk. Talk loudly. The edge. Get the edge. Go ready. You knew this would happen. Habit. You've been prepared for this. You know what to say. Talk. Shout. Shout and the fear will go. Kick it in the ass. Get the edge. Go ready. *Do it.*

Recovering, she shouted, "Don't bother opening those gates. I'm not coming in." She breathed deeply. Good. It works. The fear lessened. She raced the car motor as if to start off.

"Wait a minute," Teague said.

She shouted again, topping the dogs' ki-yi. "You just go back and tell Mrs. Crawford I quit."

"For Christ's sake," Teague said. "Donnet, will you shut them up?"

Julia called, louder still, "I won't work in a place where I have to risk my life every time I go in and out."

Teague swore. "Great," he said into the night air. "All's I need is to get the old meat ax worked up." He wheeled on Donnet. "Call them off, goddammit."

"It's another scent," Donnet said.

"My ass," Teague said. "Stop them. Say whatever you have to say but stop them."

Julia shouted, "Goodbye, Paul. Nice knowing you. I'll write to Mrs. Crawford and tell her where to send my wages."

"Goddammit, hold it, willya?" Teague said. He turned to Donnet. "Will you shut 'em the fuck up? Goddamn piss-assed dog trainer."

"Screw," Donnet said. "I'm telling you they pick up another scent. In the car. Take a look. Go on, take a goddamn look."

Teague pulled gun from holster. "If you don't shut 'em up I'll shoot them the goddamn dead, and *then* I'll have a look."

"You haven't got the balls," Donnet said. "You know what the boss paid for them hounds?"

Teague shoved the gun into his ribs. "Shut 'em up," he said.

Wavering, Donnet said, "It's another scent."

Teague cocked the gun. "I still hear 'em," he said.

Reluctantly, Donnet called to the dogs. *"Otto-ici, otto-ici."* The dogs reduced the brawling to low snarls and took a place on either side of Donnet.

Julia breathed deeply and readied herself for the next move. She reached for a white knitted sweater on the seat beside her. She held it up. "Can this be what's bothering them? It's my boyfriend's. He forgot it."

Without conviction, Donnet said, "Hah, you see? I was right." The sweater represented a face-saver and he quickly accepted it.

Teague opened the gates manually, swung them wide and walked over to Julia's car. "Boyfriend get overheated, did he? Big doings in the back seat?" He poked his head into the car. His breath was heavy with the smell of whiskey.

"You shut your nasty old mouth, Paul Teague," Julia said.

Teague leered. "Partial to beddy-byes myself. Do my best work there."

"Do I go through or don't I?" Julia said.

"Go ahead," Teague said.

"You tell Donnet to stay right there and hold on to those animals until I'm in the house, hear?" Julia said.

"It's okay," Donnet said. "I give 'em the word, so don't worry."

"Thank you, but I will worry, if you don't mind," Julia said. "You'll hold on to them until I'm inside the house, and I mean *inside*. You'll know when I turn on the light."

"Go ahead," Teague said.

"He's not holding the dogs," Julia said.

Teague turned to Donnet. "Will you stop acting like a goddamn shit?" he asked.

Donnet clutched a dog collar in either hand. Julia accelerated and zoomed past them, slowing to bear left at the driveway fork. The turn completed and her car no longer visible from the gate, she speeded up again in an effort to gain as much time as possible. The edge, she told herself. But not too fast. Slow again. No screeching of brakes in the courtyard. It might waken Mrs. Crawford.

The back door. Stop the car. Position it just so. Run back to the trunk. No, wait. Turn off the ignition first. Go back. Get the key. *Now* to the trunk. Insert the key—hurry, find the opening—there.

The trunk lid yawned open. Joe Dev bounded out, a phantom in black trousers, black turtleneck sweater, black ballet slippers. In one hand, his tools, wrapped in black muslin, a package the size of a rolled-up newspaper. Unhesitatingly, he ran for the back entrance so thoroughly described and photographed by Julia: take the two steps, hedge on either side, remember the warp in the door that makes it necessary to pull before the latch will respond to the turn of the doorknob.

Joe Dev was in.

Down at the front gate, Donnet leaned over the dogs and hissed, *"Keet! Keet!"*

Teague, shutting the gate, said, "No, wait. What the fuck are you doing, you stupid bastard."

The dogs raced off.

It happened in the span of seconds. In the tiny back hall, Joe Dev made a quarter turn to his right and found the stairway which elled upward. He moved noiselessly in the vacant darkness, counting steps as he went.

The second floor. Eleven steps to the next landing. A turn. Seven paces to the next stairway. A newel post. The start of another ell. Now, eleven steps to the third floor. Turn left.

The third floor. Directly under the roof. Stifling with superheated air. Move with a hand lightly caressing the right-hand wall, finger-search for doorframes, doors. Three doors. Four. He found the knob.

Joe Dev was in Julia's room.

Unaware that the dogs raced up the driveway, Julia banged shut the trunk lid, turned briefly to make certain she'd left the car window open, then dashed to the back door. She opened it, reached in and switched on the lights. Courtyard and stairway went aglow. Julia shut the door and started upstairs.

The Baluchis, one trying to outrun the other, tore up the drive and hurdled a privet hedge.

Julia froze on the fourth step of the stairs. The car keys were folded in her moist palm. She'd forgotten to replace them in the ignition lock. She'd have to do it now. If not, Teague and Donnet would come after them. The terror exploding within her again, she started back, opened the door and ran blindly toward the car. She saw and heard the dogs, almost upon her. Cursing hysteria, she sprinted back to the door, entered and slammed it shut.

The dogs leaped into the car through the open window, their combined bulk and frenzy interfering with their effort. Through a fondue of snarling and scrambling sounds, they tore the sweater to shreds. One leaped back out, the other followed. They attacked the trunk lid for a moment, then, their bay climaxing to the death knell, charged to the back door.

Julia ran to her room. In the blackness beyond, Joe Dev's arms awaited. He said, "Turn on the lights in here. Maybe they look up, you know?"

She turned on the lights. "Joe," she said, and showed him the keys. "I'm scared. Just purely numb. Hold me."

The dogs continued to bay.

Quivering, Julia said, "What do you think, Joe?"

Joe Dev remained silent. Julia started for the window. He said, "No," sharply. They listened. Presently they heard the two men nearing the house, their voices raised in argument. A car door opened, then slammed shut. Voices again: Teague cursing Donnet. The dogs yelped their full repertoire.

All sounds faded. Silence. Joe Dev and Julia waited and listened. They heard the back door opening and closing, then footsteps on the stairs.

"Teague," Julia said.

"Look," Joe Dev said, "we go like this. If I have to I kill him. I try only to knock him out, though, and take his gun. Then you run down first. You throw the switch to open the front gate—not from the hall, the kitchen, it's closer. Then you stand still and *I* go first. I open the back door and I shoot the dogs. The other guy too. I got no picks with him, I gotta kill him. Then you come and we go to the car. Understand?"

Julia nodded.

Joe Dev said, "Who's that? The old lady?"

Julia listened. Mrs. Crawford had intercepted Teague on the second landing to demand shrilly an explanation for the commotion. Mrs. Crawford mollified to silence, Teague's footsteps grew louder on the stair. Louise's voice piped inquiringly, and Teague responded that nothing was wrong and for her to go back to sleep. Louise's door banged shut.

Teague knocked.

"Who is it?" Julia said.

"It's me," he said.

"What do you want?" Julia said.

"Open up," Teague said. "I gotta talk to you."

Julia looked at Joe Dev. He shook his head. Julia said to the door, "Well, now, that's most interesting."

"Come on, open up," Teague said.

"Not very likely," Julia said.

"I gotta have the keys to your car," Teague said.

Julia pretended surprise. "What?" she asked.

"The keys to your car," Teague said. "You can't leave it out there blocking the driveway."

Julia looked at Joe Dev. He nodded, then slipped into the closet. Julia opened the door.

"Hi," Teague said. His eyes flashed from her face to her breasts.

Julia handed him the keys. "That was a nasty thing to do, setting those damned dogs on me before I had a chance to get in the house. You promised you wouldn't."

"Donnet," Teague said. "He's that kind of a shit."

"Damned beasts," Julia said. "I hate them."

"Gave the order to kill," Teague said. "Not you. Your boyfriend."

"My boyfriend?" Julia said.

"Yeah," Teague said. "Donnet's still uptight about things. I don't blame him much. The way them animals took on, you'd swear he was in that car with you."

"Honestly," Julia said.

"In the trunk," Teague said. "Hiding in the trunk. Can't fool those hounds about a scent."

"Rats and rattles, why wouldn't there *be* a scent," Julia said. "It's my boyfriend's car, been running it better than two years."

Teague grinned. "You oughta see what a chewing job they did on your boyfriend's sweater. Looks like elbow macaroni."

"Somebody'll have to pay for it," Julia said. "Thank you very much and good night."

He clomped one foot in the door and prevented her from shutting it. "You got a real pretty make on you," he said.

"You take your damned foot out of my door," Julia said. "If you came up here to do that kind of plantin' you're going to harvest a thin crop."

"So you got a boyfriend," Teague said. "A big strong girl like you can always use a little extry."

"You'd best take yourself off, Paul Teague," Julia said. "If you don't, Mrs. Crawford'll come rarin'."

"It's early," he said. "When things quiet down, why don't you come over to my place?"

"Oh, surely so," Julia said. "Your place—with Donnet's ear to the wall."

"You say when and where," Teague said.

"Well, it certainly wouldn't be in *your* place," Julia said. "If I did—mind you, I'm not saying I would—but if I did, it'd be on the outside."

"When?" he said. "Your next day off? Thursday, huh?"

"I'm not sayin' yes or no," Julia said. "Shoo."

He reached for her. "A little feel, just a little feel."

"You shoo," she said. "Paul Teague, you are full of the Old Nick."

She pushed him out the door.

CHAPTER **17**

They spoke in half whispers. Joe Dev said, "Look, no chances, understand? If I got my picks I go hungry before I let you take a chance." He bit into the turkey sandwich.

"I'm careful, Joe," Julia said. "I waited until everybody was out of the kitchen, and I didn't take very much."

Between bites he looked at his watch. Nine-seventeen.

Julia said, "You've scads of time."

He nodded.

He had slept his entire first day in the Cugarman house—a light sleep, the disciplined part of him tuned in and alert to sounds and voices beyond the locked door.

"Tell me about the people downstairs," he said. "The housekeeper, Mrs. Crawford, all day long I hear her squawking, now I hear nothing. Got a voice like a siren."

Julia said, "She's gone to Covington to visit her daughter. She left right after the dinner cleanup."

"How far is Covington?" he said.

"A half-hour or thereabouts," Julia said.

"She comes back tonight?" he asked.

"She didn't say, but I'm sure not," Julia said. "Wouldn't leave her much time for visiting."

"The Dutch girl," Joe Dev said.

"Same as always," Julia said. "In her room with her Berlitz." She laughed. "Donnet's still teaching her dirty words and telling her they're something else. Tonight at dinner he pointed to the rhubarb and said, 'Hey, Gerta, pass me that pussy pie.' Mrs. Crawford gave him a look that like to slice him down the middle."

Joe Dev smiled. "Yeah, huh? What about the cook?"

"Gone to bed," Julia said. "Her arthritis is fiercing her, she said. Once she's asleep she's asleep."

"The other girl," Joe Dev said.

"Louise is out walking with Teague," Julia said.

"Jesus Christ, her too?" Joe Dev said.

"Oh, no, Joe," Julia said. "It's really something to see them together. She's like a little sister to him."

"Is he boozing tonight?" he asked.

"No more than usual," Julia said. "He'll be back around ten to lock up."

Joe Dev looked at his watch. "Yeah," he said. He forced down what was left of the sandwich. He hated mayonnaise, and Julia had slathered it on. He made ready to go. Julia tilted her head and offered her mouth. "Scads of time, Joe," she said.

He fulfilled her expectations with false fervor. It seemed to him that insecurity made her insatiable, she felt the need to prove herself over and over. When, as now, his passion had to hurdle the barrier of preoccupation, he responded dutifully. He lay back, his body an offering. Her skills were many. She roused him, he performed, and then, breathless, she asked the question: "Was it all right, Joe?"

"Boy, I'm telling you," he said. "Nobody gets it better than me."

"Really, Joe? Truly?" she asked.

Joe Dev said, "Teague."

"What?" she said.

"He just came in," he said. "The girl, too."

"I didn't hear anything," she said.

He said, "It's a good thing you got such a nice ass, because your ears, they're not worth much."

Julia giggled. Joe Dev shushed her. They listened to Louise climb the stairs to the third floor. Her room was at the far end of the hall. She entered, closing the door noisily.

"Teague is setting the alarms now, right?" Joe Dev said.

"Yes," Julia said.

Joe Dev crossed to the window and looked down on the lighted courtyard. He heard, faintly, the opening and closing of the back door. Teague appeared and strolled idly toward the garage apartments. Almost simultaneously the Baluchis came silently out of the night and pranced across his path. One of them paused to water a yew, then both dematerialized in the surrounding blackness. Teague lingered before the apartment door to suck one final drag from a cigar stump. He tossed the stump into the bushes. He entered the apartment. A bit later the lights in the courtyard went out.

Over his shoulder, Joe Dev said, "The signal for the kitchen door is in his room? That what you said?"

"Yes," she said. "He'll turn it on now, and if anybody goes in or out an alarm goes off in his room."

Now Joe Dev felt her naked body against his back, warm, demanding. He turned. She kissed him. He said, "No, don't start up again. It's time."

He slipped into the all-black outfit and snapped burglar tools to his belt. He padded noiselessly down to the second floor. He listened at the cook's door. Her snoring sounded like a stew pot at full boil. He proceeded to the first floor and the tiny hall that separated kitchen from butler's pantry. He found the alarm box. It was of metal, unconcealed, and it housed four switches marked INT, EXT, SAFE, FIRE. He recognized the system's order, simple, efficient. One switch activated the exterior alarm, the second guarded against entry into the house through doors or windows, the third, presumably, would rouse house and police if anyone were to wander into the forbidden area of the safe. An orange monitor light glowed NORMAL under the fire-alarm switch. The fire detector was the type which had thermal units anchored to the ceiling of every room in the house. The units would react immediately to temperature changes and sound an alarm when heat conditions became abnormal. A master control panel warned of fire inside the house, clanging bells outside. Joe Dev noticed that extra wiring had been attached to the unit, indicating that an alarm also sounded in the local firehouse. None of the wires—fire or intruder alarms—were exposed. They squirmed into the wall behind the box.

He deactivated all systems. Free to move about, he

soft-footed it to the basement. In the ceiling directly above the pantry-hall area, he located the four wires. A six-inch length of them lay exposed to bypass a beam before they again disappeared into the flooring. He had hoped to find them arranged fanlike, thus finding a clue to the direction in which the number three wire wormed its way to the safe, but all four were neatly lined up.

He paused and looked long on the face of disappointment before rejecting the idea of cutting a hole in the flooring. Noisy, and he might sever a wire. He would have to locate the safe by a systematic search of the likeliest places.

He spent the better part of the night in the study, applying pointed patience to every surface and every object. Every book on every shelf became subject to swift but thorough scrutiny, every drawer was removed from every piece of furniture and its contents examined under the flashlight beam. He didn't find the securities or learn the whereabouts of the safe but he learned much about Daniel Cugarman. If his domain personified the man, love of neatness and order, elegantly expressed, gave evidence to the personality. The contents of the desk drawers—correspondence political, personal, household accounts, employee records, landscaping plans, heating and lighting costs and other statistics to which a man of wealth normally assigns an underling—were meticulously arranged; they identified themselves with the snap and precision of a platoon roll call.

Detailed elegance abounded. Even postage stamps were pampered by the antiqueness of a lapis snuffbox, and cloisonné artistry graced the common paper clip.

It was obvious, too, that those who served the personality dared not violate the orderliness. The daily accumulation of mail lay carefully stacked atop the desk, junk mail deleted, the personal and requests for charity donations carefully separated. Joe Dev flicked through the stack of personal mail. The pink envelope with a Chicago postmark was there, awaiting Cugarman's return.

Searching the desk, Joe Dev laughed. He suppressed the laughter and reduced it to a wheeze. Jesus. This Cugarman. The guy (Joe Dev didn't know the English equivalent) was *un sempliciotto astuto,* a cunning simpleton. Look at this goddamn desk, all crapped up with carving, eight feet long almost, like something you expect to find the Pope sitting behind; the bottom right-hand drawer is three inches shorter than the others. Only another *sempliciotto* like Teague could miss it. You don't even have to measure to realize the drawer's too short for the desk, you can see it with your bare eyes.

Joe Dev removed the drawer, reached in and slid aside the secret panel. Hidden in it was a stamp collection, five thousand dollars in one-hundred-dollar bills, an envelope, a chamois bag and two jewel boxes. A pearl necklace gleamed against the black velour on one box, a diamond bracelet against the other. Joe Dev surmised there were rings in the chamois bag even before he opened it to find eight of them—diamonds, emeralds, star sapphires. The envelope contained six safety deposit box keys.

Joe Dev inspected the loot. *Sempliciotto astuto,* no question about it. The money—fake. Feel the goddamn paper, even in the dark. The jewelry—fake, every piece. You don't need no jeweler's glass, you can tell by the weight. Like the bracelet, that many stones gotta make the weight. This don't. The pearl necklace—fake. Real necklaces don't have on them five-and-dime clasps. And who needs to be an expert to know the stamps are phony? The keys? The guy's gotta be kidding. The keys are supposed to make a dumb trick look good, like there's millions stashed away in safety deposit boxes? Maybe to a dummy, yeah, it looks good, but not to anybody knows his bone from a banana. Goddamn sketch, that's what.

He replaced the bogus treasure and resumed his search while playing a question-and-answer game with himself. Something needed explaining. This Cugarman guy, an oddball. Why, Joe, huh? Why? Why a goddamn secret compartment it's not too easy to find but not too hard to find, either? And loaded with crap. Here's a joe with dogs and guards and maybe fifteen thousand invested in electronic alarms and he fills a secret compartment with junk like that. Why? For burglars, no? But wait a minute, take it easy. Not for burglars. A burglar breaks in, he makes a quick grab and goodbye. He doesn't have all night to look for secret compartments. Gotta be something different. Sure. The secret compartment is for the goddamn guards, guys like Teague, Donnet and those other dummies, guys on the inside, guys that got plenty of time and can go through a room like a goddamn monkey goes through his fur looking for bugs. Sure. Gotta be that. You find the junk and take off and what happens? You wind up dry, or either you get busted for shoving queer, or either you take lumps from a fence don't like jokes. And the beauty part—you listening, Joe?—the beauty part is Cugarman gets rid of a crook and it don't cost him one goddamn nickel. *Sempliciotto astuto?* Maybe no, huh? Think it over, Joe-Boy, don't put this guy down. He's ready for the dummies and maybe he's ready for you, so don't put him down in your mind.

A half-hour before dawn he returned to the pantry hall and activated the switches. He went up to the third floor. Julia lay awake. "Why don't you sleep?" he said.

"I was worried about you," she said.

"Go to sleep," he said. "You don't sleep at night you won't be worth nothing during the day."

She asked, "Did you find it, Joe?"

"The safe, no," he said. "I found a secret compartment in the desk, though. The bottom right-hand drawer. You pull it out and in the back there's a panel that slides to the left."

"What's in it?" she said.

"Cash," he said. "Five thousand. The jewelry and other stuff, it's hard to say what it's worth. I make a wild guess I say maybe twenty thousand."

"Jewelry?" she said.

He nodded. "Diamonds, pearls, stuff like that," he said. "Maybe it could go to twenty-five thousand. I'm no expert at figuring those things."

"But, Joe," she said, "isn't that what you wanted? What we came to look for? Five thousand cash and maybe five times that in jewelry, isn't that what we came for?"

"No," he said. "That stuff it can be traced. I don't want any part of it." He laughed, amused. "Jesus, you're a greedy bitch," he said. "You oughta see the look on your face."

She laughed too. "Just a little piggy is all."

"Why do you love money so much?" he said.

"Money'll do anything," she said.

"And you do anything for money, eh?" he said.

"Well, not anything," she said.

"My father used to say that money, it's no good," he said. "Money's got no eyes, no mouth, no ears, no heart, no soul, nothing. You look at it, it don't look back. You talk to it, it don't answer. You love it, it don't love you, so the less you have to do with it the better off you are. Maybe that's why he died broke, he didn't want to have anything to do with it."

"Shoot, Joe," she said. "I don't want to carry on no conversation with it, I want to spend it is all."

"Go to sleep," he said.

"But, Joe, honestly now," she said, "are you sure? About what's in the desk, I mean?"

"I'm sure," he said. "That stuff is danger. New money, the serial numbers go one-two-three. And jewelry, you not only got the cops after you, you got the insurance company. And then you run around looking to make a deal with some fence's looking to screw you. No, what we came for is in the safe—wherever it is—so I keep looking for it until I find it. Okay?"

"Whatever you say, Joe," she said. "I was only thinking about us, our place, the restaurant."

"Fine," he said, "fine to think about that. That makes you go ready. But don't be greedy."

"Will you answer me one thing?" she said. "I don't want to sound pokey but what are you searching for?"

He sighed. "What am I searching for?" he said. "The safe."

"No, I mean what, in the safe?" she said.

"Stocks, bonds," he said. "You go to sleep now."

"In a minute," she said. "One more question?"

"Yeah?"

"Suppose you don't find the safe?"

"I know what you're hinting," he said. "The answer is no. Even if I don't find what we came after, we leave this place without the stuff in the desk. With nothing."

"With nothing?" she said. "Nothing at all?"

"Don't drop dead," he said.

"Seems a waste," she said, "to leave thirty thousand dollars."

"No waste," he said. "Don't worry. The stocks and bonds, they're in the house. I got a guarantee on that."

"From who?" she said.

"They're in the house," he said.

She slept. And while darkness and silence filled the house, he sat by the window and watched the moon race past flying clouds. He wasn't sure why he had led her to believe the contents of the safe were genuine; the lie had been animated by instinct, the active principle being self-preservation. Too, truth merits a reward; always, there has to be a payoff. Withholding truth, expecting reward, becomes a habit. He thought, Here you are in this goddamn strange place and the only front protection you got is your brains and a greedy bitch who sells her ass for a buck. Maybe she sells her soul too, how do you know? So no truth. Say only what your heart and your mind tells you. You treat her like everybody else until you're sure otherwise. Don't tell her you're worried about this job, she's scared enough already. Don't tell her how this guy Cugarman shapes up so goddamn tricky. Stupid-tricky, everything you don't expect. He's got more money than he knows what to do with and he still screws around with stolen goods. Why? More and more money? Trying to beat Rockefeller's no kicks because you can't win. According to Julia, the people downstairs say he's a very nice man, nothing out of the way about him, he's good to everybody. The Dutch broad, she says he's a goddamn saint. Yeah, huh? Bullshit. Saints don't hire wrongos to work for them. Saints don't turn Baluchis loose on you. Saints don't have no source for counterfeit money. What makes the guy tick? He's ready for Teague and he's ready for you, Joe-Boy. The sky could come down on you any time, some hidden alarm, maybe, you can't be sure. It's a tough one, Joe-Boy. The whole thing's gonna be tougher than you thought. You thought once you got in you'd find the safe, open it and goodbye Indiana. If you got enough time you can open any safe, unless it's one of those big fuckers, but you gotta find it first, and Cugarman isn't the type guy'd put it where you can find it one-two-three. He's the type guy has the wiring run *under* the floor of the cellar. Who the hell ever heard of anything like that? You gotta go through the whole goddamn house. The safe's here, all right, the number three wire proves it.

You'll find it and you'll open it. Just pray it isn't one of those goddamn acoustic jobs where the temperature changes if you open it, and the next thing you're saying hello Mister Policeman. That's Cugarman. He's ready for the dummies and he's ready for you.

Joe Dev reviewed meticulously the details that had formed his strategy, a strategy which did not include escape from the Cugarman house. He dismissed thoughts of escape as vagrant, premature. One step at a time. When you're ready to go, you study around. Like you're lost in a strange forest and you're naked. What do you do, eh? What can you do? You use what you find. You study around and you discover how to keep warm and how to eat, and then you give part of your brain to the question how you're gonna get out.

But the strategy for making the bonds his received full thought and nagging care. He went over it again and again. It *had* to work. Poor Bruno, poor Toni, if it didn't. He sighed. Bruno shouldn't've got mixed up with those Sicilians. Sicilians aren't real Italians. You can't figure them. Christ, that goddamn island was raped by every sonofabitch had a rowboat to get there, everybody mixed in there for a while, killed the men, banged the women and took off with the loot. Guys like Frankie Shoeshine and them, they got the heart of barbarians, not Italians. You go south of Naples and you don't know who the fuck you're dealing with. Could be a Turk, an Arab, an African, any kind of crazy mix. Goddamn sketch.

CHAPTER **18**

The first night set the pattern for the second. As Joe Dev prepared to go below, Julia said, "Joe, couldn't we leave? I mean after tonight, if you don't find it? Thirty thousand's enough for me."

"Holy Jesus," he said impatiently. "Leave? I haven't even figured how I do that, and you're goosing me out. Slow down, baby. Take it easy. Fear and hope, remember?"

He prowled the second floor. Cook slept. He listened at

Mrs. Crawford's door. An unidentifiable sound originated from within. He squinted into the keyhole. Mrs. Crawford rocked in a rocking chair, reading and mouthing a Bible lesson.

In the pantry-kitchen hall, Joe Dev deactivated all alarms. He began a systematic search of the library. Just after midnight he heard Teague enter the house.

Teague made only the slightest of sounds: key inserted in the lock of the kitchen door, knob gingerly turned, the footstep. But Joe Dev heard, and he shot out of the library and across the living room to the center hall. At the dining-room entrance he held up fearing that, in his haste, he might topple a piece of furniture. He listened while refreshing his memory as to its placement. It was fishbowl still. He considered his position. If he lost the race to the alarm box, if Teague reached there first and discovered the entire system inoperative . . . *thud.* Joe Dev tensed, reflected on and dismissed a dozen reasons for the sound. The *thud* rang with overtones of the metallic. The bolt on the kitchen door. Teague was still at the door listening for household activity.

Doubling his stride, Joe Dev crossed the dining room to the butler's pantry and into the hall. He spotted Teague approaching, his frame silhouetted against the light from the kitchen window in the background. He was headed for the alarm box.

The race went to Joe Dev. Eyes on Teague, he groped for and replaced the switches. Only enough time remained to step back two paces, to stop, to lower his head. Now his hair and his clothes blacked out his presence. He froze in attack position, torso aslant like a discus thrower, knees slightly bent, hand across chest prepared for the knifelike thrust. If Teague flashed a light the hand would smash into his throat, crush bone and tear cartilage; he would go down without even a cry.

Teague halted before the box. Joe Dev heard him breathing, caught the smell of him, of stale tobacco smoke that clung to his clothes, of gun oil and the sweat-stained leather holster. The next moment might make of Teague a long-term invalid.

The refrigerator motor clicked on. The total silence magnified it to an explosion demanding Teague's attention. For a fleeting instant he turned toward the kitchen. In that instant Joe Dev backed away into the pantry.

Teague flashed his light and deactivated the alarms. He returned to the kitchen, making more noise than he should; he hadn't learned that ancient center flooring creaks, while the sides, untrodden over the years, remain tight and unyielding. He used the kitchen exit to the center hall. Joe Dev heard him climbing the front stairs.

Julia lay awake. "What's wrong?" she asked when Joe Dev slipped into the room.

"I almost bunked into Teague," Joe Dev said. "He's down there, searching around. Stupid bastard. Gonna steal some of Cugarman's underwear or junk out of the attic."

"Joe, you'd best not go down again tonight," Julia said.

Joe Dev said, "Hey, what kind of a nut is this Cugarman?"

"I've told you all I can find out without people getting suspicious," she said. "I keep bringing him up in conversation, you know? Keep people talking about him. They say—"

"Yeah, yeah, you told me what they say. And I told you what I think. Now double what I think. He's a goddamn nut, that's what."

"Why do you say that?" Julia asked.

"Look," he said, "you know that end table in the library, the one next to the blue chair? Got an ashtray on it, birds flying? You know that table? It's a piece of furniture, right?"

"Yes," she said.

"It's a safe," he said.

"Joe, you found it," Julia said.

"Look, let me tell you and maybe you'll understand about this nut. This end table only *looks* like furniture. It's one of those goddamn safes cost maybe seventy-nine-fifty. The front of it—with the carving?—it pulls open and there's the door of the safe. Got a combination dial on it no better than you find in the locker room of a gymnasium. Goddamn sketch. Took me less than ten minutes to open it."

"Joe," Julia said.

"Don't get excited," he said.

"Joe," she said. "Tell me. Lordy, tell me what you found in it."

He laughed. "John Wayne," he said.

"What?" she said.

"Fucking Cugarman's a goddamn nut, I'm telling you," Joe Dev said. "A fourteen-carat gold nut."

"You're acting a bit nutty yourself," Julia said. "Stop laughing."

"Listen," Joe Dev said, "in this safe there's this picture of John Wayne, all framed nice. You know—the cowboy movie actor?"

"You're joking," she said.

"Cugarman's joking, the goddamn nut," he said. "No wonder Teague got all burned up when he found it."

"Joe, you're not making good sense," Julia said.

"You pick up this picture," Joe Dev said, "and you look at it and there's this fucking actor, he's got a gun pointed at you, and on the top of the picture, over his head, there's this white space with the writing, like in the funny papers, and it says, 'Hands up.'"

"Shut," Julia said. "You'll wake somebody."

"I can't help it," he said. "Goddamn nutty dope."

"Joe, stop laughing," Julia said. "Stop it and listen to me."

"I'm listening," he said.

"Joe, it could be so simple," she said. "Thursday is my day off, they expect me to drive out of here. I could drive out with—"

"The stuff in the desk," he said.

"Will you please let me finish," she said.

"We don't take the stuff in the desk," he said.

"Let's. Please," she said. "Rats and rattles, don't you realize that if they find you here, if Teague finds you, you'll be shot dead. He'll kill you, Joe. It uncomforts me, Joe, it purely does, thinking about it."

He held her. "Look, baby," he said. "That don't happen to you. If they find me, I'm on my own, see? You're in the clear. Nobody knows you got me in here. When I go out of this room and I go downstairs I leave nothing here that's mine. My clothes, my tools, they search this room they find nothing to prove I ever come here. I figured that out up front. I don't put you in no goddamn danger."

"It's such a big house," she said. "We don't have forever. How long can you go on searching?"

"I understand what you say," Joe Dev said. "Wednesday Cugarman comes home. With him in the house it's gonna be a whole new deal. Maybe good, maybe bad, who knows? I'll have to study around when he gets here. One step at a time."

"Joe . . ." she said.

"No."

"Maybe if we—"

"No," he said.

"You're keeping something from me, Joe," she said.

"Hey, you're not gonna start *that*," he said.

"I'm not stupid, you know," she said. "I've been taken for many a thing, but never, *never* has *anybody* said to me, 'Julia Sue, you are as stupid as a log.' And that's what you're saying, Joe. Or thinking."

"You wanna finish?" he said.

"Anybody who turns his face away from thirty thousand dollars has got to have *something* on his mind, something he isn't about to discuss with anybody else."

"Like more than thirty thousand?" he asked.

"That's for you to say," she said. "Shoot, I thought we were partners. You said we were, that we'd play this hand together. Isn't that what you said? Yes, you did. I remember plain as can be. And you're not, *you're not,* Joe. I don't want to make a grievance of it, but you're keeping things from me. I'm prepared to wear myself to a shadow and you're not paying me any never mind atall."

"Move over," he said.

"No," she said, "you'll be putting me off with that nimble tongue of yours."

"Move over, for Christ's sake," he said.

He lay sideways beside her, his mouth against her ear, his hand caressing, stroking. "Listen, I gave you my word. We're partners. If Joe Dev gives you his word you can put it in the bank and draw interest." He considered telling her the truth. The nonexistent treasure filled her thoughts and honed the edge of greed, it justified immediate flight, it represented a nuisance. He decided against it. Truth would not reassure her, and the nuisance would be replaced by a sense of futility which might demoralize. No, he recognized the fabric of her uneasiness, he'd experienced similar misgivings an hour after he had arrived in Indiana and had been briefed on the Cugarman job. "I don't go in a place has only one door," he'd said to Bick Anson. "Even a dumb animal lives in the ground has a hole to go in and one to come out. Right now I got only one door. And if somebody locks it, what?" That's the reassurance Julia required, needed, a second door, an escape door. Whether she used it or not mattered little; having it was imperative.

He said, "I swear to God, baby, I got no idea what we gonna walk away with from here. Maybe it's a big one, I trust your judgment. But what's the big rush? Give me a chance to search around. If I strike out, okay, then we consider different. But why complicate now?"

"It just seems so *foolish*," she said. "Thirty thousand."

"Sure," he said, "but only a little bit of that's in cash. I'm not the type guy fools around with jewelry, with fences. I already told you that. That's for guys like Teague."

"Teague?" she asked. "Why?"

"He's an ex-con, he's got connections. He knows what to do with a piece of jewelry's burning his hands. He knows who to go and make a fast deal and not get screwed in the bargain. Understand? You and me, we try to unload that stuff, it's like we're walking around without drawers, it's gonna be one big fucking heartache, and maybe we even come out dry. You want that?"

"Of course not," she said.

"So okay," he said. "Partners. One plays for the other and the both of us play to win. There he goes."

"Who?" she asked.

"Teague," he said. "He's leaving."

"I swear, Joe Dev," she said. "You've got ears like—"

"Shh," he said.

"I don't hear him," she said.

"That's because you're not listening, you're talking," he said.

A moment later, Joe Dev leaped from the bed. "He's gone," he said.

"Are you going down again?" she said.

"Yes," he said. "We do like this. By Monday night I finish

up downstairs. Tuesday I start on the second floor. Cugarman's bedroom first. We gotta operate different when I'm on the second floor. I don't have time to get to the alarm box before Teague—I mean if he takes it in his head to pay another visit and do more stealing. So Monday we do like this. You come down with me and you stay in the kitchen. If you see Teague coming, you turn on the water in the sink. Somebody turns on the water in this house, you hear it all over. You mind losing a little sleep?"

"It's better than lying here brooding," she said.

"Okay," Joe Dev said. "Teague, he's gotta do the same like me. He's gotta come in and cut off the alarm before he goes burglar. If he finds it already cut off he's gonna wonder. So you stay by the kitchen window. The minute you see him, you turn on the water and you fix the alarm switches. If you get caught in the kitchen, you say you went down for a glass of milk or something. What do you think? Sounds okay? Any suggestions?"

"No," Julia said. "Sounds fine."

"Okay," he said. "You sleep now, but when I come up, you better be ready for me."

"You." She giggled.

He left, confident that he'd set things right. Julia Sue didn't need the truth, she needed two doors, front and back. Now she had them.

CHAPTER **19**

A sign over Jo-Jo's pie case read, "Don't knock our coffee, you may be old and weak yourself someday." Little Neffie stared at the sign and stirred sugar into his second cup of coffee. He hoped he wouldn't have to order a third. They weren't kidding. Damned stuff tasted like a rusty cent. He consoled himself with the thought that you can't have it all. The air in Jo-Jo's, although heavy with rancid grease, was cooled; he'd found a parking place directly in front; from where he sat he could look through the window, over the hood of his car, to the entrance of

Saint Luke's Hospital; too, Canal Street being a one-way thoroughfare, tacking himself on to Wendell Cooney presented no problem. So far so good.

Decision time came ten minutes later. Little Neffie looked forward to the hot humid outdoors with increasing unease. The Panama hat he wore lay like a torture weight over a still-tender scalp. Without it, however, the skullcap bandage gave the crown of his head the look of half an eggshell and provoked curiosity as to the reason for it. He wasn't ready to discuss his washroom experience, not with anyone.

Little Neffie was pleased when a police car pulled up in front of the hospital. He recognized the driver, Barry Bushman, a veteran of the Uniontown force and an old friend of Cooney's. Cooney must have been waiting in the lobby. He came out a beat after Bushman's arrival, limping, his arm cradled in a sling. He crossed to the car and eased himself in. He looked angry.

Little Neffie followed them to the police station on Manchester. Cooney and Bushman entered together. A half hour later Cooney came out, alone, and rounded the precinct house to the parking lot. Little Neffie could tell by the way Cooney's coat hung in back that he now packed his police revolver.

Doing an adequate job of one-arm driving, Cooney tooled his own car out of downtown traffic to Route 15, then turned west and went on to Peru. He stopped before a small house on the edge of town. He knocked. A young woman answered the door. She wore jeans and a shirt whose lower half was knotted above her navel. Cooney entered. Little Neffie noted the name on the mailbox: Brewster. That'd be Jory Brewster, state trooper, the one who had come upon Cooney, unconscious, in the rain.

Twenty minutes later Cooney headed back toward Uniontown. When he swung south on 15 instead of north, Little Neffie surmised that he was headed for Luke Bishop's place near Treaty. And he guessed right. Luke Bishop interrupted the staking of tomato vines for a half-hour talk with Cooney. Little Neffie waited.

Cooney appeared angrier still when he left Luke Bishop's. Driving faster than he should, he doubled back to Uniontown. In traffic again, his maneuvering was less controlled; impatience with lights and other delays faulted his judgment. On the corner of Union Avenue and Petersen he barely escaped colliding with a bakery truck, and after an out-of-the-window exchange with the truckdriver, he proceeded south to Bick Anson's house on Miami Street. He spent ten minutes with Anson, who sunned at poolside, gulped two gin and tonics and then, with even less adroitness than before, drove to the Indian's farm west of the Eel River. The Indian's prune-eyed wife, Lydia, directed him to the west pasture where the Indian was putting his Tennessee Walking Horse through its paces.

Little Neffie parked in the shade of an elm and put the binoculars on them. He saw Cooney climb awkwardly over a fence and half run out to the Indian. Little Neffie adjusted the focus on the glasses. He smiled. In response to heated questioning suggested by Cooney's fast-moving mouth, the Indian kept shaking his head. He said little, a word now and then; otherwise it was the shaking of the head No and the dumb blank expression. Suddenly the Indian frowned, as if trying to remember something. Cooney came alert, expectant; he waited, swallowed, wiped perspiration from his face with the sleeve of his jacket. Little Neffie smiled again. Dumb sonofabitch was pooping out, he left the hospital too soon, was doing too much.

At long last the Indian said something. It recharged Cooney. He turned, and shouting something over his shoulder, raced back to his car.

Little Neffie stored the binoculars in the glove compartment. That'd be it. Cooney was wound up and going real good, the rest he'd do himself. Time for lunch, a leisurely one.

At three-fifteen that afternoon Little Neffie parked the convertible down the street from the Club Kisco, in Wabash, and strolled casually in. Cooney was wedged into the corner seat of the bar, anxiously eyeing the door. He waved Little Neffie over.

Little Neffie said, "Hi, Wend, how's she going?" He sat and ordered a beer.

Cooney said, "I've been two hours finding you. What the fuck're you doing here?"

"Me and the wife agreed to disagree," Little Neffie said. "Moved out of Union and put up at the Green Star, on State

Road. I gotta get the hell outta there, though. Too near the junction. Traffic all night long. You know the place? There's a stop sign right in front, see? And you hear the goddamn trucks. They come, stop, start up, pull away. All night long, come, stop, start up, pull away. I keep dreaming I'm being run the fuck over." He acknowledged the arm sling. "I heard you got stove in a while back. They said you'd be in the hospital a good spell. How come you're out?"

"What'd you hear?" Cooney said. "And from who?"

"Christ," Little Neffie said. "Who remembers? A guy hears things, you know. They were talking there, a while back, about your accident. Somebody." He slanted his glass and poured beer into it.

"Look, you sonofabitch," Cooney said. "You and the rest of the pricks call themselves friends've been laughing it up over what happened to me. Yeah, laughing. Don't turn on no goddamn dumb look, not for me. Understand? Okay. You wanna live dangerous and laugh, okay, go ahead and laugh. Only watch out. Don't give me no 'accident' crap because fancying it up is just another way of laughing, leastways that's how I take it."

Little Neffie beckoned to the bartender. "Give this fucking bigmouth another drink," he said. And when the glass was refilled, he said, "You said you're looking for me."

"Yeah," Cooney said. "The Indian put me on to you. I asked around and they told me I might find you here."

"You found me," Little Neffie said.

"I'm trying to get a line on the guy snuck up on me with that pipe," Cooney said. "You said you heard things. Hear anything about who?"

"Jesus, no," Little Neffie said. "I mean, I wasn't paying attention, you know? A thing like that, though, the guys around the precinct house oughta be able to help you. Christ, you've got the whole goddamn police force, and you need me?"

"I talked to the guys," Cooney said. "Talked to Jory Brewster, too."

"Don't believe I know him," Little Neffie said.

"Trooper," Cooney said. "Lives over to Peru." He pronounced it 'Pair-oo.'

"What about Luke Bishop?" Little Neffie said. "He's watchdog over to that end of town. Knows everything and everybody. A mouse pees on somebody's carpet and Luke gets wind of it. Talk to him?"

Cooney nodded. "And I've been trying to get Stacy on the phone, oh, four, five days now. He's out of town. Be away for a while."

"Bick? Iron Face?" Little Neffie said. "Try them?"

"Yeah," Cooney said. "Look, I'll refresh you. You said something to the Indian about a foreigner of some kind being in town—a Jew or a Greek or something."

"I did?" Little Neffie said. "Jesus, I don't remember. Oh, hey, wait a minute, yeah. An out-of-town dude. Don't recall I said 'foreigner,' though."

"The Indian mentioned it," Cooney said. "He said he was talking to you and you said something about this guy. Out of Chicago, maybe, he said you said."

"Lemme see if I can sort it out," Little Neffie said. "Now you mention Iron Face kind of brings it back. It was over to the Room, seems like, two, three weeks ago. That about right?"

"Yeah," Cooney said.

"I can't be true certain," Little Neffie said. "Jesus, there's two things drives me up the walls about toting forty years—forgetting, like from one goddamn minute to the other, you know? That and the goddamn reading glasses. Christ, how I hate going for those goddamn things every time I wanna see something up close. And the puttin' down and the losing 'em and the goddamn looking for 'em—Jesus."

"Fuck you," Cooney said. "Took me all goddamn afternoon to find you and you spiel me that shit."

"Big man," Little Neffie said. "Big policeman. Don't talk to me like I'm somebody you got in the holding pen. I come on tougher guys than you."

"Will you for Christ's sake just tell me about the guy," Cooney said.

Little Neffie worked his fingers between his buttocks, and said, "Sorry, Wend. The impression I got, though, was that this guy was in town for some action in the Room. Nothing out of the ordinary, you know? What I don't understand is why you're screwing around with asking this guy and that guy about something they *may* know—like me, for instance—instead of going right to the people what *do* know. I'm talking about the Stocker woman and the broads was around when it all happened. Shit, you slip that black cunt a twenty and she'll stand on her head, sing 'We Shall Overcome' and fart all at the same time."

"I can't go there," Cooney said. Mutely gesturing, he asked the bartender for another drink.

Little Neffie said, "I guess you've got your reasons, only it don't stack up sensible, as I see it."

"I can't," Cooney said.

"Subject's closed," Little Neffie said. He reached for his change on the bar, and then he stopped and a funny look came into his face. "If I ain't the fucking idiot of the world," he said.

Cooney looked at him.

"The fucking idiot of the world," Little Neffie said. "Of course. The broad."

Cooney said, "Do I know what you're chitterin' about?"

"The broad," Little Neffie said, "the one that died. I almost forgot about her. That it, Wend? I don't know why I didn't think of it before, but like I say, things keep slippin' away from me."

"What about the broad?" Cooney said. "What've I got to do with some whore dying with a bad kidney?"

"Games," Little Neffie said. "Shit, you want games you play by yourself. See you around."

"Lemme buy one," Cooney said.

"You're breaking my ass, big policeman," Little Neffie said. "I don't need it. Look at me, sittin' here like I'm on the goddamn civil service, like you, or I'm somebody's pad. I got a living to make. I don't even want this beer, it's a courtesy to you I'm nursing it, which I ain't gonna continue to do."

"Will you stop being so goddamn touchy?" Cooney said.

"Me touchy?" Little Neffie said. "I'm touchy? Jesus."

"The broad," Cooney said. "Run it out for me—what you're thinking."

Little Neffie pointed a finger at him. "Just remember you asked. Don't go hassling me in the middle of a sentence. Fucking farmer. This town's full of fucking farmers gotta chew

THE DEVALINO CAPER ... 135

the eraser clear off a pencil to figure out two and two. Mud on the shoes, mud on the brain. Where I come from you wouldn't last ten minutes, not ten fucking minutes. It come to me while I'm sitting here letting you take up my time. You didn't figure on the broad dying, Wend. That changes things, don't it? A guy beats up on a whore, what the hell, people figure she had it coming. But if she dies, hey now, that's something else again. That's murder one—two, maybe—if you can ante up for the right lawyer. So it's only natural you should be shittin' scared of going back to the scene of the crime—"

"Aggh," Cooney said.

"Going back to the scene of the murder, that's opening up a can of peas. Everything's quiet now, nobody's looking for you, nobody's asking questions, right? So why make waves?"

"I didn't say anything about going over to the Stocker woman's place," Cooney said. "You did."

"I take it back," Little Neffie said. "You want my advice, stay the fuck away from there."

"All I asked was, did you know anything about the guy."

"Forget the guy, too," Little Neffie said. "Look, Wend, do I have to advertise in the yellow pages? You know how I make out. Brains. Trust my judgment. I ain't infallible but my track record's something I'll match against anybody's. Forget this whole thing. Stay clear of it. Forget about the guy mussed you up. Experience, chalk it up to experience. Guys laugh, they gotta do it behind your back. What the fuck's it to you if they laugh as long as they don't do it to your face?"

"Who's laughing?" Cooney said.

"I don't recall saying anything about anybody laughing," Little Neffie said. "You're the one. Even said I did. Called me a prick and all for doing it. Which I ain't and you know it. I'm a friend and I'm advising you. There ain't no steam rising from the dunghill right now, but the underside could still be warm. You go turning it over and you got big trouble. First thing you know somebody'll be whispering things to the D.A. and they'll be doing an autopsy and questioning the Doc and those broads'll be on the witness stand testifying about what happened and, oh shit, you want me to sing it? Use your fucking head."

"Look," Cooney said, "how about you go over there?"

. . . **136**

"Where?" Little Neffie said.

"Harriet Stocker's," Cooney said. "Put a fright into her. Find out who the guy is."

"No way, Wend," Little Neffie said. "Wouldn't touch it. It's a sizzler. Bye-bye."

"Wait a minute, for Christ's sake," Cooney said.

"You're messing with a murder charge," Little Neffie said. "Me, I'd rather listen to them laugh for the rest of my life. Ha, ha, ha. That ain't so bad, is it? Ha, ha, ha."

"Sonofabitch," Cooney said.

"Big fucking policeman my ass," Little Neffie said. "Fucking farmer is what. He's getting away with murder and that ain't enough. He's gotta get even. And why? Why? Because a few dumb jerks're laughing behind his back. Can't leave well enough alone. Gotta hiss and yawn at the same time. Ha, ha, ha, Wend. Get used to it. Sticks and stones and all that shit."

"Sonofabitch," Cooney said.

Little Neffie left the Club Kisco and crossed the street to Gackenheimer's Drug Store. He lingered in the doorway until Cooney came charging out of the bar like a fighting bull headed for the arena center, then he entered and dialed a number on the pay phone.

The Indian said, "Hello."

Little Neffie said, "On his way."

CHAPTER **20**

Harriet opened the door, sucked in breath and said, "What you want here?"

He intimidated her with a stare. She stepped aside. He entered the living room, sat. Harriet shut the door.

"Who's here?" Cooney said.

Harriet didn't answer.

Cooney said, "All tongue, aren't you. Well, I'll change that."

"Ain't nobody here," Harriet said.

Cooney looked toward the staircase.

Harriet said, "Nobody. Julia, she left better'n two weeks ago. For keeps. Gone off somewhere. Alice, she driving the new girl down to the bus depot."

"New girl?" Cooney said.

"Come up from 'Nap Town," Harriet said. "Didn't like it here none, which is fine 'cause I returns the compliment. She the type want to sit around all night in a wrapper. Not here, she don't sit around in no wrapper. My girls dresses up pretty."

"Aggh, shut up," Cooney said.

"You ask me about the new girl and I tole you," Harriet said.

"I didn't ask for no goddamn rundown on how to run a cat house," Cooney said.

"What you want?" Harriet asked.

"I'm sorry to hear you saying that, Harriet," he said. "Asking me what I want tells *me* you want trouble."

"I don't want no trouble," Harriet said. "I don't give question to nothing or nobody."

"Ever see a cow walking on ice, Harriet?" he said.

She stared and waited.

"Hell of a thing," he said. "Watching the damned critter skittering this way and that, trying to stay up, and then going down. Boom. Breaks a leg usually—or the spine. Real terrible thing to watch. Real fucking terrible. Sort of like if I was to walk up to you and kick your legs out from under you. Christ, a tub like you, weighing just as much or more'n a cow, you'd hit the goddamn floor in a way that like to split you clear in half. Happens every day to women around the house, accidents. They stand on a chair that tips over, they trip on the stairs, slip on a wet floor, anything."

Harriet sat down.

Cooney laughed. "That stops me, Harriet," he said. "That stops me. I'm in no condition to yank you outta that chair, not a tub like you. Doctor says I gotta take it easy for a while."

"I don't want no trouble," Harriet said. "You leave me alone or I'm goan call the po-lice."

"Taking into account my condition and all," Cooney said, "let's try something else. You ever had a gun pointed at you? It ain't like seeing it on the television or in the movies, bang, bang,

bang, shoot 'em up. That's just a lot of fucking noise, means nothing. When you *really* get a gun pointed at you, you shit. I'll show you."

Harriet looked at the gun. "Jesus God," she said.

"You see?" Cooney said. "See how it is? You shit. People think it's nothing. Good guy looks at the gun in the bad guy's hand and he kind of laughs it off, kicks it out of the bad guy's hand or some stupid thing like that. Ain't true and you know it now, right? You shit. Right? Answer me."

"Yessuh," Harriet said.

"Nothing for you to worry about, though. The way a gun works is, you gotta release the safety catch first, this little thing right here. See? Like that. Release it and you're ready to shoot. Now I'm ready to shoot. The thing of it is, though, you can do it all at once or in two steps. Point it like that and squeeze the trigger—"

"Jesus God," Harriet said.

"—in one shot, like," Cooney went on.

"Good Jesus God," Harriet said.

"Or else," he said, "if you just want to get *ready* to shoot—I mean be real ready—you cock the fucker. There. Now it's cocked. Now it's ready to go. This here's a thirty-eight. At this range I wouldn't be surprised if the fucking bullet turned you and that chair clear over, got that kinda force. The tiniest squeeze . . . bang."

"I'll tell you," Harriet said. "Jesus God, I'll tell you."

"His name," Cooney said.

"Didn't give no name," Harriet said, "not to me, he didn't, no name atall. He just some john come in to get hisself a piece, didn't bother to give me no name."

"Never saw him before?" Cooney said.

"Nossir," Harriet said, "never saw him before that night."

"Where'd he come from?" Cooney said.

Harriet stared at the gun, and said, "I dunno. I dunno where he originate if that's what you mean. South, it come to my ear, like. Southern. Talked Southern. Somewheres south."

"Somewheres," Cooney said.

"Yeah," Harriet said. "Passing through, he said."

"Tell me how it happened," Cooney said. "Everything. From the beginning."

"How it happen?" Harriet said. "Yessuh. How it happen. Sure I can tell you, tell you from beginning to end. I recollect it was raining, night of that big storm it was, raining cats and dogs. Lord, I ain't never seen such a full rain. Well, this here fella, he come in outta the rain, and he has a couple—bourbon mash— and he talkin' and joyin' hisself pretty good with Alice—took to Alice straight off—and then, oh yeah, then come this here power failure? Whop. Just like that, the lights goes out and I hears you calling out from Helen's room. 'Harriet, Harriet,' you says, and I comes stumbling in here outta the kitchen where I was fixin' myself a snack. I takes my blood pressure medicine that time of night and the Doc he say it go down easier with a little something, so I was in there fixin' myself this snack and I comes stumbling in here . . ."

"Harriet," he said.

She held her breath.

"Harriet, I'm gonna kill you," he said.

"What you want?" she pleaded. "Ain't I telling you? What you want?"

"What I want is no fucking lies," he said, "that's what I want. No, shut the fuck up and listen. I'm warning you. I know some of it and that's how I know you're lying. So what I'm gonna do is, I'm gonna steer you in the right direction, and if you don't stay with it straight, you're dead. I mean cold dead. Understand?"

Harriet moaned and nodded.

"The sonofabitch was a foreigner," he said.

"Yessuh," Harriet said. Nervous fingers found a flat fold in her dress and insisted that it become a pyramid.

"A Jew," he said.

Harriet sobbed spasmodically.

"Wasn't he?" he said. "A Jew?"

Tears glistened on her rounded cheeks. "I don't want to get nobody in trouble," she said. "I don't. I don't."

"Oh, you don't," he said.

"He was a decent fella," she said, "come in here and behave

hisself, treats the girls like ladies, pay up handsome and all. But shit, I got no call to pro-tect no stranger, not against you. I ain't goan get myself killed for no goddamned sheeney."

"I'm waiting," Cooney said. "Start with his name."

"Shit on you, mister," she said. "Scarin' me that way you doin', damned thing pointing at me. What you think? Here my senses be flying every which way, and you sets there saying you waiting and what'm I supposed to do, not be scared? Recollect every little in-ci-dent clear as noon? What you think?"

"Did he have a name?" Cooney said.

" 'Course he had a name," Harriet said. "What kind of a question is that? His name. He mention his name, all right. Lemme see . . . no, that weren't it, it weren't Ollie—short for Oliver, that is, but it start with an 'O.' I'm sure of that. Oscar, that's it. Oscar, he say his name is, and he says like everybody call him Ossie. I knew it started with an 'O.' "

"Oscar," Cooney said.

"Yeah," Harriet said, "Ossie for short. He say call him Ossie for short. From Terry Hut, he say he come, runs a dry goods business. Don't see how it'd be any trouble findin' him if you got a mind to—Oscar, Terry Hut, dry goods business, easy as peeling a hard-boiled egg. Dark-complected fella, dark eyes. And the nose, the way his nose hook on the end like his do, I could tell straight off he was a sheeney fella."

"And his name is Oscar, right?" Cooney said.

"That's right," Harriet said.

Cooney said, "That does it, Harriet. I gotta kill you. I gotta kill you."

"I tole you, didn't I?" she said. "Jesus God, ain't I tole you?"

"I'm gonna count to five," Cooney said, "and I'm gonna count fast. Won't be no time for you to go thinking things up. The only way you can get it said is if you say it faster'n I can count to five."

"What you want me to say?" she said.

"One," Cooney said. "Oh, and Harriet . . ."

"Yessuh?"

"If you tell me he's a Greek I'll put the bullet right in your fat gut. It'll kill you all right, it'll take longer is all. And when I'm through with you I'm going after the sonsofbitches put you up to all this bullshit. I ain't figured out what it's all about, but I will, and *they're* gonna get the same as you."

She said, "Whuh?" Surprise placed her hopelessly beyond reach of words.

"Best thing you can do for yourself," Cooney said, "is to tell me why, how, where, when and who. I know about Neffie. Now I do. He's gonna get it first. I'll backtrack from you and leave every goddamn one of 'em dead."

"What you talking about?" Harriet said. "I don't know nothin' about nobody putting me up to nothin' and I don't know nothin' about no Greek."

"Two . . . three . . . four," Cooney said.

"No, no, don't shoot," she said. "I'll tell you, I'll tell you." She spoke the words knowing that he meant to kill her. She'd mingled too long with the depraved to disregard the lessons taught, the wisdom gleaned from the associations. A sense of doom flooded over her. Yes, Cooney would kill her. It mattered little what she said. Even if she told the truth about Joe Dev, his arrival, arranged by Bick Anson and the Indian, his mysterious departure, Wendell Cooney meant to kill her. "Pulley," she said.

"Who's Pulley?" Cooney asked.

"I dunno his whole name," Harriet said. "Jim Skeans sent him here. Jim Skeans from the Buick agency, in 'Nap Town.'"

"Go on," Cooney said.

"That's all," Harriet said. "Everything is just like I tole you only now you knows who the man is. Mr. Pulley. He don't like what you doin' to Helen so he says to me to put out all the lights and when you come out he goan whop you good."

Wendell Cooney forced himself to his feet—slowly, lethargically, his energy drained but his anger achieving a mindless momentum.

"Up," he said. He motioned wearily with the gun.

"What you *want?*" Harriet bawled.

"On your feet," he said.

She rose.

"Up the stairs," he said.

"What for?" she said.

"Up the stairs," he said.

Like a tug wallowing in the water Harriet crossed to the stairway and began the painful climb.

Step, brace the bad knee with a cupped hand, bring up the other foot, pause, rest.

He meant to kill her. How, she did not know, but he meant to kill her. There sprung forward from the depths of memory one early morning with Jamesie. That moment with its mounting apprehension of death was identical with this one. "Give it or I'll kill you," Jamesie had said, quietly too, like Cooney. She'd been surprised by his expertise—only thirteen and already he'd learned how to keep a fist jammed against the stomach wall while the thumb and forefinger of the other hand, at the throat, doled out only enough breath to remind that life is precious and that the choice of life and death was his.

Step, pause, rest.

The "it" which Jamesie demanded was six dollars and twenty cents. She hustled all of Saturday night for it—at twenty-five to fifty cents a throw. Twenty-five–fifty was the high–low price. You bargained for the in-between pennies. Bargaining was part of the night's work, the toughest part, it made the difference between good or bad earnings, and there was only one night in which to make it—Saturday.

Step, pause, rest.

How did Cooney mean to kill her? A bullet? Would anybody hear? Would anybody come? Jamesie's fingers had spelled out his intention clearly. "Give it or I'll kill you." His creamy-pink tongue had curled on the word "kill" and the "you" blasted forth the smell of prohibition gin which Willy Hooten mixed, cut and soothed with glycerine in his mother's galvanized laundry tub and sold for a quarter a pint.

Another step. Pause. Rest.

No doubt about it. Jamesie wasn't just talking. He would have killed her. He was desperate. She'd heard all night, up and down The Street, how Jamesie made a bet with Kitch Washington without the money to back it up, and lost. You didn't do that, not to Kitch, nobody did. Kitch sent out word that if Jamesie didn't pay off he'd cut off his cock, shove it down his throat and tie a gag around his mouth. Now it was dawn, Sunday, and Jamesie wanted her money or her life. Sunday.

Damn. Every man on The Street was clean busted and would stay busted until next Saturday noon when the factory handed out the weekly wages. For the remainder of the week every bankrupt black ass would be rooting around trying to scrounge enough for a drink or a pound of week-old fish; they'd smoke cigarette stubs impaled on toothpicks while idling and dreaming of next Saturday night and then sleep themselves into merciful oblivion. If she gave Jamesie the money she'd be busted too, and her only talent for earning more, worthless, because nobody could pay. She'd maybe have to work Town and take a chance on being shagged by a gang of white kids. Damn.

Step. Pause. Rest.

Jamesie had given her a choice. She'd have withstood a beating to hang on to her money, but die? No. She resigned herself to a week of no cigarettes, no gum or Coke or matinee movies, no hamburgers at Simsey's stand where the ketchup wasn't kept under the counter, no lording it over the improvident ones. "Give it or I'll kill you." The moment, the certainty of death, was the same, but Jamesie had given her a choice.

Jesus God, the top of the stairs already? The ascent had always seemed interminable, and now there she was on the landing and Cooney was pushing her forward one step, going past her and saying, "Turn around." *Already?*

A new outburst of tears and sobbing sounded like a cold motor refusing to start. "I gotta go to the bathroom," she managed to sputter.

"Turn around," he said. He was still quiet, tired.

"I gotta go, I tell you," she said. "I gotta."

"I said turn around."

She looked at him. "You goan kill me," she said. "You made Helen die and now you goan make me die."

His face white with fatigue, he said, "It was too fucking ugly, Harriet. It's not my fault it was so fucking ugly. Turn around."

She turned. The circle complete, she saw how she would die. It was as simple and real as a nightmare. The flight of stairs was now a sickening chasm. She would be dead, mangled by her own bulk, before she hit bottom. If any life lingered, Cooney would stomp it out. Jesus God, I'm goan die.

Unresisting acquiescence to death caused her system to release its warm juice; it flowed against her cold flesh. She shivered. It was the ultimate reality until she heard somebody asking if anybody was there and she felt Cooney tense up behind her. His clawlike hand dug into her arm and pushed her aside.

"Anybody here?" the voice asked once more. And Cooney, who took her place on the landing, stared and waited to match the voice to the man.

Presently he appeared. It was a uniformed policeman—Eugene Bang-Jens. He held a gun. It was at full cock.

"Gene," Cooney said, "what the fuck're you doing here?"

Bang-Jens looked up. "Sarge? That you?" he said. "I got a call over the radio about a disturbance here." He faced Cooney squarely as he spoke.

"So that's it," Cooney said. "So that's it."

Bang-Jens raised his arm and fired. Harriet did not have the strength to shout motherfucker as Cooney stumbled and rolled down into the chasm, but she thought it.

Bang-Jens leaped over Cooney's body and took the stairs two at a time. "You saw what happened," he said to Harriet. "I come in, he's beating up on you, I tell him to stop, I tell him he's under arrest, I ask him to surrender but he won't. He pulls out his gun. I have to shoot him in self-defense. Right? That right?"

"Yessuh," Harriet whispered. "Just how I seen it."

"Okay," Bang-Jens said. "I'm gonna rough you up a little bit so's to make it look good, his beating up on you, and to show you what you'll get more of in case you go shooting off your mouth."

"Yessuh," Harriet said. "Thank you."

CHAPTER **21**

Joe Dev cursed failure on Saturday and Sunday night and again on Monday. "The guy doesn't leave his mark on anything," he said. "He's neat, neat as a pin. Everything in place."

"Mrs. Crawford says he goes rarin' if it isn't," Julia said.

"Nervous people do that," Joe Dev said thoughtfully. "People who gotta have everything in place, so goddamn perfect, I mean, they're uptight. Cugarman's uptight and he's tricky-stupid. That's all I know about him so far. I'm not inside his head yet."

"Joe, Mrs. Crawford and cook've been here for years and years. I keep asking about Mr. Cugarman, pretending I'm curious, you know, and they say he's the *nicest* man."

"Yeah?" Joe Dev said.

"Not at all uptight, not to their mind," Julia said. "They say he's sweet and gentle and generous."

"Yeah, you told me," he said. "A saint. Listen, I found out more about Cugarman in three days than they did in their years and years. Goddamn sketch, that's what. Don't even know who they're working for."

It was nearing ten o'clock, and they prepared to go below. Teague would lock up shortly. Julia said, "But, Joe, what does it matter what he *is?* Why do you have to know things about him?"

Joe Dev laughed. "Why? Because the sonofabitch, he hides something from me—those bonds. If I can get inside his head and figure out what makes him tick, then maybe I get some idea like, you know, where he hides the stuff. Takes patience, good eyes and a fast brain." A memory provoked laughter.

"What's so funny?" she said.

"Hey, I remember one summer, in Venice it was. I'm only a kid, see, and I'm looking to do myself a little good. And there's this old lady, everybody says she's got a nice piece of cash stashed, so I'm studying around trying to find it, and I keep coming up dry. Okay. Then I notice that every time she goes out—to go shopping, like, or take a walk, you know?—she's like scratching between her legs. Women don't do that, you know. Men yes, but not women. Women're ashamed to do that around people. And that's when I go inside her head. I say to myself that I'm so scared I'm gonna be robbed when I go out of the house, I'm gonna hide my money in my underdrawers, and I'm not scratching because I'm itchy, I'm scratching around to make sure the goddamn money is there and I haven't lost it. Right? Okay. I say to myself I gotta have patience. Those goddamn drawers, they gotta come off sometime. She's gotta wash them, no? What does she do with the money when she washes the drawers? If she drops the bundle between her tits, good, there's always a way, you know? So I check around when she hangs clothes out to dry. And you know something about those drawers? She's got a pocket in them, sewed in nice, with a button. You listening? A goddamn button. That's when I give up on her. If she's got a pocket and a button on one of them, then her goddamn needle's been working on the extras too. Right? The money goes from the dirty drawers to the clean ones and it's always between her legs. Am I gonna go after it there? I gotta think twice. Not with Cugarman, though. Cugarman's got pockets and he's got buttons hiding his stuff, and it's not between his legs. It's here, in the house. I gotta get inside his head. Tell me what you think and I'll tell you what you are."

Julia frowned. "Joe, maybe there isn't a safe," she said.

"Gotta be," he said. "It's wired. That number three wire. That's for the safe."

"You said that if you didn't find it, we'd consider other things," Julia said.

Joe Dev ignored the longing that fathered the statement. "Tonight, maybe, when I search around his bedroom I'll know more about him. And maybe the safe is there."

They proceeded quietly down, Joe Dev wearing the black outfit, Julia in nightgown and robe. She remained in the kitchen to stand watch; he sped up the center stairway to the second floor and Cugarman's bedroom.

As with the rest of the house, the doors were thick, the ceilings high. Taking into account the bathroom and dressing alcove, the bedroom spread to the size of a tennis court. A long and tedious night lay ahead.

Julia looked out the kitchen window and listened to the night sounds. Moonlight dazzled, the air hung cool. She was troubled. A half-hour alone and she grew more and more so, imaginings and fears tended to deplete confidence. So little time remained for Joe Dev to find the securities; he *was* keeping something from her; he would *not* leave with the contents of the desk, and neither Teague nor Donnet would be fooled by another escape in the trunk of her car. Plans were muddled, vague, nothing about them soothed. The few positive thoughts which intruded were swarmed over and smothered by negative ones.

Anxiety prodded Julia to the penultimate question: What was to become of her if Joe Dev failed, was caught; if, as he said, she came out of the escapade clear of complicity and free to go it alone?

The ultimate question—and the answer—struck with paralyzing excitement. Even as she stepped out of her slippers and rushed barefoot into the center hall to listen for Joe Dev, and not hearing him, and then on to the study, the plan blossomed and flowered with naturalness inherent only in the simplest of phenomena. Recalling the directions which Joe Dev had passed on, she opened and pulled out the bottom right-hand drawer of Cugarman's desk and groped for the secret compartment. Her hand grasped the treasure item by item—money, jewelry, stamp collection. She left the safety-deposit keys, replaced the drawer.

Returning, she listened in the center hall for Joe Dev, then back to the kitchen to check on Teague. Only crickets disturbed the night silence.

She went swiftly to her room. There she counted out a thousand dollars and stuffed the bills into the pocket of her robe. All else she secreted in her suitcase, locking it and hiding the key under the innersole of a shoe.

More and more heartened by the reasonableness of it all, she barefooted it back to the first floor to make certain Joe Dev had not heard. Hyperventilated and aware of an oncoming dizziness, she reversed steps to the kitchen. Her mouth was gritty-dry. She got a glass from the cupboard and almost turned on the water faucet before realizing the consequences of such a move. She substituted milk for the water, drinking it before the comforting coolness of the opened refrigerator. She waited and calmed a bit. She stepped into her slippers, picked up the house phone and dialed three numbers.

Teague said, "Yeah?"

Julia said, "Hi."

"Who is it?" he asked.

"My, my," she said. "So many lady friends he can't tell one from the other."

"Oh," Teague said, "Miss rats and rattles. Where are you?"

"The kitchen," Julia said.

"Doing what?" he asked.

"Looking to see if the dogs are out there," Julia said.

"Yeah? What else?" he said.

"Nothing," Julia said. "Just standing here with the telephone in my hand. What're *you* doing?"

"I'll tell you what I ain't doing," Teague said.

Julia laughed.

Teague said, "Why'n't you come over here and we'll do it," he said.

"The dogs," Julia said.

"I'll come for you," Teague said.

"All right," Julia said.

"Wait," he said. "Before you open the door. Know where the alarm box is?"

"The what?" she said.

"In the hall, past the kitchen," Teague said.

"Oh," Julia said, "that li'l old electric box thang?"

"Yeah, that thang," he mimicked. "Now here's what you do. You stand in front of it and you count from left to right. There are four switches. The second on your left is the one you want. Disconnect it. Pull the switch down. Got it?"

"Doesn't take a Solomon to do that," she said.

"I'm on my way," Teague said.

She waited outside the kitchen door. When Teague appeared from shadow into moonlight, two disquieting shapes accompanied him, circling and crossing his path. The dogs must have joined him the moment he stepped out of the garage apartment.

Teague said nothing, merely noted that she wore robe and nightgown and that the robe tied loosely. He embraced her fully with one arm, his hand resting under her breast, and led her across the courtyard to the garage, then up the stairs to his apartment. Stale smoke hung heavily in the dark. He shut the door, turned and yanked her to him. Her body gave up richly of her perfume.

"Easy," she said. "Don't tear my nightgown."

"Hurry up," he said.

She shrugged out of the robe, untied a ribbon and let the nightgown cascade to the floor.

It occurred to Julia that Teague, easily aroused, behaved like so many of her johns. He reduced the sex act to an exercise in self-gratification, an orgy for one, the women he mounted a mere vessel to catch the discharge. She acquitted herself as for a customer, sensing Teague's surprise and pleasure at the variation of movements and undulations going on under him.

At rest, Julia spoke first, pretending the agony of ecstasy. "Mercy, aren't you something," she said.

"Yeah?" he said.

"You're more man than *I've* ever had," she said. "Rats and rattles, I had no *idea* what could happen to a girl."

He laughed.

"I'll settle for you any old time," she said. "Is it still on, for my day off, I mean?"

"Sure," he said.

She moaned with rapturous delight. "I'm so glad I came to work here. We can be together lots, can't we?"

"Just so's we're careful," he said. "The meat ax'll fire you if she catches on."

"I know. She warned me," Julia said. "What was the other girl like, Paul? Better than me?"

"I never seen the likes of you," he said. "A goddamn shimmy dancer. Where'd you learn to screw like that?"

"It's you made me behave so shamefully," she said. "Truly, I don't know what came over me. I wanted you s'bad, and you were so wonderful . . . Oh, I *am* ashamed."

"Don't be," he said. "And don't worry about us getting together. We'll work it out."

"I wish there weren't any bosses," she said. "I wish we didn't have to work, ever."

"I don't know anybody who don't feel that way," he said.

Julia said, "If I were rich I'd never stop moving around. I'd keep traveling from one place to another, googlin' and meeting different people." She propped herself up on one elbow. "Do you have one of those striped suits, Paul?"

"What the hell," he said.

She laughed. "I'd purely love to see you in one of those striped suits. You know—the thin stripes with the itty-bitty flare on the trousers? And a cut up the back of the jacket? My you'd be beautiful. You have the body for it. Mercy, my, but you do."

"Stripes're not my style," he said.

"Don't you dare go contradicting me," she said. "You'd be beautiful."

"Okay, okay," he said. "Mr. America."

Julia sighed. "Damn money. I wish it'd never been invented." Her fingers caressed his body, gliding downward.

"Gimme a minute," he said. "I ain't caught up yet. Christ, you're really charged, ain't you."

"It's you," she said. "It's your fault. Truly, I had no *idea.*" She concluded that he was incapable of a second start, and she was relieved. Time pressed. She had to return to the house before Joe Dev came looking for her. "We shouldn't, though," she said. "I've got to get back."

"Stick around," he said. "Have a drink."

"I don't want any," she said. "But let me get you one."

She poured, then sat on the edge of the bed and watched him drink.

He said, "Real pretty make on you, especially shinin' like you are, in that moonlight. Remind me of a trout I caught."

"I like that," she said.

"Prettiest trout you ever saw," he said.

"Well, then, I forgive you," she said. She took the empty glass from him. "Paul . . ."

"Yeah," he said.

"Paul, is it true that you've been in prison?" she asked.

"Who told you that?" he said.

"Shoot, the house is full of gossip," she said. "I don't remember who."

"Yeah, I've been in prison," he said.

"What'd you do, honey?" she said. "Wasn't killing or anything like that."

Annoyed, he said, "No it wasn't anything like that. It was armed robbery."

"Shoot," she said. "I'd do that myself if I thought I'd come away with enough and never have to work again. I swear I would."

"You would, huh?" he said.

"Wouldn't you?" she said, "if you were sure you wouldn't be caught, I mean?" She set the glass aside and rolled over on him. "Yes, you would, you lazy good-for-nothing. Don't think I'm not mindful of your shiftless ways. I look out the windows and I see you. A lazy dog in the sun, that's what you are." She combed his hair with her fingers.

He laughed and said, "Okay, you win."

"Want to?" she asked.

"I said if you'll give me a chance . . ."

"No, not that," she said. "The other thing."

She felt him go tense. He freed himself of her weight and rose on one elbow.

"What're you getting at?" he said.

"Paul, you've got to believe that I've never done anything wrong," she said. "I mean, I've never been in trouble of any kind, the police and such. You know? Even now, mercy, I may talk heaps about what I'd *like* but I'd never *dream* of doing anything, well, I mean, anything considered wrong."

"An angel, huh?" he said.

"I'm not claiming the purity of pines. I've got my faults same as anybody," she said.

"Keep going," he said.

"Go where?" she said. "What makes you think I'm going anywhere? Maybe I'm just talking, rambling on about how nice it'd be never to have to work again."

"Okay, ramble," he said. "I'm listening."

"Well," she said, "here we are in this great big house, lorded over by a man's got millions upon millions, and you and I, we've got no more chance of making a good life—you *do* understand what I mean by a *good* life—no more chance than we have of seeing a cat with wings."

"You ain't through rambling," he said.

"Paul," she said, "do you like me enough so's we could be together awhile?"

"No complaints so far," he said.

"No, truly," she said.

"You know damned well," he said.

She said, "Paul, there's a lot of money in that house."

"Yeah? What do you mean by a lot?" he said.

"I'm not gospel sure, but thousands. Thousands and thousands," she said.

He remained silent, waited.

She said, "I know where it's hidden."

"How would you know that?" he said.

"By keeping my eyes open," she said, "while I do the cleaning."

"You talking about a safe?" he said.

"I'm not talking about a thing, not until I'm sure," she said.

"You brought it up," he said.

"Now wouldn't I appear a silly if I just spooned out everything I know, everything I feel, and after us only being together just this once. Shoot, I've made a big enough fool of myself already."

"No you ain't," he said. "It's like you said. Sometimes two people join good, click like. Ain't no explaining it. It happens. And when it does, the two people're obliged to go one hundred percent, one with the other, else none of it's worth a damn."

"Oh, Paul," she said, "I'd be pink proud to be walking beside you, say, in New Orleans or Nashville, or Miami, even, you wearing one of those thin-striped suits, and me—what'll I be wearing?"

"The way you are now's fine with me," he said.

"Fool you," she said.

"Chicago's my pick," he said. "I know people in Chicago serve up the best of everything. Fella and a gal could have a time there. Takes bread, though."

"Fella and a gal?" she said. "You referring to us?"

"Who else?" he said. "The people I'm talkin' about, they're way up there, on the top. I wouldn't show up with no pig on my arm."

"Paul, I hope I'm not about to do anything foolish," she said.

"Do it and see," he said.

He watched her silver-green form cross to the door where

the nightgown and robe lay heaped. A moment later she was back and pressing something into his hand. "What's that?" he asked, knowing, the feel, the crispness familiar; and when she made no answer, he bounded from bed and strode to the window. He examined the money in the light, counted it. "Jesus Christ," he said. He leaned over her. "Where'd you get this?"

"There's more," she said. "Much more."

"Where?" he said. "How much?"

"You'll know when I meet you in Chicago," she said.

"What?" he said.

"My first weekend off," she said. "You tell me where and I'll meet you."

"Seems like you've done a bit of figuring," he said.

"I'll meet you and I'll bring the rest of the money and the jewelry," she said.

"Jewelry?" he said.

"Diamonds, emeralds, a pearl necklace," she said.

"God Almighty," he said. "How much? Tell me how much?"

"Five thousand cash," she said, "Lord knows how much the jewelry's worth."

"Should be more than five," he said. "I figured about ten."

"Five," she insisted.

"And the jewelry, huh?" he said.

"Yes," she said.

"Jesus Christ Almighty," he said.

"All right, Paul?" she said.

"How come?" he said. "How come you're taking me in on this?"

"I told you," she said.

"Why don't I take it all with me?" he said.

She smiled. "I trust you, but not that much. Shoot, I may be making the biggest mistake of my life as it is, blurting everything out just because of feeling about you like I do. No, you take the thousand and go. If I'm to wind up in the ash heap, like for instance, there I am in Chicago and Paul Teague nowhere to be seen, well, you understand."

"I'm taking a big chance," he said. "I shuck out of here, Cugarman gets here tomorrow, finds me gone and the first thing he's gonna do is look for his goods. He don't find it, what happens?"

"They'll come looking for you," Julia said. "But I think you know how to take care of yourself."

"I don't know as I want to go on no wanted list," he said. "What about you? What'll you do?"

"I'll come back here," she said.

"I see," he said. "You play it cozy and innocent, and me, I've got the fucking hounds on my heels."

"What good will it do for both of us to be in trouble?" she asked. "I'll come back and after a while I'll quit and come find you and we'll have us a high old time."

"The jewelry," he said. "I'll have to go to St. Louis to unload it. I know people there can handle it."

"You make all the arrangements," Julia said. "When I get there with the jewelry you can make a deal, and we'll share the money."

"Seventy-five–twenty-five," he said. "I'm taking all the chances."

"I've already taken my chances," Julia said.

"Just because I screwed you good, huh?" he said. "That's why you're doing this? Expect me to believe that?"

"Paul Teague, you are not only insulting, you're missing the brains of a gnat. What do I know about disposing of jewelry and a stamp collection?"

"A stamp collection?"

"Lord knows what *that's* worth," Julia said.

"Christ Almighty," he said. "I read where one of those things sold for half a million. Cugarman, he goes for nothing but the best."

"Will you, Paul?"

"Christ Almighty," he said.

Joe Dev worked until almost dawn, his hopes waning with the night. Walls, furniture, floors, light fixtures, the clutter of ornaments, all refused to deliver up a clue to the cache. He applied himself to the dressing room alcove and bathroom with simian curiosity, touching, eyeing, dismissing; no object escaped a hasty inspection. He learned a little more of the man

Cugarman. A strand of hair clinging tenaciously to the brush revealed white hair; he used no cologne or aftershave lotion; did not shave (was that possible?) and washed with glycerine bars; he had no need for, or could not tolerate, patent medicines. The bathroom cabinet gave space to neither aspirin nor bicarb, it contained a supply of the glycerine bars; and hidden behind the bars was a pistol, a Colt .45 automatic. Joe Dev knew it for a deadly weapon, designed for personal defense. He replaced it, checked the toilet tank, then moved on to the bedroom closet, an eight-by-eight walk-in.

Cugarman loved color, dash, style. Hats, shoes, sweaters, suits excluded neutrals from their midst; only brilliance rated space on hook, hanger or shelf. Joe Dev inspected the right and left wall—plaster, solid. The shelves and drawers filled with neatly stacked haberdashery—nothing. He parted a row of jackets hanging on a chromium pole and flashed his light on the back wall. Wood. He tapped; it did not indicate a hollowness beyond.

It was done. The safe was not in Cugarman's bedroom. Resisting an oncoming sense of failure, he arranged everything as he'd found it and shut the closet door. He pondered his next move. Cugarman had installed a modern safe with an electronic alert. Where? In some matters people are dutifully stupid and obvious. Traditionally, a safe is never housed in a kitchen, a bathroom, a hall, a closet—areas neglected by an intruder—it's always the living room, library, study, bedroom—the master bedroom, usually. For Joe Dev, the logic behind this departure from tradition brought puzzlement and frustration. It was Cugarman logic, devious and unpredictable.

He crossed to the window and looked out. The western sky took reflected light from the east. He left.

Julia waited anxiously at the center-hall entrance to the kitchen. "Joe," she said expectantly.

"Nothing," he said. "Zero."

She took his hand and tried to lead him off. "Hurry," she said, "it's late."

"No," he said. "You go. I got four more bedrooms to search upstairs."

Horror sharpened her whisper. "You can't," she said. "Not now."

"Now," he said. "Today."

"Joe, you're crazy," she said. "In daylight? You've got to come through the kitchen to get to my room. Someone'll see you, sure."

"I'll be okay," he said.

"Joe, give it up," she said. "There isn't any safe."

"You better go," he said.

"No," she said. "It's time to end it. Don't you see what you're doing? You're risking everything. People're in and out here all day long. If they see you, you've no place to run to, not outside, not inside. If it isn't the dogs it'll be Teague and Donnet. You'll be caught."

"I came to find that safe, and that's what I'm gonna do," he said.

"Damn it, there isn't any safe," she said. "There can't be."

He went suddenly silent, stunned into comprehension.

She searched his face and frowned. "Joe, what is it?" she asked.

"Wait," he said. He went to the basement door, under the main stairway.

"You can't, you mustn't," she said. "Joe, we must get back upstairs. Please, please, you'll ruin everything."

"Wait," he said.

He knew what he'd find. It was Cugarman logic. Goddamn, god*damn* this Cugarman.

In the basement he climbed atop a box and inspected the four wires that wormed out of the flooring. He pinched the number three wire between thumb and forefinger and pulled. It came free, six inches of it. He stared at its frayed end and swore. The wire had tricked him into searching for a nonexistent safe. Goddamn this tricky-dumb sonofabitch Cugarman.

He poked the wire back into the flooring. He went back upstairs. Wordlessly, he and Julia fled to the safety of her room.

"Oh, Joe," she said, "what'll we do?"

"Sleep," he said.

"No, I mean—"

"I know what you mean," he said.

"Well?" she said. "Does it mean you won't be leaving tomorrow?"

"That's right," he said.

"When?" she said. "How long're you figuring on staying?"

"Who knows?" he said. "Until I find the bonds or until I figure I got no more chance to find them."

"But Mr. Cugarman'll be home tomorrow," she said.

"I expect him, too," he said.

"What about Thursday?" she said. "It's my day off. It'd look queer if I didn't take it."

"Take it," he said.

"What about you?" she said.

"I don't know yet," he said.

"You'd stay here alone?" she said.

"I don't get lonesome," he said.

"No, I mean—"

"I know what you mean," he said.

"Joe, have you *any* idea how you'll get out of here?" she said.

"Not yet," he said. "One step at a time."

"Joe, I'm thinking that you're not going to find those bonds," she said. "I'm thinking they aren't even here. I'm thinking that it's time for you to get out while the getting's good."

He shook his head. "I got one more trick to play," he said, "and I need Cugarman to play it."

"I don't understand," she said. "Trick? What trick?"

"The letter," he said.

"Letter?" she said. "What letter?"

"Oh, I didn't tell you?" he said. "It's on Cugarman's desk, downstairs, a letter in a pink envelope."

He explained about the letter.

Julia said, "I can't catch my breath with you," she said. "How's the letter going to change anything?"

"Use your head," he said. "Say it's you. Say you get the letter and it tips you off that one of the bonds you got stashed is phony, it's hot, it's danger. What do you do?"

"But the letter is anonymous," she said.

"Makes no difference," he said. "You get it, you read it, and then what do you do?"

"Well . . . I *suppose* I might believe it," she said.

"Okay, then what?" he said.

"I'd check," she said.

"You're skipping something," he said. "Before you check, what do you do?"

"Joe, I don't understand," she said. "Truly, I am *so* confused."

"For Christ's sake," he said. "You're sitting in a goddamn chair, you open the letter, you read it. Right?"

"Yes," she said.

"Then what do you do?" he said.

"I'd go check," she said.

"This time you said *go*. You *go* check. Where?" he said.

"To wherever I've got the bonds . . ." She stopped.

"Ah, it's not only daylight outside, it's daylight in your head too," he said. "When Cugarman reads that letter, he's gonna go to the hiding place of those bonds. And when he does, we're gonna be watching."

He rolled over. "Now I sleep," he said.

CHAPTER 22

Mrs. Crawford sizzled with excitement. "He wants a cup of tea," she said to Julia and the others seated at dinner. "Hurry." She supervised the making of the tea, her bustling an uninterrupted carom. "He's in a fine good mood," she said. "Didn't think he would be, what with Teague making off so mysterious and Donnet presenting himself at the airport in a dirty shirt." She glared at him. "Disgraceful."

"Never heard of such a thing," the cook said.

Donnet turned to Gerta and smiled brazen disregard for the rebuke. Inwardly he worried. He resolved to clean up after dinner.

The tea tray ready, Mrs. Crawford inspected it and said to Julia, "Take it and follow me. Good a time as any for Mr. Cugarman to pass on you." Her gray watered silks rustling, she led the way down the hall to the study door. She knocked.

Julia thrilled to a disquieting excitement at the thought of meeting Cugarman for the first time. Her heartbeat slowed, then quickened. It was like waiting in line to buy a ticket for a fearsome roller coaster ride.

Mrs. Crawford didn't wait for a response to her knock; she entered. Julia stepped in the door. She saw two white hands sorting the accumulated mail.

Mrs. Crawford said, "This is Julia."

Julia wavered between fascination and disbelief. Before her sat a sliver of a man, a skeleton contained in electric-blue slacks and orange blazer over a chocolate-brown print shirt that did violent battle with a viciously striped tie. A ballpoint pen in his mouth slashed across albino skin. A bony hand removed the pen. He looked up. The eyes that met Julia's were the color of underripe cranberries. His face, nestled in a cloud of cotton-candy hair, a pearl in a wad of gauze, revived a childhood concept of a mischievous elf. Every aspect of the face suggested benignity until a wispy smile formed crookedly on an elastic mouth, exposed one tooth longer than the others and transformed him into a caricature, an actor in werewolf makeup.

Julia found courage of voice. "Welcome home, Mr. Cugarman," she said.

He nodded and smiled the tooth into the open a second time.

Julia followed Mrs. Crawford back to the kitchen. Shaken by the nearness of the moment which meant success or guilty flight, she joined the others at the table and pretended interest in the food. Louise caught her eye: the game. Julia shook her head slightly. Not now. Not now. She wondered if Cugarman had opened the pink letter.

Donnet sipped the last of his coffee and announced he was going to feed the dogs.

"Don't go getting lost," Mrs. Crawford said. "The boss wants to talk to you."

Donnet made no reply. He left. Mrs. Crawford muttered, "Smells. Just like them dogs. Worse. I'd be glad as fruition if he disappeared too." She helped herself to food, adding, "Julia, mind the kettle. The boss'll want the teapot hotted up."

Julia went back to the study with a carafe of boiling water and poured it into the teapot. Cugarman did not look up. Her eyes darted to the pile of mail. It did not show the pink one. She delayed leaving and tried to spot it; delayed too long. He looked up. Flustered, she said, "Can I get you anything else, Mr. Cugarman?" He shook his head and twisted his mouth into the smile. It seemed to Julia that it was a knowing smile, sly, suggestive of a seventh sense, of a reader of minds. The cloak of innocence grew heavy to shoulder. She cautioned herself not to look down to the desk drawer she had rifled. She returned to the kitchen, pausing in the pantry to rid herself of clawing anxiety.

Mrs. Crawford said, "The boss talk to you?"

"He smiled," Julia said.

"A fine good mood, same as always," she said. "I can't understand why, Teague running off and him having to call in the police."

"The police?" Julia said. "Why the police?"

"Why not, I'd like to know," Mrs. Crawford said. "Lot of valuable goods in this house. Mr. Cugarman'll know what's missing soon's he finishes his dinner and has a look around. Oh, you can bet there'll be a good search and a lot of questions asked. You don't think Teague just took himself off, do you? Reckon not. A crooked tree throws a crooked shadow. The little things he's been pilferin', that's expected, the boss figures that as part of wages. Told me so himself. But when somebody ups and plain goes like the mist, ho-ho, you can be certain something valuable's missing. Ain't nobody can put anything over on the boss. Got more gift than twenty, he has, and more eyes than the Bible's got begats."

Julia remained silent.

Mrs. Crawford said, "Set a place for the boss's dinner."

"Do I have time to run upstairs a minute?" Julia said.

"What for?" Mrs. Crawford asked.

"It's sort of personal," Julia said.

"You're supposed to tend to your personals during your afternoon free time," Mrs. Crawford said.

"This is very personal," Julia said. "You know."

"Hurry," Mrs. Crawford said.

Julia ran up to her room. Joe Dev was gone, the bed empty. Her mind flared and conjured up the worst: he'd found the money and jewelry in her suitcase. She flung open the closet door, kneeled, looked for the shoe which secreted the key to the suitcase.

A hand snaked around her neck and sealed her mouth. Joe Dev said, "Shh," and released her. He loomed disturbingly, questioning, in the black outfit. "What are you doing?" he said.

"I want to change my shoes," she said. "These're hurting." She spoke as she changed. "Where have you been?"

"On the second floor," he said. "Studying around."

"Joe, it's dangerous, you mustn't," she said.

He frowned. "Hey, all of a sudden you're a ball of nerves," he said.

"Why wouldn't I be?" she said. "Joe, he's come home, he's here downstairs."

"And that makes you blow your cool?" he said. "You knew he was coming, no?"

"I'm not used to this sort of thing," she said.

"You're sure that's it? Only that?" he said.

"Well what else, for heaven's sake?" she said.

"I'm asking you," he said.

She shook her head impatiently. "He's going to call the police," she said. "Because of Teague making off."

"So what?" he said. "You're clean. Nobody touches you."

"The references," she said.

"Everybody fakes up references," he said. "They can't touch you, they can't prove nothing. If they started up with everybody fakes a reference, boy. You were living a bad life and you decided to straighten out, so you fake a reference to get this job. Believe me, they'll cry and then they'll bless you with holy water."

"I have to serve his dinner. I wanted to tell you about him. Joe, he's queer. I mean odd, strange."

"Tell me something I don't know," he said.

"Joe, he's not funny," she said. "I *mean* it. I'm scared, real scared of him."

"Why?" he asked.

"I don't know. It's the look of him," she said. "Joe, he's an albino."

"You mean one of those people missing skin?"

"He's as white as a bedsheet," Julia said. "The car came

back with the windows blacked out, and the minute he was in the house Mrs. Crawford drew all the drapes and turned on the lights."

"I swear to God," Joe Dev said, "there isn't one thing about this guy that's straight. Not one. Look, don't worry. Everything goes like I expect, we'll be out of here tomorrow."

"Do I ever look forward to *that*," Julia said.

"Where is he?" Joe Dev said.

"In the study," Julia said. "Joe, he's reading the mail."

"Watch him," he said. "Everybody through eating?"

"All but Mrs. Crawford," Julia said. "And cook's still there."

"Donnet?" Joe Dev said.

"Gone to feed the dogs," Julia said. "He's to come back. Mrs. Crawford says Mr. Cugarman wants to talk to him."

Joe Dev said, "Okay, listen. When Cugarman goes in the dining room to eat, you put out the lights in the hall, understand? And in the living room, on the other side. All the lights you can, put them out."

"All right," Julia said. "Unless somebody says I shouldn't."

"Nobody hollers if you put out lights," Joe Dev said. "Only if you leave them on."

"I'll try," she said.

Someone walked up the stairs. Joe Dev said, "Louise. That's her step." They waited until the sound of her faded down the hall. "Okay," Joe Dev said. "On your way."

She hesitated. "Joe," she said.

"Hey, come on, baby, hang loose, this is it," he said. "Go ready."

Cugarman didn't look up when Julia stepped into the study and said, "Dinner, Mr. Cugarman." His spun-sugar head remained lowered over the mail. Julia dared not inch forward another step to look for the pink envelope; there persisted the fear that guilt would babble its way into her face. She went out to the center hall and into the dining room. She waited, standing next to the chair he would occupy at the head of the table. She felt sick.

A never-ending two minutes passed before he appeared, the alabaster purity neutralizing the colorful clothes. He stood taller

than she'd imagined, a tallness which emphasized the twig-thin-
ness, the broomstick wrists. The bony fingers clutched the
remaining mail. She tore her eyes from it. She pulled the chair
back for him. He looked at her. He nodded, their eyes touched
briefly. His stayed uncommunicative, lifeless—pink marbles
lacking depth. She had never feared a man, even when harshly
used. Artful femininity tranquilized, rendered men docile. But
this man, the strangeness of him stripped her artless.

He sat, placed the pile of mail beside the service plate and
chose another letter, a white envelope. Grateful that he hadn't
smiled again, Julia went back to the kitchen. Mrs. Crawford,
eating her belated dinner, eyed her to make certain she
performed as instructed. The cook placed a tureen of soup on
the serving tray. Julia added the ladle, wondering how the man
could tolerate hot soup when the temperature ran into the
eighties.

"Croutons," Mrs. Crawford said.

Julia came back for the croutons. She carried the tray
through the tiny hall to the butler's pantry, shouldered the
swinging door, entered the dining room. She placed the tray on
the sideboard, ladled out a plateful of soup and set it before
Cugarman. The croutons went to the upper left of the plate.
Mrs. Crawford had emphasized that detail, the upper left.
Despite herself she nibbled a glance at the mail. A flash of pink
brightened the stack. She hoped not to be there when he opened
it.

She remembered the lights. Circling the table, she crossed
to the center hall, darkened it and the living room beyond. She
prepared herself for comment. Cugarman made none. He
continued spooning soup and reading. It seemed to her—she
felt—that he turned and watched her go. She dared not look
back.

In the kitchen Mrs. Crawford said, "He'll buzz when he's
finished. Don't speak unless spoken to and no rattling dishes,
mind."

"Yes, ma'am," Julia said.

Mrs. Crawford put her empty plate on the sinkboard. "Back
in a minute," she said, and left. Julia watched her go into the
back hall and up the stairs.

Cook spoke. Facing the hot broiler oven, she advised, "I'm turning over Mr. C.'s chop." She pointed vaguely with a spatula to the adjoining oven. "Potato's in there getting crusty. Mr. C., he don't like potatoes mealy on the inside or mushy on the outside. Vegetables're simmerin'."

Julia prepared the tray: plate and cover for the lamp chops, another for the vegetables, one for the . . .

Julia sucked in breath sharply. Joe Dev, a shadow, light-footed in from the back hall. Passing her, he shushed her with a finger to nose, stole a look at cook, whose back was to him, and vanished through the exit to the center hall.

Julia forced tempo back into her breathing.

The cook sensed a presence. "Who was that?" she asked, turning like a teetotum, not knowing where the presence had come from or had gone.

"Nobody," Julia said, "I didn't see anybody."

The cook refused to let go. "Donnet, maybe," she said. "Gerta?"

"No," Julia said. "He's outside with the dogs. I can see him. And Gerta's at the back door. Mrs. Crawford's gone up to her room."

"Huh," the cook said. She wiped perspiration from her face. "I could've sworn."

Joe Dev secluded himself in an oasis of darkness beyond the light spill from the dining room. From his vantage point he viewed and analyzed the physical characteristics of the man at the dining room table. Goddamn freak, he decided. He matches the freaky things he does—phony stuff in secret compartments, John Wayne. . . . Freaky outside, freaky inside, inside that snowball head, freaky eyes perusing a letter but like he sees nothing with the eyes. (Hey, it's a white letter, not the one Bru put in the mail.) Another thing. This guy plays up the freaky, fluffing up the hair like that, dressing like a goddamn clown. Jesus, he's gotta be one big fucking mess. Good mouth for lip reading, if he works the upper lip. Some people, they got a lazy mouth, they talk and the upper lip it's like it's made out of wood. They say a word like "girl" and you're out of luck. Just try and make it out. I think maybe this guy hates people, staring at him always, reminding him he's freaky, that he's alone, on the outside. He plays up the freaky and tells himself he's special, but that doesn't work for him. A nigger gets edged out too, because he's black, but at least a nigger can go find a thousand other niggers and feel at home around them. Cugarman, how many guy's he gonna find that look like a goddamn snapshot negative? This guy, he's like the freak works that carnival in Naples, the one's got a third hand growing out of his chest. You stand there and you die laughing because he makes the fingers of the hand wiggle bye-bye.

One thing, though. Better for this guy to hate you than to like you. This kind of wrongo, his hate is more better than his friendship. Because look: if a guy's away for a whole month, when he comes home telephones're supposed to ring all over the place. "Hey, Cuge, you got back. How about getting together and maybe having a few?" *Something*. This guy comes home and it's like they shut off the service. Hey, the letter . . . he's making a move . . .

Finished with the letter he had been reading, Cugarman placed it to one side and reached for another. Pink.

Pink. Terrific. Beautiful. Just in time for the show. A seat in the front row.

The pantry door behind Cugarman swung open. Julia came in with a tray, her buttocks giving liquid motion to the white uniform.

Joe Dev smiled. Don't bother shaking it up for this guy, baby. I got a feeling he's got a number two ziti macaroni where his cock oughta be.

Cugarman leaned back in the chair and postponed opening the pink letter while Julia cleared the soup service and served the lamp chops. Delicious, Joe Dev thought. But his appetite's gonna go fast when he reads that letter. Move it, Julia. Shake your ass the hell out of there. Okay, Cuge, let's go. Now.

Cugarman blinked at the food before him. He placed the pink letter on the table. He picked up knife and fork and sliced into a chop, tasted, approved, sliced off another bite, chewed. He put knife and fork down, extended a skeletal hand toward the mound of letters to his left, drew it back, remembering the pink one to his right. He fingered, slit it open, and read while sucking a loose particle of meat stuck in his teeth.

Okay, Joe-Boy. Now. Watch the sonofabitch.

Cugarman folded the letter, slipped it back into the envelope, put it in his pocket. He picked up knife and fork and continued with his meal.

Stiff and motionless, Joe Dev's limbs quivered with fatigue. His eyes glued to the diner, he lowered himself to a comfortable squat. Cool, he thought. This guy's ready for anything. It's okay. Cool doesn't mean he's got no curiosity. A boat doesn't sink until water gets on the inside. This guy's got a leak in him now, that letter shot holes in him. Jesus, he eats slow. You decide to watch this guy put away a meal you better bring your fucking razor, because before he's through you're gonna need a shave.

Cugarman dipped fingers into the breast pocket of his blazer and produced a watch whose chain attached to the buttonhole. The pink marbles focused on it, and then he let the watch slide back into the pocket. He rose and stork-legged it to a window. Like a stage manager counting the house, he peered through a slit in the drapes. He returned to the table and resumed his meal.

Julia served sherbet and tea and left.

Mrs. Crawford entered, wearing a seldom-seen smile. She spoke. Joe Dev could scarcely hear her. But facing him as she was, he saw her say, "Did you enjoy your dinner, Mr. Cugarman?" Cugarman turned his head and looked up at her. His response was lost. What he said wrinkled Mrs. Crawford's tissue-paper skin into another smile. She said, "She's a decent . . . respectable . . ." Cugarman said something and she said, "I'm very careful . . . allow . . . your house . . . yes . . . told him . . . my advice, if you don't mind . . . police." The white head made a negative motion. Mrs. Crawford shrugged and said, "You're the boss . . . let me know when . . . waiting outside."

She rustled out. Cugarman dug thoughtfully at his armpit. He stared blankly at the dessert. He drummed chalk-stick fingers on the tabletop. He stared some more. He checked the time.

Joe Dev took it all in, confused. What's the guy waiting for? And what's with the sneaky looks outside? There, now he's doing it again, like he thinks somebody's out there, like the place is staked out or something. He knows that can't be. He's got the protection. So why's he looking? Now the letter. He's reading it again. Don't wear it out, skinny, it says the same thing like before. Go look. Wherever you got the stuff stashed, go take a look, make sure about the hot one. Goddamn, there's Julia again. Freaky's gonna say something to her. Balls. He's standing in front of her. I can't see him or her. What'd he say? And where's Julia going now? Christ, here the guy comes, right straight at me.

Joe Dev roused himself suddenly to a dilemma. Would Cugarman go up the stairs or stay on the lower floor? In either case he'd need a light. If Joe Dev remained hidden and allowed Cugarman to go upstairs he might lose him. To follow him in full light would be foolhardy.

Junking caution, Joe Dev flew up the darkened stairway. He gained the landing and turned a corner simultaneously with the coming on of the lights. He waited, listened for footsteps on the stairs. After a nervous interval, he chanced a glance around the corner. He saw no one. He'd lost Cugarman. Damn. The thought that Cugarman might be on his way to the hiding place filled Joe Dev with an unruly urge to go back down, at least halfway, to look over the banister down the hall. Cugarman hadn't gone into the living room; Joe Dev could see that the room was dark. The library? The study? The kitchen? The cellar? He resisted the urge to go down. Anyone blundering into the center hall would catch him in full light, like a prima donna making an entrance down the grand staircase of the castle.

Joe Dev heard voices. They rose from below and behind him: the kitchen entrance to the hall. Julia's voice and another, a man's, one he hadn't heard since the night of his break-in. Donnet. The voices faded. He waited. Presently Julia walked down the hall. With a guilty gleam she could not disguise, she turned off the hall lights. She withdrew into the dining room. A beat later the dining room, too, was in velvety darkness.

CHAPTER 23

After Donnet had fed the Baluchi hounds and they lay contentedly nose-on-muzzle before the lean-to, he showered, changed his shirt and sought out Gerta. Among the problems imposed by his voluntary exile was the impelling force of his manhood. The domestic helpers who came and went, it seemed to him, returned from their days off with sexual fires burnt out, the embers banked. Lacking looks, charm or even subtlety of approach, he was unable to fan midweek passions. Need prodded, however. He found Gerta standing at the back door, wistfully eyeing the twilight scene through the screen. He said: "Hey, Gerta, you know nooky, hah?"

"Nooky?" Gerta said.

Donnet faked surprise. "What? You no know nooky?" he said.

But his tone betrayed him. Gerta said, "Ah. I know vot you vant. Go vay."

"Come on," Donnet said, "we'll take a walk."

Like the others, Gerta yearned for the freedom of the outdoors, but she looked at the dogs and stirred uneasily. "No," she said.

"You waitin' for the worms to get it?" Donnet said.

"Vot iss voirms?" Gerta asked.

Donnet performed the suitable pantomime with his fingers. "Chomp, chomp, chomp, nibble, nibble," he said. "Like when you're dead and underground."

"You not talk nice," Gerta said.

"Come on," he said, "I'm only joking, you know that. Look, I tell you what. Bring your book over to my place. Ve do your lessons and then ve make luff? You like luff, hey?"

"I no come," Gerta said. "No, I correct me. I do not come?"

"You afraid of the hounds?" he said. "I'll gentle them down. Know where to come? I moved into Teague's apartment because the alarm is hooked up there. First door on the top of the stairs."

"I do not come," Gerta said.

"Okay, if you don't want to learn nothing," Donnet said. "You're gonna be a greenhorn the rest of your life."

"I nó be greenhorn," Gerta said. "No greenhorn."

"It'll be dark in a little while," Donnet said. "Nobody'll see you, not even the old crow. I'll bring you back when I lock up and nobody'll know the difference."

Julia appeared in the back hall and placed a protective arm around Gerta. "Mr. Cugarman is ready to see you," she said to Donnet. "He's in the library."

"In a minute," Donnet said. "Can't you see I'm talking?"

"Mercy, my," Julia said. She led Gerta off, saying, "Stick with your Berlitz, honey."

Donnet released an oath only he and Julia understood. He went in.

Joe Dev was unable to see Cugarman from the hall. Cugarman settled in a library chair, his back to the door. Donnet, standing deferentially before him, faced Joe Dev squarely. Distance made the conversation inaudible and lip reading difficult. The timbre of voices came through, however. Cugarman's voice brought surprise. The sparrowy chest did not suggest tuba tones.

Between intervals of Cugarman's muffled resonance, Joe Dev saw Donnet say, "Honest, I don't know, boss . . . took off, like I told you . . . Yessir, Mr. Cugarman, I keep forgetting . . . Mr. Cugarman, Teague . . . talk in the kitchen . . . take anything?" Donnet whistled. "Holy Maloney, what a haul . . . Puts me in a spot, boss, I mean Mr. Cugarman . . . Mrs. Crawford said . . . call cops." In response to a muted peal from Cugarman Donnet smiled. He said, ". . . glad to hear." He paused, considered. "No . . . nothing strange . . . same . . . well, you know Teague . . . a makeout . . . new girl." He listened. "Molest? He banged her if that's what you mean . . . last night . . . apartment . . . oh, an hour, like." He smiled lasciviously. "Plenty of time to molest . . . Teague . . . angles . . . working on her . . . played . . . big . . . dogs, last Thursday . . . I remember . . . her day off . . . pulled a gun." Cugarman drum-rolled a question, and Donnet's expression turned fearful. "Oh, no no, boss . . . Mr. Cugarman . . . nobody past . . . sweater . . . Teague putting on an act . . . the new broad." Fear melted to relief, after which he frowned and the fear returned. "You mean tonight . . . about the lockup." A rumble from Cugarman caused Donnet to shake his head sadly. He said, ". . . driving around . . . night . . . dangerous . . . picked up . . . I run over a cat, even . . . trouble." Obviously unhappy with Cugarman's reply, he added, "Yessir, I'll leave right away . . . Yessir, I'll tell her . . . way out."

Joe Dev backed off and jack-rabbited it to the dining room. He was about to enter when somebody turned on the lights: Mrs. Crawford, checking to see that Julia had cleared properly. Joe Dev retreated and raced up the stairs. Midway, he stopped. He leaned over the banister. He caught a glimpse of Donnet shambling out. Behind him came Cugarman.

Cugarman turned into the center hall. Joe Dev rocketed up to the landing, veered left and waited for a light to flood the stairway; it did, and he heard the swish-swish of Cugarman's double A's scraping the carpeted stairs. There was no escaping him. If Joe Dev attempted flight along the upper hall, he'd never make it to one of the bedrooms. He flattened himself against the wall. Only one thing could save him, the unsuspecting state of mind which blinds one to all but one's destination when in familiar surroundings. If Cugarman's destination was his bedroom, he'd turn right on the landing and, hopefully, a strange presence to his left would go unnoticed.

Stone-still, Joe Dev watched Cugarman turn right, eyed the rear of him, noting that he moved briskly on ridiculously thin legs, stiltlike in motion. He entered his bedroom.

Pressing his luck, Joe Dev dashed to the far end of Cugarman's bedroom door and took cover to one side of a table. He put his ear to the wall and heard, faintly, a knob turning. Cugarman had gone into the bathroom.

He came out in less than half a minute and started for the stairs. His destination predetermined and purpose uppermost, he looked neither to right nor left. Joe Dev thought, No water flush. Means only one thing. He went into the bathroom for that pistol. Sonofabitch.

Cugarman rounded the stair turn, and Joe Dev caught him in profile. He was smiling.

Assaulted by doubts, Joe Dev moved stealthily back to the

landing. Where had Cugarman sent Donnet? If after all the planning, the risks, if after mercilessly sandbagging Julia into helping him, if after a month of sweat and strain the securities were not in the house, Mr. Bickford Anson would have some tall explaining to do. He'd guaranteed they were in the house, paid a bundle for the information.

Sifting and winnowing thoughts, Joe Dev said to himself, So okay, Cugarman sends Donnet out and maybe Donnet comes back with the securities. Balls. Trust Donnet? Not Cugarman. Doesn't make sense. No good, start over, Joe-Boy. Okay, start over. The gun. Why the gun? Maybe he's expecting somebody. He's got danger coming and he needs heat to back him up. Maybe that's why he kept peeking out of the window. No, that's no good either. From the dining room you don't see somebody coming from the front of the house. From the dining room you see only the garden. Who's he looking for in the garden? I'll tell you who, Joe-Boy. Nobody. He's looking for nobody. The peeking out of the window, that's a fucking puzzle. All you can do is wait and see. Everything depends on the next few minutes.

He put from his mind that which he'd learned about Julia, her visit to Teague's apartment. He'd sift through that treachery later. But how about that, huh? Jesus. He smiled wryly.

Someone was below the stairs, in the kitchen-pantry entrance, a duo of voices he could not identify. One voice grew louder. He craned his neck over the banister, then drew quickly back, recognizing the rustling of the watered silk. Donnet had said, "I'll tell her on my way out." It explained why Mrs. Crawford hurried to the library. Cugarman had asked to see her.

Trapped at the top of the stairs, Joe Dev nevertheless slackened the tendency to forced haste. He reasoned that little would happen while Cugarman and Mrs. Crawford were together, unless she too knew where the securities were hidden, and that seemed doubtful. But when the silk whispered its way back and Mrs. Crawford left as he had come, from under the stairs, he tensed again. What of Cugarman? Where was he now? Fierce determination to keep his target in sight moved Joe Dev to a reckless head-on tilt with disaster. He descended the stairs, squandered twenty precious seconds hidden beside the grandfather clock, checked for a clear field, then leaped nimbly to the next point of cover, a jog in the wall necessitated by the hall closet. He studied the length of the corridor. Light spilled from the open library door. Cugarman? Still there? Only another reckless gamble could supply the answer. Slippered feet never violating a great stillness, Joe Dev edged up to the doorjamb and peered in. Cugarman leaned calmly against a bookshelf, thumbing through a magazine.

Joe Dev half heard, half sensed a stirring behind him. He spun around. Julia stood in the pantry door frantically beckoning him closer. He went. She clutched his sleeve and yanked him into the pantry. The swinging door creaked shut.

"Where's Donnet?" Joe Dev said.

"Gone to 'Nap Town," Julia said. "Mr. Cugarman sent him to his office for the mail. Mrs. Crawford just finished speaking to the watchman of the building."

Incredulous, Joe Dev said, "The mail?"

"Yes," Julia said, "and his reading glasses, his spares. He forgot the others on the plane. Donnet was madder'n blazes."

"How you doing?" Joe Dev said. "Scared?"

"Frazzled," she said, "weak as a bled calf. Joe, I've got to go, that's what I wanted to tell you. Mrs. Crawford said Mr. Cugarman wouldn't need us tonight. She said everybody's to go to their rooms. Real snitty about it too."

"The mail, huh?" Joe Dev said. "And reading glasses."

"I've got to go," Julia said. "Mrs. Crawford'll be listening for me to go past her floor."

"The others?" Joe Dev said. "They're up?"

"Yes," Julia said. "Everybody."

He suddenly shoved her toward the kitchen. "He's coming."

Scrambling out, Julia tripped. Joe Dev caught her before she hit the floor. His arm circled her waist, and he helped her through the kitchen and into the back hall. She started up. He said, "No," grabbed her arm and pulled her into hiding under the stair ell.

Cugarman's entrance into the kitchen was followed by silence, a full half minute of it, and Joe Dev wondered why he hesitated. Looking out the window again? Julia trembled. Joe Dev placed a soothing hand on her arm. Her flesh felt cold to the touch. He squeezed to alert her of Cugarman's approach, and presently the toothpick frame stood with its back to them. Cugarman squinted through the screen door. He listened. He turned the pink eyes on the stairway, scanned all in his vision and, satisfied that no witness looked on, he opened the door. Quick strides took him into the black night.

"Holy Jesus," Joe Dev said. "Now I know."

"What?" Julia said.

"Why he kept looking out of the window," Joe Dev said. "He's been waiting for it to get dark. Jesus, what a jerk I am. Donnet, he sent Donnet to Indianapolis to get rid of him. The mail and the glasses, that's bullshit. He wants Donnet out of the way."

"Why?" Julia said.

"Why? For Christ's sake, because he's got the goddamn bonds stashed outside. Jesus Christ, this puts me right in the shithouse. Outside. Could be anyplace. He's got the whole fucking world, and if I follow him the sonofabitching dogs'll chew me up"

"Joe, don't ask me to go," she said. "Please. I couldn't."

"Don't worry, I'm not gonna. It's no use. It's all over for us, baby," he said.

"Do you think he's gone to the garage?" she said.

"That guy's bunk could be anyplace—the garage, the garden, the woods. Sonofabitch could be out there with a shovel digging. No, I take that back, that's not his style. I don't believe he bunks anything underground. If you tell me he stashed the goddamn bonds in Donnet's mattress, that I consider. Jesus, if it wasn't for the goddamn dogs."

"Joe, don't you go out there," Julia said.

"Don't worry, I got my head in place," he said. "No, it's over. We been screwed. So now we do like this. You duck upstairs. Me, I'm gonna break out of this place tonight, as soon as everything quiets down. Tomorrow you meet me at the motel. Okay?"

"Yes, Joe," she said.

"Hey, if anything goes wrong, you know," he said.

"Don't let it, Joe. I couldn't bear it if anything happened to you. Don't let it."

"I got a big interest in that myself," he said.

"Good luck," she said.

He muttered, "Yeah," but she didn't hear him. She'd fled.

Joe Dev exhaled long and hard; angrily. He dared not open the back door. The dogs might pick up his scent. Even to remain under the stair ell involved risk. He took refuge in the hall closet, a central position from which he could see Cugarman returning, if he returned. The enclosure hot and airless, his vision limited to a narrow slit in the door, he sweated and waited.

Cugarman reentered the house as quickly as he'd left, a package snugged under his arm. It was about the size of a folded newspaper and wrapped in plastic. He walked briskly to the library. He shut the door.

Joe Dev smiled. He was back on track. The package no doubt contained the bonds and Cugarman was checking for the bad one. Allow ten minutes to check and to wonder what in hell that warning letter meant, and then . . . well, one step at a time.

Cugarman reappeared in even less time than Joe Dev allowed. The package under his arm, the long tooth exposed, he tracked out. Joe Dev did not follow. He stayed in the closet and studied the luminous dial of his watch. Exactly three and a half minutes later Cugarman returned, without the package, and climbed the stairs to the second floor.

The decision to stay in the closet while formulating plans for his next move prevented a calamity. The bell-like clittering of the pantry-door spring announced someone's approach. He shut one eye and looked through the slit with the other. Gerta tiptoed by, barefoot, and went up the stairs. Joe Dev gave her enough time to gain the landing, then dashed midway up the stairs and framed her figure between two spindles. She turned right and continued along the upper hall to Cugarman's bedroom. She didn't knock.

CHAPTER **24**

Joe Dev opened the broom closet, eyed the contents, selected a dust mop, unscrewed pole from mop and threw back the mop. He spun a rubber band around the tip of the pole. When it was taut, he inserted a match under it, and the match became an incendiary extension of the pole.

He worked swiftly, making the best of the little time available. Escape had to be attempted before Donnet returned and locked up. At the moment the house was not electronically alerted. Cugarman was enjoying Gerta's chubby charms and the other women had withdrawn to their rooms.

In the living room Joe Dev lifted the telephone from its cradle and placed it on the table. Then, carrying the lamplighter contrivance like a torch, he sprinted to the second floor hall. He struck a match. He lit the match at the tip of the pole. He raised the pole and applied its heat to the thermal unit bolted into the ceiling. A chain reaction ensued: the thermal unit relayed the message of fire to the master control panel; the master control device notified the alarm locater in the main hall and pinpointed the origin of the fire—the second floor; the alarm locater triggered a burst of unbelievable sounds, like the braying of a herd of scalded donkeys; a duplicate locater installed on the domestics' side of the house repeated the braying; the exterior system alerted the local fire department while setting off gongs which shattered the stillness of night for a quarter of a mile around the house. Coincident with this chain reaction, the Baluchis, responding to unaccustomed noise, howled and aimlessly circled the grounds.

Joe Dev was back in the hall closet before the first mutterings from Cugarman and Gerta. Through the slit he glimpsed Gerta racing frantically past, buttoning up as she went, a vague ballerina rushing onstage after a quick costume change. In the kitchen she collided with Mrs. Crawford. The housekeeper, in sleepy panic, screamed, "It's upstairs, it's upstairs."

"Yah," Gerta said.

"It's a fire, you idiot," Mrs. Crawford said. She barely made herself heard above the braying and the clanging.

Louise and Julia swung around the back stairway and into the kitchen, followed by the cook, who breathed heavily and whimpered. They rooted there, numbed, exchanging inquiring glances, not knowing quite what to do, and stared at Mrs. Crawford, who kept shouting the fire call.

Julia picked up the kitchen phone. The simple act triggered the others. They found voice. They sounded like caged parakeets in sight of a stalking cat. Julia lifted the receiver to her ear and heard a dial tone through which she could not dial. She tried again with the same result. "It's out of order," she shouted.

Hee-haw, hee-haw.

Gong, gong, gong, gong.

Mrs. Crawford stumbled blindly into the center hall. "It's upstairs," she said. "Save Mr. Cugarman."

"Save Mr. Cugarman," said the cook.

On the second floor Cugarman walked calmly to the alarm locater on which blinked the second-floor warning light. With perfect composure he began a systematic inspection of the bedrooms. He opened a door, looked, sniffed for smoke. He ignored Mrs. Crawford, who charged upstairs warning, "It's up here, it's up here, save yourself, Mr. Cugarman."

"Save yourself," the cook called from below.

Mrs. Crawford recalled the instructions given the entire staff by the installer of the fire detector system. "No, Mr. Cugarman," she said, "get out of the house at once. Don't stop for anything."

"Not for anything," said the cook, "Get out fast."

Gong, gong, gong, gong.

Hee-haw, hee-haw, hee-haw.

Cugarman opened another door.

"No, don't open doors until you touch them to see if they're hot," Mrs. Crawford said.

"If they're hot, don't open 'em," the cook said.

Outside, the Baluchis' frenzy had peaked.

Mrs. Crawford shouted, "Everybody out of the house. Don't leave doors open, Mr. Cugarman. No, no, the draft. The smoke'll kill you."

"Watch out for the drafts," the cook said.

Cugarman opened another door.

Gong, gong, gong, gong.

Hee-haw.

"Vacate the premises," Mrs. Crawford said, remembering the exact phrase.

This time the cook did not echo the order. She and the girls rushed out the front door. Cugarman started down with Mrs. Crawford crowing and flapping behind him, her voice rising and falling. She joined the others outside.

Cugarman did not leave. He headed for the pantry hall.

Hee-haw, hee-haw, hee-haw.

Gong, gong, gong, gong.

In the pantry hall Cugarman depressed the emergency switch which silenced the clanging and braying. The din was immediately replaced by the sound of sirens and fire-engine bells. Cugarman made a gesture of impatience.

Joe Dev saw him go past the closet and out the front door. With firemen now at the gate, the hounds resumed their cries. Greatly excited, they charged down the driveway at full speed, their brawling yelps menacing the intruders. Cugarman thrust through the women and strode rapidly toward the gate to explain that a system fault caused the alarm, and not a fire.

Joe Dev sprung into action. He left the house through the back, pausing in the kitchen to choose a carving knife from the rack above the chopping block. In the courtyard, he ran straight to the dogs' lean-to. He bent into it, craned his neck upward and flashed a light. The plastic-wrapped package lay wedged between beam and roof. Tricky-dumb sonofabitch, Joe Dev said to himself. Goddamn sketch.

He ran along the path into the backwoods.

Donnet arrived, bringing the limousine to a screeching halt. He elbowed his way through the firemen and opened the gate.

Cugarman said, "Quiet those dogs."

Clutching the dogs' collars, Donnet was about to give the order. But now their keen sense warned of another presence in the opposite direction, and before Donnet could manage a firm hold, one of them broke free and fled baying up the driveway.

Joe Dev heard it coming. He froze, turned, paled. It came

on in full anticipation of justifying its reason for existence, to chop jaws into flesh, to tear, to kill. Head and tail low it bounded across the courtyard and into the deep wood.

Joe Dev remained absolutely still, erect, like a marksman evaluating his target, package in one hand, carving knife in the other. His one chance of escaping death required calm, timing. He could not see the animal, but, judging by its frantic bristling cries, it ran very close. If he failed to see it . . . One step at a time, he cautioned himself.

He saw it. It charged ahead. It was almost upon him, its hind legs cutting deep into the turf prior to the death leap. The knife, a keen blade of light, flashed upward from Joe Dev's thigh. Knife in hand, arm stiffened, the arm became a lance, and the dog was impaled by its own frenzied force. Knife penetrated chest. It fell. Its cries took on a liquid gurgling sound. Blood flooded lungs and it lay still.

Turning to go, a beam of light slapped Joe Dev in the face.

"You vait," Gerta said.

Joe Dev wheeled around, his eyes smarting against the light.

"You vait," Gerta said.

He recognized the voice. "Sorry, Dutchy," he said. "I gotta go."

The light left his face for a moment. She focused it on the weapon in her hand, a .22 caliber revolver. "You vait, hah?" she said. The voice was incongruously menacing.

"Yah," Joe Dev said, "yah, yah."

"You throw knife avay," Gerta said.

Joe Dev tossed it into shrubbery.

"I vont money," Gerta said. "You give it."

"I got no money," Joe Dev said.

"Yah, you got," she said.

"No, honest," he said.

The light flashed to the package he held. "In there," she said. "Money."

"Hey, you're screwed up, that's what," he said.

"I kill you," Gerta said. She struck an attitude of indignation. "I voirk hard. I sleep never. I listen. I hear you. I hear everybody. Everything. That man—" She spat. "I go to bed vit him." She spat again. "You give me money or I kill you."

"I don't know how you got it in your head there's money," Joe Dev said.

"Teague tell me," Gerta said.

"Oh, him too, huh?" he said.

"You put package down," Gerta said.

Joe Dev hesitated. Gerta said, "Other dog come soon."

Joe Dev loosed his hold on the package and let it fall to the ground.

"You open," Gerta said.

The light on him, he stooped and unwrapped. She centered the light on the contents. Atop a stack of certificates he saw two banded bundles of bills.

"You throw money to me," she said.

"Hey, look," Joe Dev said.

"Other dog," she said. "No time."

He underhanded the two stacks of money to her. Gun pointed, she leaned over and picked them up. The light flashed on the certificates. "Vot is they?" she asked.

"They is junk," Joe Dev said. "You already got what I want, you might as well take the junk too."

"Fock you," Gerta said. She doused the light and was swallowed by darkness.

"Fock you too," Joe Dev said to the night. "Goddamn sketch." He hastily rewrapped the securities and stuffed them inside his sweater. His own flashlight guiding him, he continued on toward the back wall, vaulting deadfalls, skirting brier. The wall in sight, he took a running jump, gripped the rim, heaved, and lifted himself over. He ran along the road, flashing the light on every telephone pole, searching for the identifying number stenciled thereon. He found pole number 213, counted ten steps from it to the brick wall and dug up the aluminum suitcase. In it was a sailor's uniform, shoes, underclothes, a duffel bag. He changed and packed the securities and his black outfit into the duffel bag. The suitcase went back into the hole. Then, the white sailor hat rakishly unsquared, duffel bag over his shoulder, he walked the back road to the expressway. He hitched a ride into Indianapolis.

CHAPTER **25**

Bick Anson sat at his usual place in the breakfast nook. The *Oxford Universal Dictionary* lay open on the table before him. He thumbed through its pages and made notes. He stopped and listened to a car come up the drive, to a doorslam, footsteps, the knock. He went to the door, released the double bolt, opened it. Alice stood there. She wore the uniform of the Uniontown Community Visiting Nurse. Anson said, "Wrong house. Nobody sick here."

"It's a mercy call," Alice said.

He stepped aside to let her pass. She carried a nurse's bag. Anson shut the door and reset the double lock.

Alice flicked hair from her face. "I'm Alice," she said. "You Mr. Anson?"

He looked at her and grinned. "I've heard about the Stocker woman's uniform," he said. "Never thought I'd see one."

Alice put down the bag. "I wish Harriet'd spring for a summer model. Christ, these things are hot."

"Tell her to think up a new idea altogether," he said. "Word about that uniform's got around. Everybody knows. A guy sees you in it, he says, 'Hey, there goes one of Harriet Stocker's whores making a house call.' "

"I'll pass it on to her," Alice said. "But do you mind if I don't say 'whores'? I mean, I wouldn't want to hurt her feelings." She hung the jacket over the back of a chair.

"Make yourself to home," Anson said.

Alice said, "Hey, is there anything cold to drink? By the way, what'll I call you?"

"You know who I am," he said.

"Uniontown's leading citizen," she said.

"You sound pretty fucking fresh to me, kid," he said.

"Bick okay with you?" she said.

He pointed to a kitchen cupboard. "Booze in there. Beer in the refrigerator." He returned to the breakfast nook.

Alice, mixing a vodka and tonic, said, "Anything for you?"

"Beer," he said.

She joined him, the beer and vodka in either hand. "You always read the dictionary?" she said.

"I read lots of things," he said. "Know what jactation is?"

"I know it isn't anything anybody'd do in church." she said.

"Witty," he said. "Witty and pretty. I like that. Only one thing I don't like about witty pretties is—" He consulted his notes and said, "Impudicity. Know what impudicity is?"

"I know I don't have one," she said. "Front or back."

"You're supposed to say no you don't know what it is, and then I make a joke," he said.

"Sorry," she said. "Start over."

"Screw it," he said. "You play cards? Lowball draw? Razz? Hold 'em?"

"Try Fish," she said. "Or Spit."

"We'll just talk," he said. "You can do that, can't you?"

"It isn't my biggest talent," she said, "but whatever you say."

"You're a sassy little bitch," he said.

"You want wit or wisdom?" Alice said. "I mean, Jesus, mister, is this a trial heat, like, for the big race? I mean, nobody mentioned anything about qualifications."

"What did the Indian tell you when he sent you here?" Anson asked.

She shrugged, as if bewildered. "What was he supposed to tell me? Jesus, I didn't come to your door with a line of cosmetics."

Anson laughed. "Iron Face was right," he said.

"About what?" she asked.

"He said you had a fast mouth," he said.

She pretended outrage. "I beg your fucking pardon, sir."

Anson laughed again. "That's what I mean. Fast mouth. A good talker."

She poked the ice in her glass. "He said he might drop by later," she said. "For breakfast."

"No way," Anson said. "This is his wedding anniversary. Big doings tonight down at the Room."

"I didn't know that," Alice said.

"We won't see him," Anson said. "I know Lydia. She's the

type's gonna recapture the romantic past—all night and right through breakfast." He tore the seal from the can of beer. "Know the Indian well, do you?"

"I guess not well at all," Alice said.

"What're you so sad about?" he said.

"Me sad?" she said.

"Yes," he said. "You say funny things but you look as sad as bull liver."

She made a sick face. "I'm gonna barf," she said.

"Indians are very sentimental," Anson said. "Know that?"

"No," she said, "but then I've never known enough of them to take a fair sampling."

"Keep talking," he said.

"You didn't get me here for conversation," she said.

"You'd be surprised," he said. "Tell me about yourself."

"Why do I have the feeling you're talking down to me?" she said.

"Balls," he said.

"You are," she said. "How would you like it if I was to, I mean, Jesus, it sounds like I'm being interviewed for a big job in the space agency or something. Suppose I said to you, just like that, tell me about yourself."

"I'd tell you," he said.

"Okay," she said. "You first. Tell me about yourself."

"Simple as squash," he said. "Everything you heard is true, so I don't have to repeat it."

"Chickenshit copout," she said. "Sounds like impudicity to me."

"You know what it means?" he asked.

"No, do you?" she said.

"For Christ's sake, I've got the goddamn dictionary right here in front of me," he said. "It's your turn."

"To what?" she said.

"Tell me about yourself," he said.

"Everything you're thinking is true," she said, "so I don't have to repeat it."

He laughed.

She said, "Do I pass, teacher?"

"You're better than the late movie," he said. "You always such a sassy little bitch?"

"I'm myself," she said. "If you don't like me, I'll try to be something different. You'll have to tell me what. I don't have much of a repertoire."

"I'll let you know," he said. "So far, okay."

"Gee, thanks," she said. "I mean, wow."

"How do you play Fish?" he said.

They played for the better part of an hour. She kept him amused and laughing and won fifty cents. She had three vodka and tonics, and when she started to the cupboard for the fourth, he said, "Slow it down. I don't want you getting woozy."

"Up yours, leading citizen," she said, and poured. "Hey, how about that swim you promised?"

"What swim?" he said.

"In your pool," she said. "Like water, you know?"

"I didn't promise you a goddamn thing, sassy bitch," he said.

"No, but the Indian said you had a pool and you wouldn't mind," she said. "I guess he doesn't figure you for the chickenshit you are."

"C'mere," he said.

"What for?" she said.

"I wanna touch your hair," he said.

She returned to the table. She sat beside him. He said, "I like towy hair."

"Please, *please* don't say it's like cornsilk," she said.

"Bitch," he said. "That tongue of yours'd be more in place on a switchblade knife."

"Hey, Bicko," she said. "Jactation. Does it mean to hand gallop?"

"No, it doesn't," he said. "It's nothing dirty. Look it up."

"No," she said, "if it doesn't mean a hand gallop it's a word I wouldn't be using."

"How old are you, kid?" he said.

"Old enough so I can't call you a dirty old man," she said.

"Tell me about yourself," he said.

"What's to tell?" she said. "I'm a living organism."

"I can feel that," he said. "It isn't what I'm asking."

"No different from any other organism," she said. "Learned that in a life sciences course. I could be a raccoon, a water bug, a tree, a leaf, anything."

"What the hell kind of a button is that?" he said.

"A button button, you dumb shit," she said.

"Easy," he said, "your sass is getting me on the raw. Unbutton the goddamn thing, will you?"

"A man or a woman," she said, "is no different from a male or female raccoon or a male or female tree."

"Jesus," he said.

"Take the leaf," she said. "It's blown onto the road by the wind, right? Cars speed past and blow it this way and that way, one side of the road to the other, night and day. Then it rains. Li'l ole leaf gets wet, flat, sticks to the surface of the road, the sun comes up and dries it and the cars start blowing it around again. Only now it's getting brittle-like, tired. It begins to shred. Breaks down into smaller and smaller pieces. Pretty soon it's like a little pile of lentils and pretty soon it's gone, disintegrated dust."

"Goddamn long-playing record," he said.

"Hey, look," she said, "are we gonna do this trick on the kitchen linoleum?"

Reaching for something on the chair beside him, he said, "Follow me." The chair was tucked under the table, and Alice couldn't see what he came up with, but the way he palmed the object while transferring it to his pocket made it clear to her that it was a gun. "Come on," he said, and led her to a bedroom flooded with mellow moonlight.

It lasted only a few minutes. He lay back, silent, hands clasped under his head.

"What's the matter, Bick?" she said.

"Nothing, why?" he said.

"Didn't look to me like you enjoyed it," she said. "I bungle things for you?"

"Not your doing," he said. "I'm kinda dinged out. I don't sleep much. Hardly ever, in fact."

"You've got to sleep some," she said.

"What the fuck do you know about it?" he said.

"I know that a person can't go on living otherwise," she said.

"Is that right?" he said. "Is that the fuck right, sassy bitch?"

"Yes," she said. "You're confused is all. They say that sometimes you think you're not sleeping but you really are."

"No shit," he said.

"Go to hell," she said.

"You ever count up to three hundred eighty thousand one hundred and seven?" he said.

"You did that?" she said.

"It's the reason I play games with the dictionary," he said, "and why I read the most goddamn boring books, hopin' to come up with a yawn, even. It's why you're here and I'm listening to your sass, it's the reason I eat so much, the not sleeping. Eatin's the only way to keep up my strength. You cook?"

"Meat-and-potatoes style," she said.

"What time is it?" he said.

"Three-thirty," she said.

"Look, you'll find a couple packages of frozen ravioli in the kitchen freezer," he said. "Go down and stick 'em in the oven."

"What about the swim?" she said. "Three-thirty but it's gotta be eighty degrees still."

"While the stuff's cooking," he said. "Put the oven on automatic."

She bounced off the bed. "I'll wash," she said, and headed for the bathroom.

"You might be kind of nice to have around," he said.

She called back, "You don't mean permanent."

"Jesus, no," he said. "You'd talk the fucking paper off the wall. For a while. You're pretty good company—"

"And clean," she said. "Score me for that. Employee washes her hands before leaving the lavatory."

"You're pretty, good company and you're smart enough to know when to stay out of the way. Think about it."

She dried her hands and went to him. She kissed him on the neck and then put her mouth to his ear. "Bick, that's awful nice. Jesus, that's nice. Sounds great. But it wouldn't work."

"No?" he said.

"I've got problems, too," she said. "And it's not, you know, like not being able to sleep. I mean, I'd be doing things you wouldn't like."

"Like what?" he said.

"Bicko, you big dumb shit," she said, "I can't do anything without a man's hands on me."

"Nymph?" he said.

"Fuck, fuck, fuck," she said. "It's like they put Spanish fly in my morning oatmeal."

"My God," he said. "Look at me."

"No," she said, "no, Bick."

"Look at me," he said. "My God, kid."

"So you see, Bicko, I'm in the right place now, at Harriet's. I'm not saying I like it—I mean, that's it. Limitations I got."

"My God," he said.

"I don't want to take on any—I guess you'd call it obligations of the connubial variety. Know what 'connubial' means?"

"Fuck off," he said.

"You're supposed to say you don't know, and then I tell you and I make a joke."

"Okay, make it," he said.

"The joke is you'd maybe walk into your garden to smell your roses and there I am under a goddamn azalea bush with your gardener. You, you're not the type who'd turn around and walk off all hurt and choked up, like. I mean, who gives a shit if your gardener gets his ass shot up? Not me. The bastard's got it coming, leading me on and seducing me like that, right under your pink azalea, but me, I'm not leading such a miserable life I want to part with it."

"Shut up," he said. "Go to a shrink. A shrink can fix things like that. It's on me."

"I dunno, Bick," she said.

"I know this shrink in Chicago," he said. "He's a fucking ace."

"You been to him?" she said. "About the insomnia?"

"How the hell can I go to a shrink and spill my guts?" he asked. "The sonofabitch'd write it all down, or record it. I know why I can't sleep. I don't need him."

"It's something we can think about," she said.

"Okay," he said. "Now go down and put in the ravioli."

"Anybody around?" she said. "Can I go bare-ass?"

"Nobody in the house," he said. "I had a cook but I blew her off. Didn't know how to fry eggs. Outside there's a guy, a guard. He might peek in the window and see you."

"You wouldn't have a dildo around, would you?" she said.

"Now what the hell would you do with a dildo?" he said.

"I'd put it on," she said, "and if your guard peeked in the window, wow."

"If the devil had a daughter," he said.

When she came back he put on a robe. The left pocket sagged from the weight of a bunch of keys, the right with that of the gun. With a towel draped over her shoulder, Alice followed him down the stairs to the living room. Sliding glass doors opened onto the swimming pool. Bick Anson worked the bunch of keys between his fingers looking for the one which opened the doors.

Alice said, "You lock it from the inside?"

"From all sides," he said. He flicked a switch which turned on the underwater lights and the floods overhead. They went out.

Alice plunged in. She splashed. "Man, oh man, what are the poor people doing," she said. "Beautiful, Bicko, beautiful. I haven't seen so much water since Skaket Creek."

"Where's that?" he said. He stood at the edge of the pool, still wearing the robe, lighting a cigarette.

"The Cape," Alice said. "You ain't lived until you wet your fat ass in the cool waters of Cape Cod Bay. I'll take you someday."

"It's a deal," he said. "You like islands?"

"Never had any," she said. "Aren't you coming in?"

"I'll watch you," he said.

"Self-conscious because of your belly, huh?" she said. "I'll shut my eyes until you're in, then I won't see it."

"I'll watch you," he said.

"Come on," she said. "It'll relax you."

He lifted the gun from the pocket of the robe, then took the

robe off. He folded it over a chair and gently placed the gun on
it. He dove in.

Alice leaped at him, circled his waist with slim legs and
raised her body high. "Eat, Bick, eat," she said. "It's better than
ravioli."

"Stop it," he said. "Goddamn it, stop."

He freed himself. Alice embraced him with one arm; the
other arm went under water.

"No," he said, "Leggo. What the hell are you doing?"

"Come on," she said. "Then you can float on your back and
make like a one-masted schooner."

He laughed. She scooped up water and splashed it into his
mouth. He sputtered and choked. She swam for the shallow end
and scooted up the steps. She leaned over. "Hey, looka me, I'm
the White Rock Girl," she said.

Anson wiped water from his face, saying, "I take it all back.
I couldn't stand it, having you around. There isn't that much
fucking energy in the whole world."

"Yanh, yanh, yanh," she said, "you can't catch me, Mister
dumb shit leading citizen. Jactating, that's what you're doing,
jactating. Up your impudicity."

She didn't know what to make of the intruder who came
alive as if from a tree trunk in the darkness behind Bick Anson;
suddenly he was there and she stared, fascinated by the
hugeness of him, by the easy loping gait. Except for a jockstrap
with aluminum cup he shone naked. Gathering speed, he ran to
the pool's edge, dove, fell on Anson and clamped Anson's neck
between forearm and bicep like a pecan in a nutcracker.

Alice screamed and watched Anson struggle. He rammed
his elbow into the man's middle. Free for a moment, he twisted
free and faced Alice. He said—hissed—"Bitch. You wanted to
swim, huh?" Then he turned to fight for his life. But the moment
he wasted cursing Alice undid him. Little Neffie had hold of him
again, had his neck scissored in a hairy arm.

Little Neffie squeezed and Bick Anson screamed sound-
lessly.

His accusation, when it registered with Alice, when she
understood his meaning, was a gut blow that knocked the wind

out of her. Finding her voice, senses crystallizing, she shouted, "No, Bick, no. I didn't have anything to do with it. I swear, Bick. Bick, Bick, listen to me. Don't think that, please don't think that. It isn't true."

Anson strained, snaked an arm and tried to cup his hand over the back of Little Neffie's neck. Little Neffie squeezed harder, wrenching, twisting.

Alice ran to the opposite side of the pool to keep Anson's tortured face in her sight. She kept shouting down the accusation. "I didn't, Bick. I swear I didn't. Please don't think that, please, in the name of heaven, don't."

She remembered the gun. She ran to the chair and grasped it clumsily in her two hands. She pointed it at Little Neffie, whose back was to her. She pulled the trigger. Nothing happened. She pulled until her finger hurt, but she knew nothing of the safety catch. Defeated, she stood there, hair streeling, wet, shivering now, mute witness to the last moment of Bick Anson's life. Little Neffie released him, waded to the ladder, climbed slowly up and disappeared in the blackness beyond.

Face down, Bick Anson bobbed in the still-turbulent water. He slowly sank. Suppressing a scream, Alice turned her head away and in doing so her eyes hit upon another horror. Bick Anson's dental plate lay on the blue-white floor of the pool.

She could not have blacked out for very long, she told herself. She was still wet. The Indian was rubbing her down with a towel and her senses tingled. Where? The living room. On a couch. She sat up and stared at the Indian. "Bick?" she said.

"Terrible thing," the Indian said. "Probably slipped and fell. Hit his head."

"What?" she said. Her teeth chattered.

"Bick," the Indian said. "He slipped in the pool. Fell. Hit his head."

"No, that isn't true," she said.

"He's dead," the Indian said. "Drowned."

"No, that isn't true," she said.

"You weren't here," the Indian said. "You don't know. He was alone. It was a hot night. He came down for a swim."

"No," Alice said.

"Get your clothes on," the Indian said. "You've been through a bad time. I'll take you to some friends of mine that'll look after you for a few days."

"That man killed Bick," she said.

"No," the Indian said, "it's like I say it is."

"No, no," Alice said. "It was that man."

"Allie, listen," the Indian said. "I'm in the top spot now. I've been working to get there for a long time. You're protected. All your life you'll be protected."

"You sent me here—knowing," she said.

"Will you for Christ's sake listen," the Indian said.

"You told me to get him outside," Alice said, "or to unlock a door. It was so that man would kill him, wasn't it."

"You'll have everything you want, anything you need, always," he said.

"You did," Alice said. "You sent me here. You knew. And Cooney, the man who killed Cooney, the man you took me to, that day in the tower. I recognized his picture, in the newspaper. After he killed Cooney. It was Gene. You did that too."

"Hurry it up," the Indian said.

"No," she said. "Bick didn't fall. It was that man."

"I wouldn't know," the Indian said. "I wasn't here. Nobody was here. Bick was alone."

"The hell he was," Alice said.

The blow was telegraphed from his eyes, she saw it coming before he raised the hamlike hand. She made no effort to turn away, took it numbly, without a cry. Tiny dots of blood welled up on her fair skin. He said, "Get it through your head that I'm trying to help you. Yes, it was me. I fixed it so's he'd die. Cooney, too, and Stacy, and anybody who'd've backed him up. Now I'm telling you, I'm saying it for the last time. You weren't here. Nobody was. He was alone. He came down for a swim and he fell."

She wasn't listening. "I hope he heard me," she said.

"You're an accomplice, understand?" the Indian said. "An accomplice. Something goes wrong you'll get it just like me and Neffie and everybody else."

"I hope he heard me," she said.

"What in the goddamn hell are you talking about?" he said.

"Bick, you big dumb shit," she said. "I hope you heard me."

"What?"

She didn't answer. She just shook her head and cried.

CHAPTER **26**

Shortly before dawn the wind shifted to the northwest and the day blew cool and clear. The dew still glistened in the sun when her car turned into the motel entrance. Waiting at the window, he saw her. He turned into the room redolent of tobacco smoke and detergent, and zipped up a flight bag which lay atop the bed. He tossed it into the closet beside the duffel bag. He opened the door and saw her stepping out of the car. He waved. She squinted into the brightness of the morning, not recognizing the figure in the sailor's uniform. He waved her in. She came alive, the green eyes flashing radiantly, the smile emphasizing her bone-prominent, minted beauty. She slipped into immense relief, shook the mass of red hair as if shaking off doubt, and ran to him. He shut the door. She held him, breathless, then stepped back to examine the whole of him. "My, look at the sailor boy," she said. "Oh, Joe, I've been so worried about you."

He smiled. "Yeah, huh?"

"Joe Dev," she said, "you are going to *fall*—I mean fall—fall, fall, fall, fall down and *die* laughing."

"That right?" he said.

"Wait till I tell you," she said. She recounted what had happened, all in a rush, high merriment modulated with snickering glee. "Why, you'd think there'd been a social instead of confusion and shouting and fire trucks and Lord knows what-all. Take Mr. Cugarman. Would you believe it, he went to *bed*. He cleared those brave firefighters—oh my, they were *so* eager—he cleared them out of there and he just as calm as you please *went to bed*. There we are, the girls, I mean, there we are setting up till all hours chewing over what's happened and all, all of us nervous and excited as kids telling ghost stories in the dark, and he is up there in *bed*. Well, Mrs. Crawford was rarin'. It's purely dangerous, she says, not to do something about it all.

And when Donnet found the dog dead? Joe, I thought she'd go out of her *head*. She marched up to his room and banged—I mean *baa-yunged*—on his door and said he'd have to call the police because somebody, *somebody*, had been on the place." She slowed and pronounced the words carefully. "And do you know what Mr. Cugarman said? He told her to mind her own goddamned business, is what he said, her own goddamned business, that there wasn't to *be* any police and that *she* was to go to bed . . . no, wait, I'm not finished. She was to go to bed *straight off*. And when she went on about it, he said *'Fuck off.'* His words, Joe, his words, talking like that to a Bible-reading woman. I was purely flabbergasted."

"What a sketch," Joe Dev said.

"Well, there wasn't much sleeping done, I can tell you," Julia said. "Cook's talking about giving notice, and Gerta, she's leaving at the end of the week, which does not uncomfort me one bit, because that pervert Donnet's been after her, you know."

"She deserves better," Joe Dev said.

"On and on it went," Julia said, "and it's almost two in the morning when Mrs. Crawford's got it all figured just as *plain*. It's Teague's doing, all of it. It's Teague who came back last night. *Teague*." Her laughter reached new heights.

"Ho-ho," Joe Dev said.

"Teague never left his keys, says Mrs. Crawford, so he's got free run of the place, he can come and go as he wishes."

"Mrs. Sherlock Holmes, huh?" Joe Dev said.

Julia clapped her hands. "Oh, Joe, that is so *funny*, Joe. Mrs. Sherlock Holmes. My, yes. According to Mrs. Sherlock Holmes, Teague had good reason to come back. Well, I ask, just as innocent as can be, I ask, 'Whatever foah?' And she answers that he came back for something important? Something he forgot? And just *had* to have or else? Mercy, I'm all out of breath."

"Relax," Joe Dev said.

"No, no, I've got to tell you, Joe," she said. "Joe, Donnet said that Mr. Cugarman told him that Teague made off with valuables worth better'n *two hundred thousand dollars*."

"Hey," Joe Dev said.

"Two hundred thousand dollars," Julia said. "My, it sets my head spinning just to think about it."

"Me too," Joe Dev said. He listened to her self-sabatoging with a grin of wonderment on his face, like a father enjoying the performance of a precocious child, and hungering for more.

"Oh, but it has been a *night,*" Julia said. "Didn't *you* give us a time, Mr. Joe Dev."

"Yeah, huh?" he said.

"And it's Teague who's taking the blame," she said. "Mrs. Crawford says it's the flight of the wicked. Teague came back for whatever it is he came back for, and something goes wrong with the fire alarm, and off he goes through the woods and has to kill the dog to make his escape. Of course, there are questions Mrs. Sherlock Holmes can't answer, like *why* did he come back and *why* would he kill the dog when the dog was *trained* not to harm him, but they're all no-account questions because Mr. Cugarman says no police and that's an end to it, period, exclamation point and close the book."

"Beautiful," Joe Dev said.

The phone rang. He picked it up. "Yeah?" And then, "Thanks." He cradled the phone. "I told them to call me when the coffee shop opened. You like something?" he said.

"I couldn't touch a bite," Julia said. "But I'll sit with you."

He breakfasted on ham and eggs; she sipped three cups of coffee. She said, "Joe, did you . . . Was there anything . . . ?"

He shook his head.

"When we parted last night, you were so disappointed I could've cried for you."

"I come away with nothing, Julia," he said. "A big goose egg."

"Oh, Joe," she said.

"I looked," he said. "I looked like hell right up to the last minute. Nothing. After that, I gotta think to save myself."

"Oh, I am *so* sorry," she said.

"Hey, you're okay, you know?" he said. "I expected you be disappointed, mad."

Her face tensed resentfully. "Mad," she said. "Shoot, we shared a smidge of bad luck is all. Mad?"

He reached across the table and squeezed her hand. "You like more coffee?" he said.

"I'll splash," she said.

They returned to the room. "I guess we better get started," he said.

"Where to?" she said.

"We talk about it on the way," he said. "I don't know for sure. When this job came up I was thinking like about Los Angeles. Maybe we go there. You like Los Angeles?"

She managed a half smile. "What'll we do in Los Angeles?" she said.

"Well, look," he said, "we don't make out here, okay. It's no use to sit down and cry. We make another stab."

"Another *stab*," she said.

"Yeah," he said. "Cugarman's not the only one got money. Lots of money around. We want the restaurant, no?"

"Another *stab*," she said. Delicately placing a hand over her diaphragm, she exhaled. "Another *stab*. Mercy."

"Something bothers you, huh, Julia?" he said.

"It's just that I don't know that I can go through that again," she said.

"Oh," he said.

"Joe, when I was standing there, in the kitchen? And cook right there? And you came through like a cat running for its dinner? Joe, I like to turn to stone," she said.

"Hey, dopey me," he said. "I don't consider. It was tough on you, huh?"

"It wasn't a ham dinner," she said.

"I tell you what we do," he said. "You be the bookkeeper, and me, I go out and get the money. When I bring enough for the restaurant you say stop. Okay?" He held up a hand and prevented the answer from coming. "Wait," he said. "Something else we gotta consider. We gotta consider maybe we split. If it's not the kind of life for you, you don't force yourself. That's no good. Split. What do you think?"

She said nothing.

He said, "Maybe we take a vacation."

"The two of us?" she said.

"No, I mean one of us goes one way, the other the other,"

he said. "That gives you a chance to think and make up your mind. We meet like, we say, in a month. How's that?"

"I don't like parting from you, Joe," she said.

"Sure," he said. "You think I don't understand?"

"A month isn't a long time," she said.

"Goes just like that," he said.

She forced sadness from her, and a show of animation accompanied the conversion. "But rats and rattles," she said, "we don't have to think about parting *now*. Why, we've got us a whole day to have us a time."

"No, Julia," he said. "It's more better if we split right away." He looked at his watch.

"Oh, Joe," she said.

"First, though," he said, "I gotta ask you, Julia."

"Yes, Joe?"

"The stuff you took from the desk," he said. "Where is it?"

She stood there, stupidly, having heard the world crash but not feeling the impact.

He said, "Don't try to unload, Julia. It's junk. No fucking good. Get rid of it or you got big trouble. Especially the money. You try to spend that and you wind up in jail. I mean it."

She said nothing.

He said, "Teague, who gives a shit about Teague? You, yes. You I worry." Through the tightness in the air, he said, "Sorry, Julia."

She lowered herself into a chair and studied her hands, her shoes, the carpet. To look up at him took more courage than she possessed. She moaned within. If he knew that much, then he knew all. All. He knew all. What did he expect now? She said, "The crazy part of it is I love you."

"Take a good look in your heart, Julia," he said.

"I love you," she said.

"No," he said. "You sold yourself on that to make yourself feel more better for what you did."

"I love you," she said.

"You tried to betray me, to fool me," he said.

"How can I make you believe what I say?" Julia said.

"Don't bother," he said. "We do the best we can in this life. I fool you, you fool me. When we through fooling though, I play square. You, no. I say I be here, I'm here. I could be a thousand miles away, but no, I'm here. You, you're still fooling."

"I love you," she said.

"Bullshit," he said. "What you did?"

"Joe, I was scared," she said. "I've always had it to figure on, being scared."

"What kind of scared?" he said. "You scared that you don't go high? That you always be a piece of shit? Okay, me too. You scared that if you don't keep scratching around they gonna step on you and squash you under their feet? Okay, me too. You think being scared was made special for you? Since they cut the fucking cord off my belly I'm scared."

"When you said you loved me, I thought it would be different," she said. "It was. The being scared changed it. Loving you didn't change."

"Look," he said, "we talk, talk, talk, and we only complicate. Let's finish. Split. You tell me where, I send you ten thousand. My own money, out of my own pocket. Maybe you don't believe that, that's okay. I don't suck you in this thing with the intention I leave you dry.

"What you said, lies." It was not a question. "All of it, lies. Everything you said that day, about loving me, lies. Lies," he said.

She looked up, the tears came. "You had Alice," she said. "Why not Alice?"

"Alice was not right for the job," he said.

"I see," she said. "You went inside my head, as you say, and you found a mixed-up, stupid, greedy, frightened bitch—"

"Hey, now, what's the use of that?" he said.

"—incapable of loving anyone," she said. "Is that what you found?"

"Hey, look, what do you want?" he said. "From the minute you walked in here I give you every chance to wash out your mouth that's full of bullshit. Every chance. I say we go to L.A. I say you be the bookkeeper. I say we think it over. I say we take a vacation. Every chance. But no."

"You damned hypocrite," she said. "The truth wouldn't 've made any difference and you know it."

"To me no difference, no," he said. "I figure maybe you feel better for what you did if you spit it out. But you don't do that. Fuck Joe Dev. All you think about is two hundred thousand and some goddamn trick you make up with Teague."

"You used me," she said. "You used the worst I've got in me."

"Listen, I'm not smart," he said. "I'll never go high. But I understand people. I gotta. People, they're the only thing give me trouble in this life."

"Damned hypocrite," she said.

"You know why Cugarman doesn't call the cops?" he said. "He's a crook. A crook doesn't call cops. So I consider that. And I consider when I come to you that you're gonna screw me first chance you get. And what happens? You're like everybody else, baby. You don't want to walk straight and you don't want to walk crooked. Down the middle only, and every once in a while make a grab, right or left, a grab, then back to the fucking middle. Jesus Christ." He hammered his fist onto the tabletop. Anger melted immediately, and he said, "You want the God's honest truth, Julia? I don't have it in me, it's like not in my nature to feel about a woman like that. I'm talking about love, understand? For me that kind of a woman isn't alive. She never was born. When I lie to you about a lake and a restaurant and a woman that's with me, that's my dream. Just like your dream is you go high in the real estate. But neither one of us is gonna make that kind of dream, Julia, neither one of us is got that kind of love to hand over."

"Joe, I have," she said. "I'd show you. I'd do anything."

"You said that once before, remember?" he said. "You talk about *love* now, baby. *Love*. Anything? For you love is like you spread your legs and that's it."

"No, damn you," she said.

"You love somebody it means you gotta like them more than you like yourself," he said. "It means you gotta trust them more than you trust yourself. It means you give them the right to make you suffer. Be honest, you ready for that?"

"I am. I was. It was the being scared changed it."

"It's not for fools, Julia," he said. "You keep believing that and you be in trouble all your life."

He remained silent and allowed her to cry a while longer,

then he said, "Where you gonna be, Julia? I gotta know where to send the ten thousand."

"You think that's all I care about, don't you?" she said.

"Maybe not now, no. Tomorrow, yes," he said.

"I don't want your damned money," she said.

"You don't want it you give it to the poors," he said. "Where you gonna be?"

Her cry echoed the wretchedness within. She buried her face in her hands and fled into the bathroom. She slammed the door shut and bolted it.

Annoyed, Joe Dev crossed to the telephone. He picked it up. A voice from the motel switchboard said, "Number, please." Joe Dev said, "Never mind," and cradled the instrument. Uniontown was a toll call. He didn't want to leave Bick Anson's number on record.

He called from the telephone booth outside the motel office. He dialed, deposited the amount asked for, heard the ring.

The Indian said, "Yeah?"

Joe Dev said, "Let me talk to the boss."

The Indian hesitated a moment, then said, "Dev?"

"Personal appearance," Joe Dev said.

"Bick's in the tub," the Indian said.

"Always in the fucking tub," Joe Dev said.

"I'll take a message," the Indian said.

"Tell him I got that paper," Joe Dev said.

"Fine," the Indian said. "Where are you?"

"Where I am is none of your goddamn business," Joe Dev said. "Where you're gonna be, that's what we discuss. A meet. I bring the paper, you bring the cash I got coming."

"A hundred of them, right?" the Indian said. "Ten percent."

"A hundred and two," Joe Dev said.

"More than we expected, huh?" the Indian said. "You're honest."

"How do you know it isn't a million four or five, and I'm holding out?" Joe Dev said.

"Why don't we meet at the field?" the Indian said. "I'll arrange for the plane to take you wherever you're headed."

"No, thanks, I'm going the other way," Joe Dev said.

"Okay, you name it," the Indian said.

"We passed a place the first day you picked me up," Joe Dev said, "a place where they sell tractors. Higbee's. You know it?"

"I know it," the Indian said. "You've got a good memory."

"Next to Higbee's, on the same side, there's a corn field. You know that?" Joe Dev said.

"I know it," the Indian said.

"I'll meet you there," Joe Dev said.

"Okay, eleven o'clock," the Indian said.

"Twelve-thirty," Joe Dev said.

"Twelve-thirty," the Indian said. "It's a big corn field. How do I find you?"

"I'll find you," Joe Dev said. "Just you and the boss, understand? Nobody else. Otherwise you're not gonna be so easy to find."

He hung up. As he walked past the motel office window the manager, engrossed in the newspaper, looked up and waved a good morning. Joe Dev smiled pleasantly and continued on to his room. The manager resumed reading. The *Star* headline told of Bickford Anson's accidental death a few hours earlier.

The bathroom door was still bolted. He called, "Julia."

She made no answer.

"Come on," he said, "I'm going."

She made no answer.

"This is the way you wanna finish it up? Okay," he said. "I send the ten thousand to Harriet's place. You pick it up there. Goodbye, Julia."

She was out and into his arms before he could pick up his bags. "Joe, don't leave me. Please, please, please, please."

He wrested free and slapped her clear across the room. She fell, sobbing. He zipped open the flight bag. The securities were gone, their approximate weight substituted by two rolls of toilet paper wrapped in bath towels. He said, "What's the matter, baby, you think I'm so fucking stupid I leave you alone for five minutes and I don't check?" He stormed into the bathroom. She had hidden the securities in the vanity. He stormed back and stuffed them into the flight bag.

Between sobs, she said, "Please listen."

"Jesus," he said. "Listen."

"A minute, please," she said.

"Start," he said.

"I wasn't going to keep . . . whatever it is," she said.

"Pretty good start," he said.

"I was desperate, scared," she said.

"That I know," he said. "You told me."

"I wanted to prove that I love you," she said.

"That's the way to do it," he said. "A knife in the back."

"No, no," she said.

"Yes, yes," he said.

"Please. You said you'd listen," she said.

"Okay," he said.

"I wasn't going to run away," she said, "I'd've been waiting for you."

"Holy Jesus, why didn't I think of that before I started batting you around?" he said.

"When you found it gone, after you were through thinking the worst of me, after you'd cursed me, you'd've come back, and you'd've seen how wrong you are. Because I'd've been here, waiting for you, and I'd've proved I love you." She lifted a tear-smeared face and screamed, "You think about that, Joe Dev. You just think about that."

"Take care of yourself, Julia," he said.

He opened the door, came back to the closet, heaved the duffel bag onto his shoulder, picked up the flight bag.

"You bastard," she said, "you dirty, evil, low bastard."

"It coulda been worse for you, Julia," he said. "You coulda met a guy comes from nice people."

CHAPTER **27**

North of Indianapolis shallow valleys and peaks bring gentle relief to the level surface, but beyond Uniontown the land flattens and remains flat for mile upon mile. Joe Dev drove past a filling station, Tootsie Pie's Good Eats, then Higbee's Tractor Sales and Repairs. He slowed and looked for an opening in the half mile of woodland which flanked Higbee's. He found it: tire-tracks, the center hummocked and weedy. He drove deep into woods littered by beer cans, crushed cigarette cartons and discarded or forgotten female underclothing. He turned the car around, nosed it toward the highway, shut off the motor. He took off the sailor blouse. He stuffed the packet of securities into the waist of his pants, then slipped into a white sport shirt which hung loose and covered the packet. He listened hard and heard none but the sounds which belonged. He got out of the car, locked it, and hiked through a density of maples, hickories and sycamores. It was hot. The sun, nearing its zenith, pierced the leaf covering and spotted the floor of the woods. A wind blew, but only in the treetops, and Joe Dev sweated.

A thousand or so yards ahead, at the edge of the woods, the corn field sprouted and spread as far as he could see. Knee-high when he arrived on July fourth, it was now head-high. He climbed to the lower branches of a maple and searched the distance on the three sides of him. He noted the roofs of barns and a farmhouse crouching low on the horizon, the highway traffic, toylike at that distance, the cow pasture far off to his left. In the foreground, the distance of a city block, he estimated, ran a narrow dirt road used by tractors and other heavy equipment. It cut into the field from the highway and ran parallel to the woods, penetrating far to the left of Joe Dev and then angling sharply toward the woods.

But it was the seemingly endless sweep of golden-tasseled corn that greedily demanded the attention, and when Joe Dev felt the wind across his face, that same wind produced a soft swishing sound—*shhhhoooooooeeeeee*—and set the field in motion, transforming it into a sea of palomino tails. Thankful for the cooling wind, Joe Dev settled against the trunk of the tree and enjoyed the panorama. It was eleven-fifteen. He'd allowed enough time to wait and watch, to make certain that the arrival of Bick Anson and the Indian was not preceded by a stakeout gang. Time well spent, he thought. Maybe he was doing things the hard way, but his instinct insisted that he not trust the Indian. His instinct for sensing treachery was a gift he never rejected. Bick Anson had Uniontown in his pocket. If he and the Indian decided to renege on the deal, they'd have him picked up, jailed and sentenced before the day was over. The packet of securities represented the edge he held. He was the second target, the securities the first, and he intended to stay in their protecting shadow.

The 1970 Mercury swung into the dirt road at twenty-five minutes past twelve. Until then he'd seen no one. A dozen yards into the road, the Mercury came to a stop. A man got out: the Indian. He made a sun visor of his hand, scanned the field, then turned and spoke to someone in the back seat of the car. He slid back behind the wheel and drove deeper into the field, hazy dust trailing. He stopped. He got out again.

From his perch, Joe Dev saw only the Indian's head and a slice of the hardtop Mercury. He waited for five minutes, eyes darting from car to highway. The front seemed clear, but he'd found the tire-track road, and so could they. He climbed down from the tree and returned to the thick woods. Halfway to his parked car, he paused and, stone-still, gave himself up to animal faculties. He heard and saw no one. He hiked back to the field. At its edge, head lowered, he ran to the dirt road at his left. Standing in the center of the road, the safety of the woods behind him, flanked by the corn field, he placed thumb and forefinger between his teeth and whistled. He heard the Mercury's motor roar to a start and presently it came into view. The Indian saw him and was about to turn left. Joe Dev held up his hand, signaling him to a stop. The Indian did not complete the turn. He got out of the car and shambled toward Joe Dev. Looking past him, Joe Dev could see another man in the back seat of the car, but his concentration was on the Indian, who came on, his hands at his sides, corded forearms hanging loose below the rolled-up sleeves of his shirt. He was unarmed.

Face to face, the Indian deadpanned a hello. Joe Dev said nothing; he stared. Finally the Indian said, "Well?"

Joe Dev said, "Well, what?"

"You bring what you said you'd bring?" the Indian said.

"Did you?" Joe Dev said.

"Yes," the Indian said.

"I don't see it," Joe Dev said.

The Indian said, "It's in the car. Bick wants a look at the paper first."

"No looks," Joe Dev said.

"Pignuts," the Indian said. "You asking us to hand over a hundred and twenty thousand? Just like that?"

"Any way you like," Joe Dev said. "Just so you hand it over."

"No way," the Indian said. "You *know* what money looks like, the paper has to be looked over."

"You got a good recommend from my people," Joe Dev said. "A guarantee I'm okay. I step out of line, the end of the world ain't far enough away from Lodi, New Jersey. So you go get the money and you come back. No looks, no talking, no bullshit."

The Indian said, "Wait," and shambled back to the Mercury. He caucused with the man in the back seat, returned. "Bick says nothing doing. He wants a look."

"Bye-bye, Mister Indian," Joe Dev said.

"For Christ's sake, put yourself in our place," the Indian said. "You call and say you've got the paper, we check, and nobody knows a goddamn thing about a robbery at Cugarman's."

"You think I haven't got it," Joe Dev said.

"Let's say we want to see it," the Indian said.

Joe Dev smiled. "I guess you got me," he said. "I try to fool you but you're too smart for me. I give it to you straight. No robbery. It breaks my fucking heart to tell you, honest. I skunked out. I come away dry. I couldn't get in the Cugarman house."

The Indian remained silent.

Joe Dev said, "No hard feelings, huh? I go now."

"Not with a million four hundred thousand you won't," the Indian said.

"No, not with a million four hundred thousand," Joe Dev said. "I haven't got it. You said so. And who's smarter than you?"

"Look," the Indian said, "put yourself in Bick's place. He has only your word. You expect him to believe you went over that wall, dodged the dogs, the alarms, and then got back out with the paper? And nobody knows about it? Pignuts."

"How I did it is none of your fucking business," Joe Dev

said. "I don't give away my business secrets. You want the
bonds, yes or no? If you want them, go back and get the fucking
money and bring it here and stop bullshitting around."

The Indian shook his head. "Bick wants a look," he said.
"He's got serial numbers he wants to check. Just a goddamn
look. Bring the goddamn paper over to him and let him have a
goddamn look. Christ."

Joe Dev considered the tenability of his position. The
request was a reasonable one, although uncalled for. Playing
footsie with the Lodi barbarians never yielded anything but
tragedy, and they knew it. On the other hand the lack of
publicity regarding his success did leave his claim open to
skepticism. What did they ask, Bick Anson and the Indian, ask,
that is, in the sense of lining him up for a kill. The Indian was
unarmed, at least not with a gun, and as long as he remained
outside the car, Joe Dev felt equal to him. Anson, however, had
a clear shot—if he meant to shoot—from the side window of the
car. There would be an interval—from the second he moved
within range of the gun and that which proved Anson innocent
of evil intent—during which he'd be wide open for killing.

Joe Dev said, "Okay, I show the bonds," he said. "That's
my big trouble. I trust everybody."

"You wouldn't trust your mother," the Indian said.

"I don't have a mother, so that's off my list of worries," Joe
Dev said.

"Let's go," the Indian said.

"Look, you don't mind, huh?" Joe Dev said. "My feet hurt.
I don't come to the car. You drive the car here."

The Indian said, "Aw, for Christ's sake."

"You got no pity for a guy, his feet hurt?" Joe Dev said.

"Okay," the Indian said. Annoyance almost crept into his
face. "You got the paper on you?"

"One step at a time," Joe Dev said.

The Indian started away.

Joe Dev stopped him with "Hey."

The Indian looked over his shoulder.

Joe Dev said, "If you drive with two hands on the wheel it's
more better. I guarantee you I get the first shot."

"I thought you said you never carry heat," the Indian said.

"You don't know what a liar I am," Joe Dev said.

The Indian started away.

Joe Dev stopped him with "Hey."

The Indian turned and regarded him with withering coldness.

Joe Dev said, "You tell the boss to sit on the other side of the seat, not in back of you. Okay? Thanks."

The Indian started away again.

Joe Dev stopped him with "Whoa, whoa, whoa, I forget something."

Face still expressionless, the Indian's eyes blazed.

Joe Dev said, "Drive slow. That's all. You giddyap now."

For a man whose bowels writhed with anger, the Indian's movements were deceptively sluggish. He betrayed himself only when he slammed the car door viciously shut.

Joe Dev saw the man he thought to be Bick Anson shift his position. The Indian started the motor, the car crept ahead and made the turn. Now Joe Dev faced the windshield.

The Mercury inched forward, closer, closer. The Indian's eyes, cooled now, stared ahead, his fingers gripping the steering wheel. Joe Dev kept alert for the danger point, when he'd be in range of a gun. Not yet. If a guncrack was to come it would come—

Now. The man in the rear seat leaned forward. Light struck his face and revealed him for an impostor. Coming up, too, his hand took the same light, and Joe Dev dove into the tangle of cornstalks, the hair over his ear singed by the heat of Little Neffie's bullet. Head down, body doubled over, Joe Dev scrambled away.

It seemed to him that he heard six shots before the silence. Little Neffie had emptied a revolver. But the guncracks picked up again, too soon for reloading. The new reports claimed another origin, a weapon with more boom than bang, louder, thicker.

Joe Dev held up, still. The killer could no longer see his target, he fired for the sake of firing, the bullets hitting a dozen yards past his intended victim. Yet he continued to fire, at what Joe Dev could not tell. He raised his body from bent knees and squinted past corn tassels. The Indian was standing on the roof of the car. He held a rifle. He saw Joe Dev. He fired. Joe Dev hit the dirt and crawled. Now the bullets boomed close by, strangely so, considering he was in complete cover. But then he stopped, realizing that in attempting flight he disturbed cornstalks and gave the Indian a moving target. After another burst the firing ceased.

Joe Dev listened for pursuit by Little Neffie. Hearing nothing, he deduced that he had run to the margin of the woods to head him off. It meant that the highway, almost a quarter of a mile away, offered the only escape route. But he dared not move. To stir would invite the Indian's fire.

The plastic packet against his stomach was slimy wet from perspiration, the sharp corners chafed his skin. He transferred it to the back waistband. He cursed himself for stupidity, for allowing himself to be sandbagged. But the oaths, a release, soon ended and he concentrated his thinking on the present predicament. He found, however, that his thoughts were a warring blend of fear and anger, the anger hot and unshakable.

Bullets whinged ten feet to the right of him, meaningless fire triggered by the hope of a lucky hit. He wished he carried matches. He'd set the securities afire before he'd allow the Indian to get them now. He thought of burying them, there where his cheek rested in the dirt. If they killed him they'd never find them. He shoved the thought from him. If he buried them, he wouldn't find them either. Revenge would be his, yes, but defeat too. Because he meant to live.

The rifle boomed again. He judged that the bullets struck ahead and to the left. He failed to understand the logic of it. Why did the Indian fire? And at what? Maybe he thought that continued random fire would score a lucky hit. Joe Dev dead. When would that crop be harvested? He'd rot there. Nobody knew where he was, nobody would look for him. He'd be found when the corn was picked—not him, his bones.

He considered waiting them out and what action that would spur them to. Maybe they'd come in after him, not the two, one; one to stand high watch, as the Indian did now. He hoped they'd do that, come to him, but he had no real belief that they would. Cunning honed sharp, they'd anticipate death in the move, anticipate his waiting for them, with a gun maybe. They

THE DEVALINO CAPER . . . 207

could not be sure he was unarmed. No, invading the field did not stack. They had the edge now, they'd wait *him* out. How long? Till dark? Eight? Eight-thirty? Not likely. Once they guessed a wait-out, they'd dream up a new strategy. So that was that. Impractical to wait them out, and yet to lie huddled helplessly, to delay, would prove deadlier still. With instant appreciation of the crunch came the admonition that his own plan of action had to be formed and introduced at once, now, while they smiled into the face of his torment.

Powdery dry dirt turned to mud in his mouth. He spat but phlegm refused to clear past his throat. From the dim distance he heard the gnashing teeth of a truck engine chewing up the highway. He scolded: Forget the goddamn highway, it's too far away, it's a nightmare run.

He rested and tried to plan ahead. The thought of the highway persisted and he kept discarding it. Then, suddenly aware that he lay on cornstalks crushed when he drove into them, the idea loomed less nightmarish. When making a run for it, he could dive to the rear for cover, into ground which would not reveal his presence because the stalks were already crushed. Why not? Go, and when the bullets strike too close, stop, go back.

He sprung into a half crouch and ran, shifting, weaving, halting, retreating, slowing and increasing speed. The bullets zinged and boomed with double fury. He felt a searing stinging pain in his shoulder blade. He held up, slewed about, flattened on the ground and crawled back over the route he'd covered. The firing continued, but the fury exploded behind him now, where he'd been a moment before. He touched the pain in his shoulder. His fingers came away with little blood. The bullet had burned, skinned, nothing more.

He rested and brooded. He estimated the gain. Five feet? Ten? How many feet in a quarter of a mile? How many times risk his life under the Indian's gun, trading five or ten feet for each risk, before he reached the highway? Stupid. Crazy. No good.

Cheek to earth, he pondered his next move. He glanced obliquely into the hot sky. The sun had begun its descent. Hope glimmered. The Indian faced the sun. It might fault his aim, might take some risk out of the forward spurts. But make sure. Wait until the sun fell lower still.

He wondered what churned in their minds. He put himself in Little Neffie's place. Were he Little Neffie he'd be prowling the edge of the woods, ready to intercept and kill. Yes, kill. Little doubt of that. The Indian craved the Devalino carcass more than the million-four; odd, considering how little had passed between them. A fire-and-water mix from the very start.

Joe Dev imagined himself in the tree again, elevated, advantaged, and in his mind's eye he saw the Indian enjoying the same advantage atop the car. A big edge to have. Big enough to make Indiana Joe Dev's graveyard.

The rifle spat again, five times, all around him. Four shots hit wide, but one powdered the earth a few feet from his ribs. Wild shooting, but a wild bullet kills too, if it hits. He rolled over on his back and got a hot golden blast from the sun; it glistened through his sweaty eyelids. The change in position soothed, however, and he did not move. It would be a while yet before that sun slanted into the Indian's eyes.

A sharp whistle sounded, a human tone. It originated from behind, from the woods. Probably Little Neffie trying to call the Indian's attention. Joe Dev flipped over, did a pushup, tucked knees under and straightened the upper portion of his body. He looked toward the car. The Indian was nodding toward the woods, acknowledging a signal of some sort. His left hand cradled the underbelly of the rifle magazine, his right hand the trigger guard.

The Indian's head snapped to, he raised the rifle and fired a volley at Joe Dev's head. Joe Dev hit the dirt unharmed. The Indian had fired too swiftly for accuracy. Had he held up for one beat, Joe Dev's skull would have splintered. Instead he scurried away, swerving, veering, five feet, ten, then back five. The hazardous exposure yielded only a few feet. Hope dimmed. Never had he felt such loneliness, such despair, such anger; the mixture choked worse than the dust he inhaled. He felt the anger most of all, hot anger that brewed a sullen passion for freedom.

He felt fear, too, and his mind strayed back to morning. Poor Julia, he thought, poor scared Julia. That's a hell of a life they gave her to live. Scared all the time. She's never gonna learn, that girl. Fear is the mother and father of everything bad. You gotta kick it in the ass or you're not worth nothing. Maybe she was telling the truth about waiting for me, to prove she loves me. But, Jesus, what a dopey thing to do, lift those bonds out of the bag. She's gotta know me better than that. A dirty low bastard, she called me. And if I get killed now, what? She's never gonna get the money I promised to send, and that's gonna make her think I really am a shit-heel. Well, listen, Joe. You weren't born to take care of somebody else. Right now take care of yourself. You got some fear to kick in the ass yourself. These sonsofbitches are gonna get to you unless you shake something loose out of your head, something that'll screw them. Jesus, this makes me mad. I do the job and then they turn around and they fuck me. But look, stop with this getting mad. Getting mad's no good. It eats you up. It's like you eat your own hands, your own body. You stay mad long enough and there's nothing left of you but bones.

Hey.

The sound caressed his ears. He listened.

Shhhhoooooooeeeeee. Shhhhoooooooeeeeee.

He listened and remembered the wind sweeping across the corn field, remembered the millions of palomino tails.

Shhhhoooooooeeeeee.

Joe Dev exulted over the sound. It explained the random shots. Of course. The Indian only blasted away when the wind played with the palomino tails and set the entire field in motion. He fired at phantoms.

Shhhhoooooooeeeeee.

Joe Dev scrambled ahead.

The gun again. But the bullets were off, way off.

The discovery was a mindblower. When the wind blew, *that* was the time to run; listen to the wind-whispers and advance only when they murmured assurance that the palomino tails were in motion, acres and acres of them, and no way for the Indian to spot him for a target.

He thought, Maybe you got them, Joe-Boy. Sonsofbitches. Maybe you got them.

He warned himself that the contest was no longer against an enemy but against himself. Premature jubilation might lead to recklessness.

The air still, he waited and embraced the thoughts that offered themselves. *Back,* one said. Go back, the way is *back.*

Holy Jesus.

Don't you see, Joe-Boy, another thought asked. They expect you to flee in the only direction open to you, the death focus of two brutally keen minds is zeroed in on your making a run for the highway. Go back. Don't run. Attack.

Shhhhoooooooeeeeee.

Now. He belly-crawled, the skin of his elbows and wrists wearing raw. *Whang, whang, whang* went the antiphonal sound of the guncracks. But death was nowhere near. The Indian fired at someone he *thought* he saw.

Shhhhoooooooeeeeee.

Joe Dev kept on, shifting direction but always resuming a diagonal approach to the Mercury. He was unable to reckon its exact position, but he knew he was drawing closer and closer to it. He stopped, rested, listened for the whisperings. He cautioned himself again. Check yourself out, Joe-Boy, make sure you got the edge. Figure what you're going to do when you get there. Put yourself inside the Indian's head.

His hair, the white shirt—no good, too easy to spot. He took off shirt and T-shirt. The shirt he put aside, the T-shirt he rubbed into the earth until its whiteness was dulled. He wrapped it around his black hair and tucked the ends under to secure it. Now his tanned body and head were the color of everything surrounding him.

Shhhhoooooooeeeeee.

The wind blew a full twenty seconds. The Indian fired a shot, and after a five-second interval, another. The wind died down. Joe Dev stopped. He heard a faint *chink.* He puzzled over it for a moment, then identified it. A spent shell falling on the roof of the car. He was close now, he could even hear the scraping of the Indian's shoes on metal when he shifted stance to reload.

He could see nothing in front of him, not yet, only a scraggly tunnel of stalks. At rest, he searched for other advantages that might be in the offing. What would the Indian see if he looked down? How far was the car from the nearest row of stalks? Joe Dev could not tell, and would not, until he was closer. One condition was certain: when the rifle boomed the Indian would be looking into the gunsights to a distant target.

It was slow waiting and slow going. He snaked ahead, careful not to disturb the stalks' prop roots with the tips of his shoes. Breath came fast and hard, hard enough to be heard, perhaps, when all was still. He prolonged exhalation to rid himself of poisons that taxed the lungs.

He wiped dirt from the face of his watch. Almost ten minutes since Little Neffie fired the first shot through the windshield. Impatience would be nibbling at confidence; he'd have to move faster, before they decided on a different strategy, a different attack.

An out-of-place color caught his eye, a swatch of black. The car tire.

Chink, chink, chink. The Indian toe-kicking shells from the roof of the car.

Now hope glimmered again. He was there. Ten feet to the car, no more. The discovery steadied him.

The whispering began and he pressed on. Suddenly he froze. The rifle was ominously silent. He wondered why. Then came the shuffling noise. Someone was coming, running. Little Neffie. Joe Dev saw his shoes when he halted beside the car tire.

They spoke quietly. The Indian said, "What do you think?"

"He's out there all right," Little Neffie said.

Joe Dev smelled smoke. Little Neffie was lighting up a cigar. "No place for him to go," he said.

"Keep him there," the Indian said. "Bishop's on his way. I told him fifteen minutes. Almost that now."

"Just about," Little Neffie said.

"Better get back," the Indian said. "He might try to get past you."

Little Neffie said, "I wish he would," and the shoes were gone.

Joe Dev sighed wearily. His earlier guess had proved out. The arithmetic of their new strategy was painfully clear. More men. Surround him. Close in.

He had to get to the Indian and he had to do it while he was occupied with shooting. What in hell happened to the wind? Why wasn't it blowing? He turned slightly to favor the bruised portions of his body and prepared for another spurt forward. He waited for the whispers. Why didn't they come? He experienced a sinking feeling. Had the wind died down for good? He concentrated on gauging the distance to the car. Seven feet, eight. Covering the distance was feasible, but what of the open space between the last row of stalks and the car? Two feet. A death trap. If the Indian were to glance down and see him, he'd lower the rifle and smash one into his spine.

Shhhhooooooeeeeee.

All his working senses terrorized into vigilance, he slithered ahead. He nursed a panic that he might not reach the car in one try and that he'd have to hold up and lie helplessly in easy view of the Indian. Sweat blinded him. Shaking of the head did not help, he had to squander a precious moment to pause and scrub with his forearm. He heard the gun thundering, not knowing or caring how many times. So long as it thundered, he'd keep going.

He scrabbled on until he achieved a gopher's view of the car chassis, and in that same moment his heart violently started. The dirt road below the car hummocked in the center. He could not, as planned, crawl under the drive shaft to the other side: to circle the car would leave him too long exposed; to stop was disastrous.

He crossed wthout hesitation the two feet of open death and rolled under the car, face upward, body parallel to the drive shaft. Exhausted, he let every muscle lie as it would. His cheek was pressed against the differential, it bled from the blow sustained when he smashed into it. Turning his face away from it, his eyes fell on total defeat. He'd lost the plastic package when he twisted in the death space.

Reach? No. The decision was ferociously emphatic. An arm in motion would capture attention much faster than an inert package. He had to play for all or nothing. That meant the Indian had to die. So long as the Indian remained alive the package was worthless.

The gun-roar continued for some moments before it

stopped, a longer burst than before, and Joe Dev concluded that the Indian's intention was not to flush his quarry but to discourage it from running, to keep it motionless, cowering, until the others arrived.

The wind fell still and the silence stretched out. Joe Dev dug his heels into the dirt—his knees rose only six inches before contacting metal—and pushed. The top of his head met the rear axle. He turned a cheek into the dirt, dug again and again, until he cleared the axle. He flattened his two hands on his abdomen, slid them palms upward and stretched. Exploring fingers found a gas tank and grasped its curved edge. He tugged, gained a full foot before he had to stretch again. The groping now was for the rear bumper. His hands found it, then released it. He worked his fingers to untense them and prepared for the move which would take him into the open.

Shhhhoooooooeeeeee.

Unexplainably the silence lengthened. He tugged against the leverage of the bumper. His body slid back. His forehead cleared the bumper and he felt the breeze across his sweat-wet face. The sun hit, and through the glare he saw the rifle muzzle.

The Indian towered on the trunk. He said, "Up."

Joe Dev pointed bleeding elbows into the ground, came erect, stood. The Indian's eyes examined him from head to foot.

"Where is it?" the Indian said.

Joe Dev shook his head. "We gotta deal, Mister Indian."

"Pignuts," the Indian said.

"Any kind of nuts you like," Joe Dev said. "We deal."

"I'll kill you," the Indian said.

"Fine," Joe Dev said. "Kill me and then go look for the bonds."

The Indian scrunched up his mouth to produce a piercing whistle.

Joe Dev said, "Hey, I'm beat. You mind if I sit down?" He didn't wait for permission but did so, stepping slightly to the left of the Indian, away from the side of the road where he'd lost the package.

The whistle summoning Little Neffie brought him loping down the dirt road from the woods. He carried a revolver in his hand. He stopped, looked at Joe Dev and flashed a smile. "Mind if I have him?" he asked the Indian. "I ain't forgot what the bastard did to me."

"He's holding out the paper," the Indian said.

"Oh, he is, huh?" Little Neffie said. "Well, don't fuck with him. What you do is, you give him a choice. Like this." He stepped directly behind Joe Dev, who sat relaxed, resting on the palms of outstretched hands like a sun lover enjoying the beach after a strenuous swim. Little Neffie rammed the revolver against the top of his head. The revolver made a ratchety sound as he cocked it.

"See?" Little Neffie said to the Indian. "A choice. Now ask him."

There was no disputing Little Neffie's logic. Joe Dev agreed wholeheartedly. Even with the knowledge that death would follow his disclosure of the package's whereabouts, the time span—a half minute, a quarter, ten seconds?—between disclosure and death added up to life. Hope crushes a rebel mind and body. To a man facing death ten seconds spreads into an eternity, and Joe Dev chose the eternity.

"The other side of the car," he said.

The Indian said to Little Neffie, "Watch him."

"My fucking pleasure," Little Neffie said.

The Indian leaped from the trunk and rounded the car to the far side. He appeared framed in the back window for a moment, was lost when he stooped to pick up the package, and seen again as he came erect. He kept the rifle lowered, muzzle down, his hand cradling the trigger guard, balancing the weapon. He came back. His forehead tightly creased, he looked at the package and turned it over in his hand. He was totally unaware of Little Neffie's hand coming up.

Joe Dev, his head bent against the pressure of Little Neffie's revolver, felt release of the pressure and, looking up, saw the first bullet hit the Indian squarely in the chest. He saw the red spurt to life. It started as a tiny well-formed disc and then smeared into a Rorschach blot on his white shirt. He saw the Indian thrown back and spun around by the force of the bullet, watched him drop the million four hundred thousand, try to lift the rifle and, not managing, sending an un-aimed bullet skyward. Little Neffie kept firing and Joe Dev saw other red blots smearing the white, five in all. The Indian reeled crazily back, back, back, back, back, in an up-and-down and sideways progress which made Joe Dev think of a tin can under the gun of a showoff cowboy. The Indian hit the ground and briefly writhed, an ant mangled under the inadvertent tread of a passing giant.

Joe Dev knew that the sixth bullet was for him. But he wasn't dead yet, he told himself. One step at a time. His hands were free and he was rested, now, and Little Neffie's mind was on the million four hundred thousand. One step at a time. Study around. If you wanna stay alive in this world you gotta keep studying around.

He reached back and grabbed Little Neffie's ankles. The sixth bullet went wild, and even before Little Neffie hit the ground Joe Dev struck him a sledge-hammer blow across the abdomen. The second blow ruptured liver meat below the many thicknesses of flesh. He died nursing the excruciating pain in his middle, oblivious to the real cause of his death: Joe Dev's fingers at his throat.

Throughout, Joe Dev never lost sight of the package of securities. When Little Neffie lay still, he picked it up and ran down the dusty road to the woods. In the car, he squirmed into the sailor blouse, started the motor and dug out. He drove to Indianapolis International Airport, stopping briefly at a gas station to wash mud from his face and hands. At the airport he turned in the rented car. A flight to Chicago was due to leave. He bought a ticket and boarded it. In the washroom of O'Hare Airport, he changed into civvies and dumped the sailor suit and duffel bag into a litter can. He caught a flight to Las Vegas. There he rented a car and drove to Los Angeles.

Only three people alive in Uniontown would remember that he had even visited Indiana. At nine o'clock the following morning he boarded a flight to Newark and resisted sleep only long enough to review again the tale he would tell: He completed the job. He delivered the bonds to Bick Anson. Anson paid him his ten percent in cash, one hundred and twenty thousand dollars. He left Uniontown. As for the tragic events that happened after he left, who knows? But how about that, huh? Jesus. What can you expect, though? With that kind of money being handled, anything can happen. People, they're like monkeys fighting over a banana. Goddamn sketch.

Joe Dev yawned. One hundred thousand would pay off the Lodi barbarians, twenty thousand would go to Bruno and Toni, and the one million . . .

Joe Dev slept.

ABOUT THE AUTHOR

A. J. RUSSELL was born in New York and
educated at New York University. He now lives in
Westchester County. He is a well-known television
writer and has won an Emmy and a W.G.A.
Award for drama, musical variety and comedy.
This is his first novel.